OUR LITTLE LIES

GEMMA METCALFE
JOE CAWLEY

BLOODHOUND
— BOOKS —

To my brother David, who I've always looked up to... both literally, and in admiration. Joe x

To Nanna, your stories made me the writer I am today. I love you the world. Gemma x

1

GRACE
NOW

This is it. This is where my story ends.

I don't expect you to condone what I've done. All I ask is that when you know the whole truth, you try to understand. After all, are we not all capable of sin in the name of love?

I once heard that love never dies a natural death. A loving heart is killed; stabbed by hurt, poisoned by betrayal, snuffed out with lies.

And a dead heart can only beat with revenge.

I'll let you in on a little secret. Nobody in this story is as they first appear. Nobody is innocent.

Least of all me.

2

GRACE
NOW

The harsh reality of the interrogation process has an immediate effect. I choke down the rising bile in my throat and fold my arms tight across my chest. The room contains no windows, holds no hope. If I stretched out, I could just about touch both of the pitted, lead-grey walls. But I don't. I sit hunched forward, my denim-clad thighs sticking to the black plastic of one of three chairs. Each seat is bolted to the floor through drab, green carpet tiles, stained and worn, like most who trudge over them, I guess – like me now, I suppose.

A female officer glares at me. What does she think I'm capable of? What *am* I capable of? I'm struck by the coldness in her pale-grey eyes. It reminds me of the ash left in a dying fire.

'This interview is being recorded. It is presently 8.32pm on Tuesday 19th May 2020. I am Detective Inspector Sally Ambrose, currently at Cheadle Heath Police Station.' She leans across the table, intertwining long, slender fingers which seem too feminine for a DI. Instinctively, I conceal my bandaged hand between my thighs and pray she doesn't ask me about it. 'Grace, you're aware of the charges against you?'

I turn my head to the wall where a riot of smudged fingerprints seem to point accusingly. 'I'm not refuting any of it.'

She allows my admission the space to breathe. 'Do you know where Daniel is?'

I shake my head, tears spilling down my face. 'I don't. Please find him. Please make him be all right.'

The detective's brow creases. 'Do you have reason to believe he's come to harm?'

I blanch. She's trying to catch me out. 'No. It's not that. He wouldn't hurt Daniel. It's just...' My gaze drops to my lap.

'Just what?' Her voice has turned ice cold.

I need to speak, to have this end right now. I can't allow *him* to take the fall, not when this is all my fault. My stomach lurches, a scream from deep inside bubbling to the surface. I need to let it out, to rid myself of the demon within, the monster that allowed this to happen: to purge. To say I'm sorry.

Our eyes lock, woman to woman.

It's time to confess.

3

GRACE

'Please God, let it be positive.' Slipping the cap back on the test, I place it face down on the edge of the bath.

Three minutes to go.

I've lost count of the number of tests I've peed on over the years; Clearblue, First Response, those crappy dipstick ones from Superdrug. Two lines for the jackpot, X marks the spot – it all amounts to the same thing when neither appears, namely that my reproductive system is about as useful as a hand-knitted condom!

Flushing the toilet, I fasten my jeans and tighten my belt to the last notch. I've lost more weight in the last six months than I care to think about. Turning sideways, I inspect myself in the bathroom mirror, wincing at the emaciated, ghost-white figure I've become; legs like twigs, jutted-out hips and sharp shoulders – of course, there was a time I'd have considered such a figure desirable, rebuffing suggestions that I was anorexic as jealousy gift-wrapped in concern.

'I'm afraid one of the long-term effects of an eating disorder is often infertility.' The gynaecologist's words had been fired at me like bullets. Only then did I realise I was actually sick – mentally as well as physically. For years I'd starved my body, and now it was wreaking its revenge.

I fought to make it right – eating well and giving myself over to counselling. Justin, my partner of ten years, was just as desperate to start a family as I was, which was a blessing at first, though over the years his heartache only added to my guilt. There's nothing quite like guilt to quash your appetite.

I glance at the downturned test, hope fluttering in my heart despite knowing the chances are slim. My period's late, three weeks and four days, though I only plucked up the courage to buy a test this morning. 'Just do this one thing for me, God, and I promise I'll never ask for anything again as long as I live.'

As a child, my younger brother, Andrew, and I attended a Pentecostal church with our mother, a born-again Christian who was the mixed-race daughter of a Black South African pastor. My heart still swells with joy when I think back to that time, Mum, Andrew and I singing our hearts out on a Sunday morning, my arms raised high and my heart thumping in time to a twenty-strong worship band, but I've long since given up on church. Andrew's death at the hands of a hit-and-run driver saw to that. Thirteen years young, his life snuffed out in a heartbeat. I was sixteen, on the cusp of adulthood but, like most sixteen-year-olds, blissfully ignorant to the horrors life can afflict. Andrew's death robbed me not only of my brother but of my innocence, faith, the belief that the world is a good place. When Mum also died a few years later, I didn't so much disbelieve in God as despise him. Yet, like many a disgruntled believer, I still cling to God when I'm drowning in despair.

I track the seconds hand on my watch until it reaches twelve. *Two minutes to go.*

A knock on the bathroom door sends my pulse racing.

'You want me to open the red or the white? It's fish, so white, yeah?'

Justin has no idea my period's even late, let alone that I'm taking a pregnancy test. There was a time he would have at the beginning, but not now. Now I'm not even sure he'd notice if I were three weeks late home from work.

'Whatever you think.'

'You all right?'

'Yeah. Just on the loo.'

'Should I stick some prawns in too, or just stick with the cod?'

Nausea claws at my throat at the thought of fleshy, raw fish. *For God's sake, leave me alone.* I swallow down the irritation. 'Just cod.'

'Cheesy mash or normal?'

I lean forward against the sink, hands splayed like starfish and take a slow breath. 'Just give me a minute, all right. I'm not feeling so good.'

'Why, what's the matter?'

Go away!

'Grace? You got the squits?'

'Good God, Justin, can you just leave me alone for five minutes!'

The sound of creaking floorboards sinks my stomach. I never mean to push him away, and yet somehow, I manage it every time.

A sudden wave of nausea brings me to my knees. I hang my head over the toilet bowl and dry retch until at last, my stomach contracts and empties itself. The sight of sick only makes me heave more, but there's nothing left to part with. Wiping the acidic residue from around my mouth, I pull myself up and stumble over to the sink to splash cold water onto my face.

Seconds later, my hand shakes as I hover over the test. A part of me is desperate to toss it straight in the bin without looking, but I know I have to face it head-on, whatever the result. Cautiously, I turn it over.

4

GRACE
TWO YEARS AGO

My brain stutters, as if unable to take in what my eyes are seeing. I collapse down onto the toilet seat and squint as I hold the test up to the light. There's a faint line, I'm sure, though my eyes could easily be playing tricks on me. I've fallen victim to it countless times before, convinced myself of a second line when it was little more than a shadow. But this time – I look again – yep, it's definitely visible.

Hands trembling, I fish the box out of the rubbish bin and scan the instructions. *A second line, no matter how faint, is a positive result.* I bring the test close to my face, breathing momentarily suspended as the enormity of the situation takes root. I'm pregnant! I wouldn't believe it if I wasn't holding proof right here in my hand – a kiss from Mother Nature, the promise of new life.

I remain in a daze for the longest time, a surreal kind of elation paralysing me. I have a baby growing inside of me. He or she will be – I quickly do the math – seven or eight weeks. My child – God, I can hardly say the words to myself. My. Child.

Cautiously, I place both hands on my stomach and make a silent promise to be the best mother I can be. Justin and I may have our problems, but there's no doubt we'll give this child the world. Shit! Justin. He still has no idea.

Thundering down the stairs, I head straight for the kitchen, keeping the test concealed behind my back. I imagine Justin's face as I break the news to him, the brief look of shock as he registers the positive test followed by the inevitable euphoria. A smile breaks out as the image takes shape. I run through the announcement in my mind. *I'm pregnant, Justin. We did it!*

'Justin!' I burst through the kitchen door and stop dead.

Justin's finger stabs at the screen on his mobile. His cheeks are flushed red, eyes hardened. 'Sorry what?' He stuffs the mobile into his jeans pocket, coughs into his fist and then, perhaps aware of my stunned silence, rearranges his face into something resembling indifference. 'Bloody hell, Grace, you shit me up then.'

'What are you doing?' Instinctively my fingers curl tighter around the test still hidden behind my back.

'Making fish pie, what does it look like?' He expels a nervous laugh.

'You look worried.' I nod at the phone in his pocket. 'Who were you on to?' The accusation is clear, though I have no idea what it is I'm accusing him of.

He snorts, his eyes everywhere but on me. 'Nothing, just work stuff.' He leans back against the countertop and visibly swallows the lie. 'What were you going to say?'

The test now feels like a red-hot poker in my fist. After a few seconds of silence, I hold it up, tears distorting my vision. 'I'm pregnant.' I can't believe this is it, the moment I've waited my entire adult life for, the words now spoken in an almost apologetic whisper. This isn't how it was meant to go.

Justin stands open-mouthed, unblinking, his face a train wreck of thoughts. 'Grace... I...' He takes the test and, in the same way I did only a few minutes ago, holds it up to the light. 'Are you sure?'

'Of course.' My voice splinters. 'You're happy, aren't you?'

He nods, unconvincingly I notice. Where's the amazement? The euphoria? I feel my chin trembling as he hands it back, my stomach twisted into knots. His eyes widen, a small smile lifting the corners of his mouth.

He's happy, thank God. I let go of the breath in my chest and allow myself to relax, to enjoy the moment. Is it possible I imagined the other stuff, the guilt, the shame? I didn't, I know, but there's no way I can analyse all of that now.

'Why didn't you tell me?' he asks, now frowning. 'Why did you do the test alone?'

I shake my head, the reason lost under all the other shit inside my mind. I've just announced I'm having a baby, *we're* having a baby, after everything we've been through; the years of hurt; the treading on eggshells around one another, terrified of saying the wrong thing; the month after month of stomach cramps, knowing, always knowing what will follow and hoping against it anyway, then the inevitable shedding of a month's worth of dreams, of imagining a life so very different. And now, now we finally have what we've always wanted, and all that Justin's interested in is why I took the test alone? 'I'm not sure. I suppose I didn't want to get your hopes up.'

He seems to consider this, or perhaps he isn't thinking of me at all, his head still caught in whatever he was doing on his phone. What *was* he doing?

Vomit burns my throat. Hand clasped to my mouth, I run to the loo and remain doubled over the toilet basin for what feels like hours, my heart and head accelerating at double-quick speed. I'm pregnant, and Justin... Justin is hiding something.

'Grace, you okay up there?'

I wipe my mouth and heave myself up. From the landing, I

see Justin is pulling his jacket off the coat rack in the hallway. He zips it right up to his chin before turning towards me. 'You got morning sickness at night? Trust you.' He does that strange, nervous laugh again. 'I have to pop out.'

'Where are you going? What about dinner?' I lean against the bannister, not steady enough to take the stairs.

'It's in the oven. Help yourself.'

'Justin? What's going on? Where you going? What time are you back?' He must sense the exasperation in my voice, but if he does, he doesn't react.

'Soon,' he says calmly, as if this is completely normal behaviour.

'You *are* happy, aren't you? About the baby?'

He glances back from the front door and I see the fleeting look of panic on his face. 'Of course. Just something I got to go and do. Back soon.'

Only he doesn't come back.

I never see Justin again.

5

GRACE
NOW

'I can imagine that was... upsetting,' says Detective Ambrose, studying me with concern.

Upsetting? Is this woman for real? Upsetting is when your pet goldfish dies or when ET phones home. It's most certainly not when your partner of ten years walks out of the door and never returns.

I grit my teeth, fed up with my feelings being picked apart. I appreciate the need for her to understand how past events led up to this, but I'm certain there's nobody on earth who's been convicted or acquitted based on what they *felt*, so what's the point?

'Upsetting, yes.'

'It would have made you really angry, wouldn't it?' she persists, arms folded over a crisp uniform. Clearly, she's had a chance to shower and change since she read me my rights last night, which is more than can be said for me; my T-shirt is crumpled from hours spent tossing and turning on a rock-hard bed, and I can only imagine how badly I stink.

'Look, have you found them yet?' I ask after a beat of silence. 'Going over the past isn't going to help anything.'

'Let me be the judge of that,' she states, not missing a beat.

I sigh, exasperated. 'Yes, okay. It broke my heart. But that isn't why...' I search for the right words. 'That isn't why I did what I did. It wasn't about revenge.'

'Grace.' Detective Ambrose looks at me the way Mum used to when I was a kid caught out in a lie. 'Be honest. You wanted Justin to suffer?'

'You don't have to answer that,' offers my solicitor after a beat of silence, as though the thought has just occurred to him. He's slumped in the chair next to me, legs stretched out underneath the table.

I look to Detective Ambrose for confirmation. She shrugs. 'Your call, Grace.'

I consider the question. Did I want Justin to suffer? 'I just wanted to find him,' I offer. 'To have him come home so we could work through whatever it was that made him leave in the first place.'

'You reported him missing, didn't you?' Ambrose scans an open folder in front of her.

My fingers curl tightly around a plastic cup of tepid tea. I want to tell her that if 'her lot' had done their job properly two years ago, none of this would have happened.

'Blame-shifting,' Mum would say if she were here. 'Take responsibility for your own actions, Grace, darling.'

My mind wanders back to that day. Six hours after I heard the door slam shut, I reported Justin missing. In truth, I knew he wasn't coming back within a few hours. I can't explain how I knew this; a sixth sense perhaps, a woman's intuition? Despite my decisiveness in reporting it, the police took three days to come and take a statement. Within minutes of hearing the circumstances of why Justin left, they'd written him off as another deadbeat dad shirking his responsibility, helped no doubt by his record of petty theft and breach of the peace from years before. They weren't interested that he'd since turned his life around, or that I, his partner of ten years, was adamant he'd never walk away from his unborn child without an exceptional reason. Of course, now I know he did have an exceptional reason. Knowing what I do now, would I have wanted him to make a different decision? It's a question I still don't know the answer to.

Back then, oblivious to why Justin had abandoned us, I pleaded with the police to investigate, inundating them with emails, phone calls and even turning up at the station. As my stomach began to swell, so did my frustration. How could they justify doing nothing? I was sure that if they would just find him and haul him back home, I could do the rest.

Though now, of course, I know it wasn't that simple.

'I reported him missing two years ago but nothing was ever done about it.' I glare at Detective Ambrose, the implication clear. 'I never knew what had happened to him, or where he'd gone. Not until two and a half weeks ago.'

6

GRACE

Daniel bangs sticky palms against the reinforced glass of the arcade's grabber machine.

'Oh look, it's got him!' The claw grips Tigger's arm with all the strength of an arthritic pensioner before swiftly dumping him onto Eeyore's head.

'Gen!' he shrieks, as the claw parks itself back into its bay. I reckon I've already put enough money in this damn thing to buy him the entire cast of *Winnie the Pooh* and have each one personally signed by A. A. Milne! 'Let's try the two-pence machines instead, buddy.'

Placing Daniel onto the threadbare carpet, I watch as he happily totters off. He's only been walking for a matter of weeks, and as he waddles back and forth, I feel a fleeting sense of sadness. He's growing up far too quickly. It seems like only yesterday that he was a chubby baby with rolls of fat and a gummy smile. Where has the time gone? It's almost two years now since I found out I was pregnant, exactly 103 weeks since Justin walked out of the door and never came back.

Feeling the onset of tears, I quickly banish from my mind the memories of that time. It's a strategy I've adopted in order to protect myself. It buries every negative emotion before it can take a hold of me. I know that if I allow myself to feel, to dwell on the past, I'll crumble under the weight of grief. I have to remain strong, for Daniel, for myself. There's no point in clinging to ghosts.

My head throbs in synchronicity with the pulsating neon lights as I feed a handful of copper into the steely mouth of a slot. I silently pray it isn't bulimic.

I came to Blackpool with high hopes, a longing to share a little of my own childhood with Daniel, to connect him with Mum and Andrew, if only by experience. In reality, it's nothing short of a shithole. Was it always this way? The stench of unwashed bodies and fried food fogging the air, while fat middle-aged men feed fat fruit machines, and tracksuit-clad teens high on testosterone and Christ-knows-what pummel leather punch balls. Where's the magic, the simple pleasures? The tang of sugary sweets and the adrenaline-fuelled chatter; the jingle of coins in paper cups? Perhaps Blackpool hasn't changed at all, only me.

Daniel points at a Peppa Pig car ride which looks well in need of an MOT.

'One go,' I say, already rummaging around in my bag for yet another fifty-pence piece. He has me wrapped around his little finger, but I wouldn't have it any other way.

A minute later and Daniel is spinning the steering wheel with all the care of Miss Daisy while I snap pictures of him on my mobile. 'Big smile for Mummy!'

'Gen,' he shouts as the ride slows to a stop.

'No, I think it's time...'

'Geeeeeeen!'

Having neither the energy nor the mental strength for a showdown, I slot in another coin and we proceed to cover the distance of Land's End to John o' Groats while Peppa squeals about muddy puddles.

Finally shoehorning Daniel out of the arcade on the promise of ice cream, I strap him into his stroller and zip his Cosy Toes right up to his chin, a northerly spring breeze making the air feel almost icy.

We set off walking along the famous Golden Mile, where the sweet smell of hot sugar doughnuts awakens happy memories of summer school trips. Blackpool, Southport or Rhyl, it didn't matter which – the summer trip meant school was out for six whole weeks.

I never liked school much. I wasn't cool or pretty enough to fit in. My red hair, wide nose and freckly skin, courtesy of an Irish father, meant I was often the butt of jokes.

I steer the buggy onto the pier, the rubber wheels on the wooden planks adding a rhythmic drumming to the melody of squawking seagulls, clinking ping-pong balls and tinny arcade music. The soundtrack transports me even further back in time, to my younger years; pulling silly faces with Mum and Andrew in The Hall of Mirrors, our waists sucked in and our eyes as big as saucers; me and my cousin, Candice, high on E-numbers and tearing up the pier wearing Kiss Me Quick hats; me as a pre-teen, feeling queasy after riding The Big One and gorging on baby-pink candyfloss.

Tears prick my eyes as each happy memory swirls in and out of focus. Dad left soon after Andrew was born, but Mum made sure we never went without. I have little memory of him from my early years, and what I do remember I'd much rather forget. He was an alcoholic, or so Mum told me years later when I plucked up the courage to ask her why he'd abandoned us. It was obvious that she felt uncomfortable speaking about his failings, as though his inability to love and care for his children was somehow hers too.

Despite Dad's absence, I always felt loved, Mum made damn sure of that. I know I'm blessed to have had such an idyllic childhood, yet I can't help but feel a sense of grief, the nostalgia of being here in Blackpool both a blessing and a curse. No matter how much I remember Mum – her wide, toothy grin or her howling laughter – it's a sad fact that I'll never again feel the warmth of her body as she holds me close or hear her rich velvety voice telling me she loves me. And Andrew, my brother and best friend, his memory now bent out of shape by the hands of time. I don't remember his voice anymore, his laugh, the markings in his eyes. I could tell you they were brown, but that would be like describing the sky as blue or the sun as yellow.

If I don't look too closely at the boarded-up cafés or graffiti-clad benches, I can almost convince myself this is the Blackpool of old, the intrinsically British seaside town where fish and chips are eaten from vinegar-soaked newspaper, where happy families stroll arm in arm, and the distant squeals and screams from the Pleasure Beach rides cascade through the red-brick backstreets and along the heaving seafront. I do look too closely though, in fact it's all I can see, the grime and dirt, the poverty. I guess the world is no longer magical for me.

Daniel, perhaps sensing my change in mood, becomes restless in his stroller. Scooping him up, I hold him close and kiss the top of his head, breathing in his sweet scent. As he wraps his chubby arms around my neck I think, not for the first time, just how much he reminds me of Andrew. Not only does he have the same easy-going nature, but unlike me, who's as pale as death, he's also inherited the same black curly hair and tanned skin. Maybe, just maybe, through this little boy I can make new, happier memories.

'How about a ride on the big wheel, champ?' I point over to the Ferris wheel which, like everything else on the pier, looks fit for demolition. 'At least if it breaks down, we'll get a nice view, hey.'

'Look, there's the tower!' I squeal a minute later as our carriage reaches the highest point. Holding Daniel on my lap, I point out the gulls as they swoop down to the sandy swathes in search of titbits. My stomach lurches as the carriage rocks in the wind, and for a second I feel truly alive. On the descent, we wave at the long line of people in the queue, and Daniel, on instruction, blows kisses to an elderly couple huddled together on a bench. Skimming the ground, we ascend once more, and that's when it happens.

My breathing suddenly becomes rapid and shallow. Everything is spinning. I need to move, to stand up, to call for help, but an invisible hand is clamped over my mouth and I can't speak. 'Daniel, Daniel!' Wedging my arm beneath his ribcage, I squeeze him tight. He thrashes around, freeing himself. 'No, no. Please.' As we begin the descent, he starts to cry, but the sound is distant and muffled. I realise a panic attack is taking hold of me and I fear I'll pass out, leaving Daniel to climb over the bars and...

The ride stops. A faceless figure releases the safety catch and pulls us from the carriage. 'Y'all right, love?'

My legs tremble as they find solid ground. For a moment I don't understand what's happened, why a crowd of people are staring at me, why Daniel is gripping tightly hold of me as if his life depends on it.

Then I remember.

I've just caught sight of Justin.

GRACE
NOW

An officer enters the interview room and gestures for Detective Ambrose to step outside. She ends the interview and excuses herself, placing a hand lightly on my shoulder as she passes. 'Won't be a minute, Grace.'

I'm grateful for this small show of compassion, even if it's nothing more than a ploy to keep me talking. When she leaves, I turn to my solicitor who's slouched back in his chair. His trousers have ridden up and I see he's wearing Simpson socks. The sight of Homer Simpson swigging a can of Duff beer reminds me of TV dinners in front of the telly with Andrew, the two of us scoffing down turkey twisters and beans from trays on our laps. Mum was no Nigella. To be fair to her, she worked all the hours God sent as a secretary as well as cleaning Grandpa's church at the weekend so home cooking was a luxury she couldn't afford, though I doubt it would have made a difference anyway. Bless her, the most Mum ever came to à la carte was spelling out our names with alphabet spaghetti. I smile at the memory, aware that the apple hasn't fallen far from the tree in that regard. 'What do you think that's about?' I ask the solicitor, who shrugs in response, indicating he doesn't know or doesn't care – I figure it's most likely both.

Detective Ambrose re-enters the room and takes her seat. She's flushed red and her fringe has been blown into a semi-quiff. 'There's been a development.'

I open my mouth, then close it again as angry voices bustle past the open door, followed by a scream, a violent, raw scream like a wounded animal. 'Justin?'

She raises her eyebrows.

My body reacts as though she's just put a gun to my head. 'Daniel? Is he... alive? Is he... okay?'

She studies me for a moment, as though reluctant to say.

'Just tell me!' I clench my hands into fists.

'Daniel is still missing.'

I have no time to react as suddenly Justin appears at the open doorway, shouting and swearing, his bare feet dragging along the ground as he's pulled along by four uniformed officers.

'He's my fucking son, you bastards!' he spits. 'Why would I hurt him?' He turns, looks directly at me, his reddened eyes pleading. 'Tell them the truth,' he cries, again and again, each plea growing more distant. Then he's gone.

GRACE

18 DAYS EARLIER

'Do you need an ambulance?'

I look up at the ride operator for the first time since he pulled me from the carriage. He's a weedy bloke, all shaggy grey hair and haggard skin, as though somebody's left him out in the sun and forgot to water him. 'No, no, I'm fine, honestly.'

'Come and have a sit down,' he says as he gently steers me away from the onlookers and over to a vacant wooden bench. 'You stay there. Had a stroller, didn't you?'

'Thanks, yeah,' I mutter.

He marches back across the pier. Heat burns my cheeks as I imagine what the other riders made of my panic attack; what if my frantic screaming caused them to question their own safety? And Daniel? Imagine if he now grows up with a fear of heights?

The familiar feeling of guilt awakens a memory long buried; Mum shuffling onto the porch, her body stooped, skin the colour of ash, a course, pink dressing gown hanging like a dead weight from her wire-thin frame; me, on the other side of the door, university textbooks stuffed under my arm, a thick pane of glass separating us. I knew Mum had been diagnosed with cancer, but the oncologists were optimistic they could cure it.

Stage One they'd said – nothing much to panic about. I'd only been away at Exeter half a term – six weeks. How had I returned to a ghost?

I didn't know who Mum was anymore, what to say to her, how to comfort her. The look of horror in my eyes must have said it all. She reached out a shaky hand, her sickly skin thin and taut over veins and bone as she clutched my arm and mouthed the words that will haunt me forever – 'I'm sorry.'

We made it as far as the hallway before I broke down. 'Tell me! I have to know!'

'There's nothing more they can do.'

I hit the ground, my entire body folding in on itself. First Andrew, and now Mum. She couldn't leave me too, she just couldn't.

'Come on, darling. Please, Grace.' A thud followed by a whimper, the sound of a wounded animal scratching at the wall.

My eyes flew open. 'No, Mum, no, no!' I crawled over to her, but despite her frailty, I couldn't scrape her broken body up off the floor. That's when I experienced my first ever panic attack.

To this day it breaks my heart that it was Mum who found the inner strength to drag herself off the floor and ring an ambulance for me. We didn't know it then, but she was six days away from her last breath, ovarian cancer robbing her of everything but an instinctual mother's strength.

After Mum died, I hit rock bottom. The pain of losing her was too much to handle, and over the coming months my mind plummeted further and further into darkness. I was dead inside, a corpse trapped in a world which no longer had purpose. I quit university as there was just no way I could focus on my studies. If it wasn't for my then best friend, Rob, who has since married my cousin, Candice, I'd never have gotten through those dark days. He saved me, in every way a person could be saved. I know without doubt I owe him my life.

'Here you go, love, this the one?' I jump at the sight of the ride guy, towering over me, one spindly hand on Daniel's stroller. I'm grateful for the distraction. I already have enough on my mind without having to revisit that period of my life – what I did after Mum died and the impact that had on everyone around me. I don't think I'll ever be able to forgive myself for that.

'Yes, that's it.' I attempt an apologetic smile, but thoughts are still firmly with Mum in that hallway. 'Sorry.' I push away the memory. 'Just got a bit of a shock, that's all.'

'Shock' is putting it mildly. One minute I was pointing down to the airplane ride and making Daniel laugh with whooshing noises, the next thing I was looking straight into the waltzers watching Justin bounce around the rotating platform and spin a car of excitable girls who shrieked and screamed in protest. There was no mistaking him, I'd know him anywhere; his gait, the way he hopped from one foot to the other, the unique way he dressed – oversized hoodie, baggy jeans, a backwards baseball cap.

I don't recall much after that, just the terror of gasping at air only to discover there was none, and Daniel, squirming in my arms and crying out.

'As long as you're all right. Shit me right up, you did.' Ride Guy's laugh quickly becomes a hacking cough. His mouth houses only a squatter's-worth of stained teeth, and yet there's something gentle about him.

'I'm sorry,' I say again, dropping my gaze back down to Daniel who is still unusually quiet. 'We'll go get ice cream soon, honey,' I whisper into his ear. This raises the smallest of smiles, though his eyes remain downcast. I lightly trace a love heart on his back while silently praying Ride Guy gets the hint and leaves us be. It's not that I'm not grateful for his help, but I desperately need to think.

'Right then, love,' he says, begrudgingly, 'I'd best be off.'

I get the impression he was looking forward to a ten-minute skive under the guise of helping a woman in distress.

I strap Daniel back into his stroller and forage a biscuit from the depths of his pram bag. 'Here you go, buddy.' He takes it cautiously, still untrusting of me. I can't blame him; I must have terrified him. With my mind a carousel of thoughts and my heart thumping in my chest, I head towards the waltzers.

9

JUSTIN
NOW

The detective saunters into the room, eyes on mine. He carries a manila folder in one hand, a mug of something steaming in the other. He sits at the table facing me but says nothing as he arranges papers in front of him like chess pieces.

I reach forward and grab his jacket sleeve. 'Have you found Daniel?'

He stops, looks at my hand on his arm with one eyebrow raised. I tighten my grip.

'Have you found him? Tell me!'

'Take your hand off me,' he says quietly.

We lock eyes for a while. I have to know if Daniel is all right. But I know I'm not going to achieve anything by antagonising him. I let go.

He straightens the spread of papers, making sure there are equidistant gaps between each, then switches on the digital voice recorder on the desk and introduces himself as DC Gorman, resuming the interview with Justin Roberts.

I flop back in my chair. 'I just need to know if he's okay, where he is.'

'There's no news yet,' he says. 'Maybe *you* can help us find him?'

'Me? How do *I* know where he is?'

DC Gorman weighs me up, his suspicion obvious. 'What have you done with him?'

'I haven't done anything with him. Why would I?'

'You were the last person with him.'

Images of earlier today tumble through my mind like a kaleidoscope – listening for a breath; my hands frantically pumping up and down; a crowd of faces; having to leave; running; panic; gagging...

'Let's go back to why you walked out on Grace two years ago,' continues the detective.

'And my friend? Is *he* okay?' I interrupt.

'You just answer the questions, and I'll make sure I find out. How does that sound?' DC Gorman's voice is patronising, weary. 'Now, why did you walk out on Grace?'

'I didn't want to, but things had become complicated between me and her.'

'Complicated. Like how?'

'Just... awkward. Everything I did, I did to protect Grace.' I say it with all the conviction I can muster, but in truth, I wonder if it was more about looking after myself. I lean forward, put my hands flat on the table. 'You are still looking for Daniel, though, right?'

He ignores the question again. 'Awkward. In what way?'

'We both weren't being honest with each other.'

'How were you not being honest?'

'Are you still looking for Daniel? Yes or no?'

He rubs his hands up and down his cheeks and sighs. Like me, it's obvious he's not getting what he wants to hear. But he's not going to.

'Yes, we're still looking for him. But something tells me you know more than you're letting on. If you know anything about where Daniel might be, about what could have happened to him, you have to tell me right now. This is serious, Mr Roberts. Do you have any idea of the charges you're looking at?'

'I'm telling you everything. I don't know what else you want me to say. I have no idea where Daniel could be. All I know is that he could be out there dying somewhere and you're dicking around asking me the same things over and over.'

'And I'll keep asking you all night if you don't start telling me what really happened. It's your choice, Mr Roberts. I'm going nowhere.' He crosses his arms, indicating he's ready for a long wait.

I feel the rage rising, but there's nothing I can do. I shake my head and stare him out as he repeats the questions again with theatrical weariness.

'So your girlfriend told you she was pregnant. You walked out on her. Why?'

'Because if I hadn't, she'd have lost everything.'

'What would she have lost?'

'It's complicated.'

'So you keep saying.'

Our eyes lock. The silence is tangible. He decides he's not going to get more along that line and switches tack.

'You went to Blackpool. Tell me again, why Blackpool, and why for two years?'

'I've told you already! I knew a mate from when I was growing up there. Said I could stay with him for a few nights. He sorted me out with a job, on the pier, and I just never went back.'

'For two years.' He taps a pen on his chin. 'For two years you never went back?'

'Correct.'

'And you never saw Grace again?'

'Nope. Not till that day in Blackpool.'

JUSTIN
18 DAYS EARLIER

'Nine tickets, love,' I shout over the music.

The largest of the three giggling girls passes me a sweaty fistful of stubs, and I slam the safety rail down into the latch. 'Oi, mister, you nearly had me nose off then.'

'I bet that's not all he wants to have off,' says another.

I force my best smile before giving their waltzer car a neck-jarring spin and moving on to the next customers.

Buzzing vibe, easy money and plenty of beaver. It's a fanny magnet, a breeze. That's how my mate, Garth, 'sold' me the job of working the waltzers. Only it isn't; the 'buzzing' vibe is an ear-splitting hammering of eighties songs; the money is crap, and I wouldn't touch 'the beaver' with a sterilised bargepole, even if I wanted to, which I don't. What I do want is normality, or at least anything but this, but right now I have no choice.

I weave my way through the cars to a smart-dressed dad who is carefully seating his two young kids between him and his wife, reassuring their worried little faces that all will be okay. 'Hold on to your mum and dad now,' I say to the kids, then give the car the very gentlest of spins. The ride is only half full, so I lean on the painted, psychedelic central booth and wait to see if there are any more takers. I watch the family as the car rotates slowly, revealing and concealing their smiling faces like a G-rated peep show. The man catches me staring and I smile instinctively, but it's a smile that hides an envy.

Other families on the pier stroll up and down, some holding hands, some holding cans. I feel resentment growing when I see one young couple leaning on the ticket machines, both tapping on their phones and ignoring a glum little girl with blonde ringlets staring up at them. Bring your daughter on a family day out then spend all your time with your head in a screen! Tossers. I want to go over and tell them, but they'd probably just think I was going to mug them. I mean, look at me. Who wouldn't think that? I look down at my torn Reeboks, my oily hands, and my ripped jeans. Regret and shame surface again as I trace the scar that runs from my forehead to my right cheek. This is not who I am.

It should have been so different. If I hadn't been forced to leave, it would be me taking my family out, not stood here on the wrong side of the neon. The thought makes me wonder what my child looks like now. I tried to look Grace up on social media, of course, but she never got the whole social sharing thing, didn't see the point in letting the world know what she had for lunch or where she went at the weekend. I'd want to know, but I guess I never will.

A pimply teenage couple sit in one of the cars. I take their tickets then retake my place at the booth and nod to see if Lee thinks we should start the ride or wait. He holds up his hand, signals three more minutes, and goes back to reading *The Sun*. My phone buzzes in my back pocket. 'For fuck's sake,' I mouth, shaking my head as I jab out a response – *No Garth, I'm working. Get your own bloody beer.*

A foghorn sound blasts through the speakers and makes me jump as Lee hits the sound-effects buttons to try and attract attention one last time. Out of the corner of my eye I see another person step onto the ride, silhouetted by the coloured, flashing spotlights that Lee has set into a frenzied dance. *Saddo*, I think, *who goes on the waltzer alone?* I push myself off the booth to direct them to an empty car, but the figure strides past them all and carries on straight towards me. I lift a hand to shield my eyes from the blinding beams criss-crossing the ride and get a glimpse of a woman, a redhead. She's not alone as I first thought, she's carrying a child. My phone clatters onto the metal floor as a finger points directly in my face.

It's Grace.

11

JUSTIN
18 DAYS EARLIER

Her lips are moving fast, her eyes manic like a rabid dog, but I can't hear what she's saying.

I try to say something, but my mouth dries up. As if in a hallucinogenic dream, my entire focus zooms in to her angry face, its colour changing rhythmically with every beat of the bass. Venom spits from pursed lips that form angry shapes but whose words are drowned in a cacophony of sound. And below Grace's chin, in her arms, a boy looks up, open-mouthed, mesmerised by the kaleidoscope of colours and noise around him. My son! This has to be my son!

'Jus!' Lee is shouting from the booth, making a circular motion with his index finger to tell me the ride is starting.

I hold both hands up, mouthing, 'Wait, wait.' He shrugs his shoulders questioningly. The banging music, the explosions of colours, the swirling of the cars and the sudden appearance of Grace and my son is all too much. I feel like my head is on fire, like I'm about to empty my stomach right here and now. I grab hold of Grace's elbow and lead her behind the booth where the speakers are quieter. I can't distinguish how I feel amidst the bombardment of emotions detonating in my brain.

Grace has stopped talking but her gaze swishes like a switchblade from one of my eyes to the other. *Say something, anything*, I urge myself. 'Grace, I... I...'

Her mouth shapes the word 'what' and she just keeps shaking her head, her eyes still crazy like she doesn't believe what she's seeing. 'Justin...'

The very sound of her saying my name throws more conflicting emotions into the mix.

The finger-pointing starts again now, only this time I can feel it jabbing on my chest. The boy's gaze fixes on the tears that flow down his mum's cheeks as she screams in my face. 'Two years! Two years without a word. Do you know what I've gone through?'

I hold my hands up in defence. 'I need to explain. You have to know why I left, why I've never been in touch, with you... or my son.' I reach out to touch his shoulder, to touch my son for the first time ever. Grace shoves me back and turns her body, shielding him from me.

The jabbing finger has now curled into a fist. I seriously think she's going to punch me, but her delivery hurts much worse than that.

'Oh no. No you don't. You'll never be his dad, ever! You lost all rights to that when you walked out on us.'

I suddenly feel like I'm falling, as if all my breath, my blood, my bones have been taken away. For two years I clung to a vision of seeing this boy, calling him my son, hugging, holding, kissing him, and now I'm in free fall, frantically searching for something to hold on to as that dream evaporates. 'No, Grace. Please. You can't...'

She pulls the boy in front of her, cups his chin in her hand. 'Take a good look, Justin. This is the last time you'll ever see him.' She shakes her head in disgust again, her face a picture of pure hatred, then turns and walks away with the boy, *my* boy.

Lee opens the door of the booth and leans out. 'C'mon, we're starting.'

'Grace!' I shout. 'Please!' but she carries on walking. 'We can talk.'

Shit, shit, shit. I can't just let her go. 'Lee! Give me a pen and piece of paper, quick.'

'What?'

'Pen, paper, now!'

I scribble on the paper then give it to Lee.

'You gotta do this for me, mate. That girl with the red hair.' I point. 'Holding the kid. Give this to her and don't let her say no, all right? Go!'

'You sad git,' says Lee, tutting. 'You owe me one, yeah?'

12

GRACE
NOW

'It took me a day and a half to ring him,' I admit to Detective Ambrose. 'I wasn't going to, I hated him.' I catch myself – *hate* is a strong word, particularly when talking to an officer of the law and especially given the charges against me. 'Okay, I didn't hate him, but I was furious with him, seething. You understand that, right?'

Detective Ambrose nods.

My eyes fall down to her ring finger and I see there's a white indention where a wedding ring once was. *What's her story?* I wonder. Does she, like me, know how it feels to be betrayed? To have the person you love the most in the world abandon you when you needed them the most.

She catches me staring and sighs. Almost ashamedly, she covers the offending hand with the other. 'I'd be pissed off if it were me, Grace.'

Tears prick my eyes. It's important to me that this lady believes me when I say that I never meant to get into the situation I did, that usually I'm not that sort of person, but anger, betrayal... they can make monsters out of all of us.

'I finally made contact on the Saturday night because I was

35

desperate to know why he left me. And also, I had to know why he was hiding away in Blackpool. What had I done so wrong to force him to choose that life – a life away from me?' My voice hardens. Quickly, I remind myself that I'm still under caution and everything I say can, and likely will, be held against me. 'There were too many questions that needed answering,' I say, forcing calm into my voice. 'I had to know, no matter how much it hurt. And also...' I pause, unsure of how much I should divulge.

'Also what, Grace?' she urges. 'You have to tell me everything.'

Taking a deep breath, I admit the real reason I invited Justin to the house that night.

13

GRACE
16 DAYS EARLIER

I press my nose against the cold pane of glass and glance both left and right. Dark clouds spit at the ground while lamp posts throw lazy pools of light onto the street. Apart from this, the scene is still and grey, like an old photograph. Justin messaged over two hours ago to say he'd just caught the train to Manchester and would jump on a bus from there. Where the hell is he? How, after two years, am I *still* the one waiting?

Moving away from the window, I collapse down onto the sofa and refill a wine glass to the brim – Pinot Noir, cheap and strong, the perfect combination. The repetitive drumming of rain against the windowpane accompanies the low murmur of the television. I switch it off and drink in silence for a while, praying my self-confidence lies at the bottom of the bottle.

My phone pings.

Just jumped in a taxi. 2 mins

A rush of adrenaline sends my heart racing. Panic or excitement? In truth, the two are physiologically identical. The only difference is the emotion we attach to it. I learned this from

Justin, his fascination with the mind interesting, if not a little disturbing. I guess having an abusive childhood meant he always had an obsession with human behaviour; conscience, or lack of, what shapes a human, nature versus nurture. 'Is anyone all good or all bad, Grace?' he'd ask, his forehead creasing under the weight of consideration. I never really entertained the question, replying rather flippantly that good people do bad things and vice versa. Of course, I realise now that life's big questions are rarely answered in the time it takes to drink a cuppa.

Perhaps I ought to ask myself the same question now. Where am I on the morality scale compared to Justin? And more importantly, will the scales tip in his favour or mine after tonight?

14

JUSTIN
16 DAYS EARLIER

The taxi passes the corner shop where Grace would send me jogging for Saturday night treats on our nights in, the tiny post office where Grace would frantically rush to catch the last post with yet another belated birthday card for a distant relative; the tea shop where I would retreat after trailing round the shops after her on another quest to find the perfect soap holder, cushion cover, toast rack or other knick-knack that would 'finish off our home'.

Each place brings back a flood of memories, all good, but all making me more nervous as I measure the shortening distance to Grace's house.

'Stop here, mate,' I blurt out to the taxi driver.

'You sure?' he asks. 'The house is only just down this road.'

'Yeah, I'm sure.' I pay him and step out into the torrential downpour. I'm happy to face the drenching, but I'm not ready to face her yet. Will I ever be? My heart beats ten to the dozen as I trudge through the rain wondering what I'll say, what Grace will say, how she'll be with me, what I'll say to my son, how he'll be with me. What if he hates me, rejects me? What if they both do?

15

GRACE

Draining the last of the wine, I heave myself up off the sofa and check my appearance in the wall-mounted mirror, a huge wood-framed monstrosity that I picked up from IKEA a few years back. When it became clear that Justin wasn't coming back, I got rid of all our quirky, kitsch furniture and replaced it with flat-pack, mass-produced crap that has about as much character as Innkeeper One in Grandpa's annual nativity play. What's Justin going to make of it all, I wonder; the beige walls, the brown carpet, the trio of beechwood frames with corny quotes about life.

Dance like nobody's watching.

Life is what happens to you when you're making other plans.

Live each day as if it's your last.

I mean, what would that last one actually look like in reality? If I knew I was going to die tomorrow, I'd spend the entire day hyperventilating into a large glass of red. Not dissimilar to today, granted.

I cringe at my reflection. I've fixed my hair into a loose bun, aiming for classy chic, but in reality it only emphasises my sunken cheeks and long, bony neck. Ripping it out, I attempt to tame the mass of curls, but to no avail. Tears of frustration prick my eyes. Why do I even care about my appearance anyway? It's not as if *those* feelings for Justin are there anymore; the need for his approval, to have him find me attractive.

I know I ought to stop lying to myself, but it's difficult to break a habit of a lifetime.

I'm drawn away from my ghoulish appearance to Daniel's toy box, reflected in the mirrored glass. He's obsessed with animals, so for his birthday, I upcycled a cheap storage box and spent hours painstakingly painting on monkeys, lions and giraffes by hand. A set of wooden cars and half a track are still strewn across the carpet from where he was playing with them earlier today. I consider tidying them but think better of it. Let Justin see that life has continued without him. That we're doing fine.

I was nineteen when I started dating Justin. It was a year after Mum's death and, although I'd inherited her house, *this* house, I was living with my Aunt Clara and Candice, twenty miles away in Manchester. I couldn't face rattling around in the same house that was once filled with Mum's love and laughter. Everything was a reminder of what I'd lost, from Mum's oversized, olive-green armchair by the window which still held her indentation long after she'd been put in the ground, to the tea-stained 'World's Best Mum' mug which hung on the cup rack in the kitchen.

It was while I was living with Aunt Clara and Candice that I really struggled with my weight. Within months I went from a curvy size twelve to a sickly size six. I was little more than skin and bone, my knees only touching when I forced them to. It wasn't as though I woke up one morning and decided to starve myself. After Mum's death I developed a permanent lump in my throat which meant I couldn't swallow. Aunt Clara sent me for tests at the doctors but they soon discovered that there was nothing wrong with me, at least not physically. I'm unsure when starving myself became intentional – I guess I was just so desperate to fade away back then. What better way to do that than to physically disappear?

I first met Justin in a pub close to where Aunt Clara lived. Candice had dragged me out one Friday night against my will, something which still regularly happens despite my protests. I was wearing an oversized black jumper over flared cords to hide my skeletal form. I didn't care much for make-up in those days and, before the invention of GHDs my hair likely resembled a bird's nest. I must have looked hideous, though I remember Justin looked out of place, too, in a washed-out T-shirt and ripped jeans. Some ripped jeans were fashionable at that time but his were just old and in need of the bin. It was Candice who initially struck up a conversation with Justin, announcing rather loudly to a pub full of drinkers that she 'fancied a bit of rough'. I'd held back, not wanting to be seen. Despite Justin's lackadaisical approach to dressing, I fancied him the minute I saw him; his eyes were a deep blue-grey, like the colour of storm clouds – striking against his almost black, tousled hair which he kept pushing his fingers through in an attempt to keep it from his eyes.

It was obvious within seconds he had zero interest in Candice. I smile now at the memory of her sauntering back over to me, one manicured hand wrapped around the neck of her WKD bottle as though contemplating using it as a weapon. 'He's a puff. Has to be.'

'Reckon I could do a turn though,' Justin joked an hour later when he approached me at the bar. 'Just don't go telling my boyfriend.'

With the memory still fresh in my mind, I pour another glass of red, gulping it down like a refugee who hasn't seen water for a week.

After tonight, Justin's memory will be all I have left.

16

GRACE
16 DAYS EARLIER

Although I'm expecting it, a sudden knock on the door sends my pulse racing.

It's time.

'Thanks for agreeing to this.' Justin stares down at the ground, his bottom lip between his teeth. I remember he does this when he's nervous, an outward sign of his vulnerability. In our past life I found it cute, but now he just looks like an oversized toddler.

'I'm not doing it for you.' There's a beat of silence as we each consider what comes next. He stuffs his hands into the front pocket of his hoodie, the hood pulled tight around his face.

'You best come in then.' I step back, allowing him inside. He leans in to kiss me on the cheek and in response I make an involuntary grumbling noise in my throat, a sort of wordless rebuttal. It's awkward. There's no other way to describe it, though I'd rather be awkward than fake. At least awkwardness is a genuine emotion and not one that can be easily fabricated.

I go through to the living room and perch on the edge of the armchair. The front door latch clicks shut and the sound of wet boots squeaking on the hallway's laminate floor means at least he hasn't legged it again. *There's still time.* He hesitates as he reaches the doorway.

'What?'

'Should I take my shoes off?'

'If you don't mind.'

'You hate carpet,' he questions, as he bends down to unlace his boots. Rainwater drips from his dark fringe into his eyes. He sniffs up noisily.

'It's safer with a toddler.'

'Fair enough.' He practically marches across the room but lowers himself down onto the sofa hesitantly, as though expecting an electric shock in the backside. It's all wrong, I'm sat in his space and he's in mine. 'You mind if I?' He pulls at his hoodie. 'I'm wringing.'

'Be my guest.'

Underneath, he's wearing a plain, white T-shirt. It's too big for him and washed out of shape. I can't imagine he bought it new, more likely a dead man's cast-off from a charity shop. He's lost a lot of weight and he never really had any to lose in the first place. It makes him appear odd, as though his arms and legs are too long for his body. His once thick mop of hair has thinned and, rather than the taper and fade cut which suited his angular face, it's now a dull mess of kinks and curls.

He wrings the hoodie between his hands, further soaking his jeans.

'You want me to stick that in the dryer for you?'

'It's fine.'

His unsettled eyes glance around the room before finally resting on Daniel's toy box. 'How is...'

'You want a drink?' I interrupt, already standing.

He shakes his head. 'I'm trying to cut back.'

'I meant tea.'

'Right.' He glances up at me. 'Is he in bed?'

'You're not seeing him.' The rebuff comes out too fast.

'I didn't say...'

'I know.' *Chill it, Grace.* 'Sorry, okay, it's just... awkward.' This isn't going well, certainly not the way I planned it out in my head.

'Thanks for agreeing to see me.'

'You've already used that line,' I snap. 'Practised what you were going to say on the journey here, have you?'

'I did, actually.' The shadow of a smile flashes across his face. It dislodges the tension.

'You're a twat, you know that?' Our eyes lock and in an instant it's back; the chemistry, the desire, a bellyful of tiny explosions or whatever other flowery adjectives people use to describe the indescribable. Do I still love Justin? Am I still *in love* with him? Shit! It makes the situation so much harder; how can I now do what I'd planned to?

'You're right, Grace. I am a twat. It was a twatty thing to do.' He stops, his eyes pleading with me to let him off the hook, to forgive him without a single explanation. *It was a twatty thing to do?* What does he take me for? Anger burns like acid in my throat, yet the feeling in my stomach... what even is it? Love, lust, desire? How the hell can I be simultaneously experiencing this many conflicting emotions?

'Just tell me why you left?'

He sighs. 'It's complicated. I don't expect you to understand.' The moment has gone, the wall back up and I fear it's too high for either of us to scale.

'Don't patronise me, Justin.' My voice splinters. I'm aware I have to rein it in. Becoming emotional was never part of the plan.

'I think I will have that drink, Grace,' he says.

'I thought you said you were cutting back?'

'I meant tea.'

I suppress a smile. 'You still drink it like a kid?'

'You know me too well.'

Do I? I'm not sure I do anymore.

17

JUSTIN
16 DAYS EARLIER

I follow her into the kitchen, lean against the worktop and watch as she takes the milk out of the fridge door.

'See you're still into those crappy ready meals.' My voice makes her jump and she spills a little milk on the top. I can tell she's on edge.

'You know cooking's never been my strong point.'

That's an understatement. 'I don't know, you were pretty good at spag bol.'

The compliment goes unnoticed, her expression still stone cold.

'He's got a bit of artist in him.' I trace a finger over lumpy streaks of orange and black that cover a piece of paper. It's fastened to the fridge with a colourful magnet showing a beach scene below the name, Rhyl. Another family holiday I missed.

'It's a tiger. He loves tigers,' says Grace over her shoulder as she sponges at the spilt milk.

'You haven't told me his name.'

She hesitates. 'It's Daniel.'

I say the name to myself, over and over. 'I thought your first choice was always Noah?'

'You always said it was too churchy,' she says, pouring water over the tea bags.

'Daniel,' I repeat. 'I like it. Still biblical though. He fought lions, didn't he?'

She turns and hands me the tea. 'Right, no more stalling. Tell me why you left. Then once I know,' she says, 'you can get the hell out of our lives for good.'

Our eyes lock as I take the mug. She's not for being diverted. Can't blame her though. I've been an idiot, but not in the way she thinks. I know I'm a mess, not good enough. I never have been, despite her reassurances back when times were better. Well, finally, I've proved I was right and she was wrong. *What a victory!* Deep down, I was aware she knew that all along. When she was trying to convince me, trying to lift me out of my black hole, I think she was trying to convince herself too. But words are easy. Anyone can speak, anybody can listen. Believing is different, and I can now see in her eyes that all that belief, if there ever was any, has gone.

Despite that, there's still something in the way she holds my gaze. Something in the way her eyelids partly shield those olive-green windows to her soul that suggests there's more than just anger. Her words say she's made her mind up, but her eyes are still searching for something. But for what? The truth? For me to go, to leave her alone? Or to stay? For a night? Forever?

'I miss your brews, Grace.' *You idiot, Justin. That's it? She's in need and you compliment her tea-making ability?*

'It's really changed,' I say, now back in the living room.

'It's more practical, for a child.' She sits down.

I nod.

'Not that *you'd* know.'

I ignore the dig. 'It doesn't seem...'

'What?'

'Like... your kind of style, like it's someone else's choice, you

48

know?'

'Unbelievable!'

She's back on her feet, her finger and her words jabbing at me like a blade.

Nice one, Justin. You take off for two years then you accuse her of seeing someone else. Give that man a round of applause.

'I'm sorry, I didn't mean it like that.' But I did, of course. It would be a natural assumption for anybody with as much insecurity as I have.

'Do you want to leave? Right now!' She's pointing at the door.

'Sorry... sorry... I just...'

'You're here to answer questions, not to ask them.'

I hold my hands up in submission.

She sits back down. 'Start talking. Why did you leave?' She cups the mug with both hands in front of her mouth, concealing any reaction.

I know those lips, how they first tremble as the tears well up, then downturn like a five-year-old when she can no longer hold it in. I remember she's a cute crier, how her vulnerability was my strength, rare moments when it was my time to play the knight in shining armour.

There's no armour to hide behind right now. I take a deep breath. 'To be honest, I was shit-scared.'

I stare. She stares. Obviously, that's not going to cut it.

'You know what happened with my dad... what he did,' I continue. It's a cheap ploy, playing on my childhood and the abuse I suffered both at the hands of my parents and in care, but what choice do I have? She can never find out the actual truth. This is my one lifeline back to some kind of normal life. There's no way I'm throwing this chance away, no matter what. 'I was worried I'd end up like him.'

She speaks from behind the cup, her expression unchanged:

'You're a grown man, you can't use him as an excuse.'

I look away, remembering. My jaw tightens.

She places the cup on the table. 'You're nothing like your dad, Justin.' Her voice is softer now, like she's reassuring a child.

I'm taken aback by this sudden show of compassion, a sign that maybe she does still have belief in me. Even when I was homeless, on the edge, she would quietly talk me round from my need for self-destruction. I was unworthy, still am, but she would persuade me otherwise, albeit momentarily.

It was Grace who encouraged me to do more with my life. She told me that someone with my IQ could do anything I set my mind to. She was the one who encouraged me to put the time in on my Open University psychology degree. But it was me who ultimately decided to quit, unable to attend the in-class sessions with all those bright sparks with genuine talent and intelligence. Yes, I've always been a deep thinker, and yes, I could always more than hold my own in a philosophical conversation, but there was no way I was going to risk being shot down in front of a whole classroom. More than letting myself down, I felt I'd failed Grace, my prevailing cheerleader.

I turn back to her. She's leaning forward, legs uncrossed, her head tilted slightly to one side, eyes locked on mine. We've been here a thousand times before and each time reinforces my belief that she is quite simply the best person I have ever known.

'Your dad was a violent alcoholic,' she says, 'and you...'

'Are just an alcoholic,' I joke. Was there a slight smile? I lean in too. 'I never meant to stay away. I guess I panicked. I'd just gotten used to the idea that we would never have a kid. In my mind, I'd convinced myself that it was always going to be me and you. And then... well, you got pregnant and it was like, shit! How could someone like me raise a child? I can barely look after myself.' I sigh for effect. Every word has been practised on the way here, but now, spoken aloud, it all sounds so wooden.

The reality is that everything I'm saying is true, but that truth is just the tip of an iceberg and everything underwater is a mound of lies.

'I understand that,' says Grace, 'but why didn't you just talk to me?'

She scrunches her hair. Like many things in Grace's life, it's changed. It's much longer now, tumbling in red ringlets all the way past her breasts. She always complained about it, said it was unruly, and was forever smothering it with some dye or other. I went along with whatever she wanted – the blondes have more fun phase, the fifty shades of red period. It's nice to see her natural hair for once, a rusty auburn, the same colour as the best present she said I ever gave her, a tarnished copper bracelet I restored from a flea market. I notice she isn't wearing it. With all these changes, it makes me wonder if she was ever being true to herself when I was around, or was she trying to be what she thought I wanted her to be.

'I don't know why I couldn't say anything,' I continue. 'I just freaked. I needed space to think. Then hours became days, days became weeks, and then it was too long, too awkward. I didn't know how to face you again. I didn't think you'd want to see me. Eventually those weeks became years.'

I know how shit that sounds, how much I've missed out on the life of that beautiful child in the framed photo on the mantelpiece. I get off the sofa and pick up the picture. This boy – *my* boy – has no idea I even exist. As far as he's aware, he doesn't have a dad, just like me. The thought of that common ground kills me.

I just want my son to have the chance to do those things I missed out on when I was growing up – to kick a ball around with his dad, to be held, to be told how proud his dad is, to know that he'll always be there for him.

Grace gets up and stands beside me.

'Can I see him, please?' I ask. *Damn! Whose voice was that? So quiet, pleading, pathetic?*

'I think you should go.' She says it quietly, but it shatters the silence.

She's close, so close I can feel the heat radiating from her body. She turns towards me, her hand brushing against mine. 'This is all pointless, Justin. Please, just go.'

I don't know what to say, so I say nothing and just stare into her eyes. I see the same warmth, kindness and affection that I've seen on the pillow so many times. But I also see sadness, loss, and resignation. Is this it? Is this the end?

'We could be a family,' I say. It sounds desperate and the words hang in the air. Her lips begin to quiver.

'We can't,' she says. 'It's too late.' I can see her fighting to stop the downturn in her mouth. 'Please go. Now.'

I want to hold her, but I know she'll lose her battle against the tears and if that happens, I can't guarantee I won't cry too. I've already acted like a dick, I don't want to look like one as well, not here, not now.

I grit my teeth, then turn and head to the front door, stooping to put on my boots while I secretly bundle Daniel's picture into my sodden hoodie. 'I know I've been a complete twat, Grace, but I promise I will never let you down again. I don't want to lose you and Daniel... so if there's any way you can put all this in the past, well... I'm here, you know?'

I open the door and quickly glance back. She's still holding back the tears but I can see they're close. 'I'm sorry.' What else can I say? I've never meant anything more in my life, but it still sounds hollow. I look up at the leaden sky and consider putting my hood up against the rain but decide not to. I deserve to get soaked.

18

GRACE

16 DAYS EARLIER

I slam the door before my mouth begs him to stay, and stand in the hallway for a long time, my head and heart pulling in different directions. A part of me is incredulous at his cockiness, his belief that he can just waltz back into my life. Then there's the other voice, the one I'm trying hard to ignore.

With a heavy heart, I make my way up the stairs and into the box room, which I spent months painstakingly transforming into a nursery. Despite the constant nausea and crippling backache, I'd heaved myself up ladders to restore an old wooden cot that a member of the church congregation had donated, even kitting it out with a patchwork quilt and a knitted mobile. Although losing Justin had all but crippled me – both financially and emotionally – I was more content than I'd ever been in my life because I had something much more precious than Justin. I had our little baby boy growing inside of me, his kicks like a thousand champagne bubbles popping, a celebration of knowing I didn't have to be on my own for long.

Switching on the lamp, I allow the tears to fall. The room remains frozen in time, the smell of paint still fresh from having never being aired out; newborn baby clothes in white and blue lie folded on the dresser, freshly washed and ready to be put away. I don't want to look up at the stencil on the wall, to read *those* words, but I do anyway. Perhaps I want to punish myself for what I've done.

Every child is a story yet to be told.

Only our baby boy's story ended abruptly, his life over before it had ever really begun. I blink away tears, his name in italics beneath the quote. Noah.

It was just after I'd peeled back the sticky-back plastic on his name stencil when I felt the warm trickle between my legs. At first I thought I'd wet myself. It was only as I put my hand there and saw the blood that I knew something was badly wrong. Barely able to speak, I called the midwife, who urged me to get to a hospital. At eighteen weeks' gestation, a pool of blood was not good, not good at all.

We never made it to hospital, Noah and I. He died right here on the nursery floor, no bigger than a baby bird, perfect in every way. I held his tiny lifeless body for the longest time, my life over in every way but physically. The experts didn't understand why it had happened, only that 'it wasn't my fault'. But it was. My body, which for years had denied me the chance to be a mother, had found a new, crueller way to punish me for starving it for so long.

If it wasn't for Candice and Rob, I'm certain I'd have ended my life. They were by my side every step of the way, through the endless days of heartbreak, the denial, anger, and gut-wrenching pain that I could never describe in words.

'I'm pregnant, Grace,' confessed Candice a month after Noah's death, her eyes brimming with tears. 'We never meant for this to happen, not with what you're going through.'

I wasn't angry at them. How could I be? Their gain couldn't make my loss any greater.

Their son, Daniel, was born two months to the day of Noah's due date.

Daniel, my beautiful second cousin, the baby boy I've been child-minding for the past fourteen months.

19

GRACE
NOW

The detective's eyes are softer now, exposing her natural compassion for the first time since the interview began. I wonder whether it's an advantage or a hindrance to somebody in law enforcement, to have the ability to empathise? To see beyond the offence committed. She must witness some truly repulsive acts in her line of work, hideous human beings who would turn even the strongest of stomachs.

Am I such a human? I don't feel that way, but actions speak louder than words.

In the last three hours I've bared so much of myself to Detective Inspector Ambrose – or Sally, as I've now come to know her. I've exposed it all; the scars, lies, hurt; the more I confess, the more human she becomes. And so do I.

'I'm really sorry to hear about Noah,' she says, maintaining eye contact. That in itself is a rarity. People seldom know what to say to the mother of a stillborn.

'Thank you.' I hold back the memory of Noah. I can't allow myself to go there, not now. Although what happened to him was a catalyst for what followed, it doesn't justify it, and I'm mindful to not wallow in self-pity.

'So you had Justin believe he was Daniel's father? And you, his mother?'

'Yes,' I admit, mortified. 'I didn't set out to lie, he just assumed, that day on the pier. I guess I wanted to hurt him, but only in that moment. I invited him to the house intending to tell him the truth but...' *Why didn't I just tell him?* This is a question I struggle to answer, the one that's kept me awake at night since this whole thing began. Was it because I feared that I alone wasn't enough? Or did I just want a family at all costs?

20

JUSTIN

15 DAYS EARLIER

'Oh aye, the wanderer returns,' says Garth.

He's slumped on the two-seater, a scattering of empty beer cans at his feet. The bedsit looks just as shitty as I when I left three days ago. Actually, it looks worse, about three days worse. The gangly, pasty-white body of my naked flatmate doesn't exactly add to the aesthetics.

'D'you mind putting some strides on, mate? Last thing I want to look at in the morning are your hairy bollocks.'

'Where you been? I've been worried sick, mate,' he says, as he plucks a pair of discarded Y-fronts off the stained carpet.

'Sorry, I...'

'I'm not really worried. Couldn't give a shit, to be honest.'

'I needed some space... to think, you know?'

'Yeah, whatever.' Garth sparks up one of the three joints he's neatly lined up on the armrest. 'Be careful with that thinking lark, eh? It's not all it's cracked up to be.'

'My head's in a mess. Just seen my son... well, a picture, anyway.'

'Whaaat!' he says. 'That's heavy.'

'Been staying in the Starcrest B & B for a few nights. Needed to process it all.'

'A son! A mini Jus!' He tilts his head back and lets out a laugh. 'S'funny that.'

I ignore the bait. We've known each other that long we both know what buttons to push to get a reaction. 'Wanna see him?'

Garth removes the TV remote control, the pouch of tobacco and the glass ashtray lifted from the Bull's Head three doors down. I sit down and show him the photo.

He studies it for a while, sucking noisily at the joint through gritted teeth. 'You sure he's yours?'

'What do you mean?'

'Well... not exactly a dead ringer is he, bruv?' He draws on the joint again, the tip crackling red.

I feel the anger rising. 'He's a baby, for God's sake.' I bring the photo to within inches of my eyes. Normally I would have disregarded the opinions of this pothead in Y-fronts peering over my shoulder without even a second thought. That Garth can even see what's in the photo, or even that it's actually a photo I'm holding, is debatable.

Ever since our days together in Springfield House children's home, Garth has never been one for holding back an opinion, no matter how inappropriate or misaligned. Even more so on mornings like this, where his double-glazed vision and bloated bags under his eyes give away the fact he's been up all night – possibly nights – smoking himself stupid.

'He's got my mouth, look!' I protest, jabbing at the photo.

Garth squints from within a cloud of smoke. 'He's got a baby's mouth. Could be anyone's, that.'

I'm all for a bit of banter, it's always been our default setting as friends, but even Garth must know this isn't the time. 'Why are you being like this?' I ask, genuinely hurt.

'Like what?'

'Like an arse.'

'Just being honest, mate. You need to get a reality check. You've not been with Grace for what, two years? She'll have been with all sorts in that time. It's what birds do.'

He offers me the 'torch of friendship'. I refuse to even look at it. I also refuse to let Garth bring me down, today of all days.

'Whatever. You're risking it though, aren't you, getting back involved, like?' he says.

I shrug. I know the risk of being back in Grace's life and how dangerous that is for all of us, but how can I not be now. 'It's my son. I can't *not* be involved.'

'Yeah, well just be careful, eh.' He grabs the photo and studies it for a while. 'Look at his mitts! You know what they say about big hands.' He passes it back and holds up his own hands in front of my face. 'Look at these fellas. Never had any complaints, Jus, know what I mean?' Garth wiggles his fingers, dropping the lit joint between his spindly white thighs and onto the settee. 'Shit, shit, shit.' He jumps up and swats it off the faded brown material. We both stare at yet another burn mark. There are so many singed circles they look like part of the pattern.

Like the rest of this shitty bedsit, the settee is a disaster, just one more item of furnishing liberated from a skip or 'borrowed' from a friend of a friend and never returned. While Garth sits back down and flicks at an empty Bic trying to relight the stub, I gaze around our shared kingdom.

I've done a lot of thinking during the past three days. It's been more than enough time to know that things have to change. I have to change. My crappy life since I was forced to leave Grace is represented in this one room – the barely adequate TV, the horrific seventies sideboard, the rusty fridge in the kitchenette, the worn-out mattress in the corner, the stained sleeping bag at Garth's feet, the six-string guitar that only has five. Everything is on its last legs, and I mean *everything*, including Garth. Nothing is thought out, simply add-ons grabbed when opportunity knocked. I've been living my life reactively, acting only when the occasion necessitates. It's time to be proactive.

Garth picks up an empty can of lager from the floor, shakes it, then tosses it over his shoulder.

'Come on, mate. Just stick it in the bin. How hard is it?' I ask.

'I will, I will, don't lose your blob. Just need to roll lunch...' Tobacco flutters onto the floor from between Garth's yellowed fingers.

I stand up, scoop up the discarded can and drop it on top of last night's chip wrappers that are spilling out of the pedal bin.

'I can't live like this anymore.'

Garth carries on rolling. 'Like what?' He licks the edge of the Rizla paper. 'Like kings? Masters of our own destiny?'

'Like a couple of dropouts with no future.'

'Speak for yourself, pal.'

'I've got to get away, from this,' – my hand sweeps the room – 'From Blackpool.'

'You mean from me.'

'No, not you personally, don't start all that again.'

Garth glances up, all hurt, eyes wide under an unkempt mop of shoulder-length blond hair. I've seen that look so many times. It started out real enough. I mean, who wouldn't look hurt with all the abuse we suffered in the kids' home, him more than me. I knew when to keep my head down, when to keep shtum. But not Garth. When things started to kick off in the home either through physical fights between the kids, or just general bullying by the godawful staff, he would be the one to stick his head above the pulpit and complain, often magnifying the issue and turning the spotlight of vitriol towards himself. He soon came to the conclusion that the world was more on his side when he was the victim, either genuinely or play-acting, which has left him in a perpetual spiral of self-pity as he became both perpetrator and victim of his own misery.

'I need to sort my shit out now I've got Daniel.'

'*If* you have Daniel.'

I throw him a look.

'You also need to remember why you had to leave,' he continues.

'I'll deal with that.' God knows how, I think. If it were that simple, I wouldn't have left in the first place.

'And where will that leave us, me and you, the old Batman and Robin? You just dumping me?'

At the moment that's exactly what I feel like doing, but our bond always overcomes the many temporary fall outs we have. 'Nope, course not. Have I ever left you in the shit? When one limps, we both limp, remember?'

'Never mind limping, I'm actually dying here, Justin, you know that. Look at me! Gorgeous body apart, what have I got going for me?'

'Mate, I've told you. Cut back on the blow. That's your main problem.'

'No, that's my main friend, 'specially now *you're* deserting me. Only thing that stops my head banging.'

'Not getting a hangover might do that too. You've got to start looking after yourself. I've got to get back with Grace, be a dad to my son.'

He opens his mouth, about to interject again. I don't let him.

'I can't keep being your babysitter.'

He leans back on the sofa, crosses his legs and blows a slow, long plume of smoke. His eyes have narrowed. He's now Garth the aggressor, yet another side I've seen too many times.

'You know *your* problem, mate.' He waves the joint at me.

'Go on.'

'You're a wanker.' He brings the joint down, seemingly satisfied with this carefully considered assessment.

'That's it, is it?'

'You pretend you're a mate... when you want a place to kip, when you're on one of your shitty downers, when you want a drinking buddy, when... when...' He's counting on his fingers but has run out of things to itemise. 'You're just a wanker.'

'Fair enough. You done?'

'Wanker.'

'I get it.'

'Besides, you can't just do one and walk back into your old life. You *know* that,' he continues. 'It's a death wish.'

'Yeah, well I'm going anyway.'

Garth is right, it is a death wish, but it's one I'm prepared to take. Nothing is going to stop me being with my family.

21

JUSTIN
NOW

'So you two were close,' says Detective Gorman. 'Thick as thieves if you like.'

He smiles, happy with himself for the criminal analogy. I don't give him the satisfaction of a response.

'Seems he'd have done anything for you, this Garth,' he continues.

'We go back a long way.'

'And obviously he'd help in any way he could. That's what *close friends* do, right?' The detective draws quote marks in the air.

'Don't bring him into this. None of this has anything to do with him.'

'Really?' The detective starts leafing through the ream of papers in front of him. 'Only, in the eyes of the law, we call it aiding and abetting.'

'Aiding and abetting? He was doing what friends do. Helping me, nothing more.'

'Same thing.' Detective Gorman raises an eyebrow.

'You need to tell me if he's okay.' Thoughts of Garth lying in a hospital bed reel through my mind. Is this what it feels like to be a parent? To have that uncontrollable need to protect, to know the ones you love are safe and well? That's exactly what I did when I found out Daniel was missing. But it was at the expense of Garth's well-being. Hobson's choice, I think they call it. An impossible position. And now look what's happened. I cup my face in my hands and slump further down in the chair. *What have I done?*

'You're not family,' says the detective matter-of-factly. I feel the iciness in his comment. Apart from Daniel, Garth *is* my family and always has been, more than those imposters to whom, as a toddler, I was nothing more than an inconvenience. Even more family than Jack and Caroline who did all they could as 'caring adults', but who reminded me so blatantly that *I'm not their blood.* And yet this twat sits here smug and indifferent, and thinks he has the authority to tell me who is and who isn't my family. *Family* is just a word, a collective term for a group of people with similar DNA. *Family* in its truest sense is people with an unbreakable bond and an unspoken commitment to protect each other, no matter what, no matter when. That, by definition, is the relationship between me and Garth.

On more than one occasion in the care home he literally put his physical well-being on the line to save my skin. When Chappy, or Mr Chapman as we were supposed to call him, found an excuse to start laying into me – usually because he was bored – Garth would stand in his way, deflecting any physical punishment onto himself while I crawled into bed and cried myself to sleep, listening to the raging obscenities, and sounds of feet and fists on Garth's body. He would never make a sound, never give Chappy the satisfaction of knowing his violence was affecting him physically or emotionally. I would feel the pain, both bodily and in the fact that someone would want to do that to me, along with the guilt of letting Garth take the beating. It didn't seem to affect Garth, or at least that's what he would say. I know now it did.

I owe him so much, and now it's come to this. *I'm so sorry, mate, sorry I wasn't there for you when you needed me the most.*

22

GRACE
15 DAYS EARLIER

'Seriously, this kid's driving me crazy this morning.' Candice slings Daniel's backpack onto the floor and flops onto the sofa. 'I swear the terrible twos have come early.'

'I don't believe it.' I wink at Daniel who is already busy ransacking the toy box. 'You're a little angel, aren't you, buddy?'

He responds by launching a wooden block across the room.

'Good luck with him today, Grace, he's got the devil in him.'

I smile thinly, not comfortable with my cousin's choice of phrase.

At 6.30am, the first fingers of light are creeping through the blinds. Drawing them back, I instinctively glance up and down the street, almost expecting Justin to pop up from beneath the window. My nerves are shot. Last night I barely slept; the fear of being exposed waking me the moment sleep came. Now my eyes are stinging and I have no idea how I'll make it through the day.

'Grandpa is popping round this morning,' I tell Candice wearily. 'Wants to talk to me about Andrew's memorial.' I can't help but roll my eyes. This Sunday it'll be sixteen years since my brother died and as is customary, Grandpa will be intent on paying tribute to him with an all-singing, all-dancing extravaganza, or that's what it's become akin to in recent years. I know he means well, desperate as he is to keep Andrew's memory alive, but I can't help feeling that after almost two decades it's time to let my poor brother's memory rest in peace. 'I haven't actually seen him for months.'

'He's not changed,' says Candice dryly. 'Still believes the second coming's just around the corner.' She throws me a wry grin. 'But he's harmless, Grace, just tell him what he wants to hear, that's what I do.'

'I know, you're right. I guess I am looking forward to seeing him again. Then this afternoon I reckon we'll head to the park if the weather stays nice.'

'Park,' parrots Daniel, clapping his hands excitedly.

My heart swells with pride. 'Did you hear him?' I gush to Candice, in awe of his intelligence for somebody so young. 'He said park as clear as day.'

'Just don't get his outfit dirty,' she groans, rummaging in her handbag, a Louis Vuitton which I haven't seen before. She notices me looking. 'His outfit is Sarah Louise,' she adds by way of explanation. It means nothing to me, but I nod out of politeness.

'He looks adorable.' Outwardly, I admire the baby-blue cable-knit cardigan and bloomer set while inwardly thinking how bloody impractical it is for a toddler. Poor sod looks like he's a royal prince attending luncheon at Buckingham Palace.

'Stick the kettle on, will you, lovey.' She swipes at the screen of her phone, the latest iPhone encased in rose gold. Candice, too, is dressed immaculately in her beautician's uniform, her hair pinned stylishly into a topknot and her make-up expertly applied.

'Five this morning he's been up since,' she continues. It seems moaning is her default setting these days. It's a shame as she never used to be like this when we were kids. I don't know what's changed, perhaps it's just the stress of being a working mother. 'Not to mention twice in the night. I need caffeine, Grace. Like now!'

As I watch the kettle boil, I decide to keep Justin's return a secret from Candice. Although I'm desperate to offload, there's no way I can admit having intentionally lied about Daniel being mine and Justin's son. I'm wholly aware it makes me look crazy. Besides, Candice has never been Justin's greatest fan, labelling him 'an oddball' amongst other things. If she knows he's back, she won't rest until she's destroyed him for leaving me when I was pregnant. Fiercely loyal she might be, but she's also a tad psychotic.

'So yeah,' she says as I take the drinks back through to the living room, as though there hasn't just been a five-minute lapse. 'I'm not even sure how I'm going to make it through to lunch. Cheers, hun.' She takes a sip then places it on the edge of the coffee table, dangerously close to where Daniel sits playing with a dumper truck.

'You might want to move that back a bit.'

'You what?' She glances up from her phone.

'The coffee.'

'Oh right, yeah.' She laughs as though I've just told a joke. 'Trip to A & E today is all I bloody need.' She pushes it back a fraction.

I fight the urge to roll my eyes. Sometimes I can't fathom how Daniel has even made it through sixteen months of life with all his limbs intact. I love Candice dearly, but she'd make Ma Baker look like Mother of the Year.

'Anyway, I might be late tonight. No later than seven but you know how it goes. You've got no plans, no?'

It's more a statement than a question. I shrug. It's the 4th of May, twenty-one months to the day that Noah died and as always, I'd planned to visit the cemetery where his ashes are kept.

'I was planning on visiting Noah later,' I say, almost apologetically. 'Before it gets dark. But don't worry if you're late, I can go tomorrow.'

'God no, you must go!' She makes an apologetic face. 'Shit, Grace, I can't believe I forgot about...'

'Honestly, it's fine,' I interject. As much as it pains me to admit it, I understand that to other people Noah's death was a tragic event but one that can be 'gotten over'. He was, according to them, 'only' a foetus, never a living, breathing child. I'll be forever grateful to Candice for the support she gave me in the early days but I know I have to accept that, for her, it's now in the past. 'I can go tomorrow instead,' I say through a forced smile.

She considers this. 'Well, if you're sure.' She stuffs her phone into her bag. 'It's just I'm in dire need of a bikini wax. Think fur burger and you'll understand.' She shudders. 'Bye-bye, Danny boy. And Grace,' she adds, now standing. 'For the love of God, no sugar. He was hyper as hell when I picked him up last night and I don't have the energy after a full day's work. Ciao.' She leaves without a backwards glance.

'Come on then, buddy,' I say, once I hear her car pull away. 'How about we go and have a kick-about in the garden until Grandpa arrives?'

'Ball,' he squeals, pointing to his toy box.

'Let's get you out of this silly outfit first.' I take him upstairs to where I have a drawer full of clothes – comfy bottoms and T-shirts with all his favourite characters. Together we pick out a PAW Patrol jogger set, and I swap his white buckle shoes for a pair of trainers which light up at the back.

'Much better, my boy,' I say, ruffling his hair. 'Now, how about Mama Grace gets you a chocolate biscuit?'

23

GRACE

15 DAYS EARLIER

Grandpa steps into the hallway and doffs his trilby. 'How's my favourite granddaughter this morning?' He kisses me on both cheeks.

'I know you tell Candice she's your favourite granddaughter too, you know.' I take his trench coat and hang it on the coat rack. 'It's so good to see you, Gramps.'

He smells of pine and toffee, which kindles old memories of arriving at his cottage for the weekend; Andrew and I would cosy up in front of the television between Grandpa and Grandma, hypnotised by the curl and sway of naked flames from their open fire.

'Can't I have two favourites?' He shrugs, his smile accentuating the deep laughter lines around his dark-brown eyes. Being a Christian and running a church has given Grandpa such joy in his life. As a child, things were far from easy for him. He grew up in a poor village in South Africa during apartheid, though he rarely speaks of it. I guess it's too painful for him.

'We're your only granddaughters,' I counter, realising just how much I've missed his wit. He's aged considerably since I last saw him though. His wizened face is not so much lined but carved with deep wrinkles, and a smattering of white whiskers sprout out where a full beard used to reside. I try to recall how long it's been since I last saw him. Nine months? Possibly longer.

'Two precious granddaughters, and I love you both equally.' He winks at me in the same way he used to when I was little, normally when Grandma was telling him off for something or other. 'Anyway, what do I have to do to get a cup of tea round here?'

'Do you take sugar?' I shout in from the kitchen a moment later, feeling guilty that I've forgotten how he takes his tea. I know I should make more of an effort to spend time with him. Even Candice, for all her faults, manages to see him at least once a month.

'I'm watching my waistline, Grace,' he shouts from the living room, which is absurd because there's nothing of him. A puff of wind would blow him over. 'So just the two spoonfuls this time,' he says after a deliberate pause. I hear him chuckling to himself.

Taking through the tea, I sit on the sofa beneath the window and watch in silence as he finishes reading *The Tiger Who Came to Tea* to Daniel.

'Do you remember reading to *me*?' I ask wistfully.

'I remember it well. You and Andrew, a knee apiece, the same way I used to with your mother and Aunt Clara when they were little. No wonder I'm now on the list for a knee replacement.' He chuckles again, though I sense a slight shift in mood, the memories no doubt clouded by grief. Not only did Mum, Grandpa's firstborn, die tragically of cancer but then Aunt Clara, Candice's Mum turned her back on the church. As far as I know, she now lives somewhere in mainland Spain and never gets in touch with anyone bar Candice. And then there's the unforgivable thing I did in my late teens, which went against everything Grandpa had taught me. I'm certain he still hasn't forgiven me for that.

'So you wanted to talk about the memorial?' I ask, keen to distract myself from the darkness which has begun to fog my mind.

'I was hoping you'd choose a bible verse to read,' he says hopefully.

I swallow down my initial response, instead opting for 'I'll think about it.'

Grandpa nods, though I can see the light has dimmed in his eyes. 'You know it's your decision and yours alone, Grace, I shall never force you to.'

I nod, though we both know in reality that isn't quite true.

'Perhaps one about eternal life?' he pushes. 'John 10 where...'

'Yes, I know it,' I interject, not needing to be reminded of the passive-aggressive verse about hellfire. 'I'll be there regardless,' I say, more offhand than I mean to, 'I know it's important to you.'

My mind wanders back to the first memorial I ever brought Justin to, a few months after we began dating. He was uncomfortable from the start, sweating and wringing his hands together. Twenty minutes into the service, he shot up and ran from the church. I didn't see him for three or four weeks after that and even then, so early in the relationship, I'd have sold my soul to the devil if it meant he'd come back. When he finally did return, I tentatively broached the subject of why he fled, but he only gave me some claptrap about how it had reminded him of the Catholic school they forced him to attend as a kid. To this day, I can't help but wonder if there was more to why he didn't feel worthy of being in God's house.

'I appreciate it, Grace. It wouldn't be the same without you there.' Although Grandpa directs his words at me, he's now staring at Daniel. The likeness between Daniel and Andrew is uncanny, and I'm sure Grandpa can see it too. 'I wish Candice would bring this little one along on Sundays,' he says through a sigh, more to himself than to me. 'A child should be brought up in the ways of the Lord.'

'Perhaps I can bring him.'

'Not really your place to, is it,' he counters. 'Candice is clear she doesn't want her son following a religion.'

His words sting, but I try to not let it show. I know I'm *not* Daniel's mother, neither is he Noah, yet I'm all too aware I feed that fantasy for my own gratification.

'What's wrong, Grace?' asks Grandpa. 'Did I say something?'

Thankfully, I'm saved from answering by the sound of my mobile vibrating on the coffee table. Before I have a chance to reach over and grab it, I see Grandpa's eye flick to the screen. 'Justin?' he asks, frowning. 'Not...'

'Of course not,' I snap, swiping up the phone. Grandpa isn't keen on Justin, never has been. For all Grandpa's belief in forgiveness and redemption he seemed to despise him on sight, and I have no idea why. 'There's more than one person in the world called Justin, you know,' I continue, feeling the need to ripen the lie.

'Who is it then?' he asks, his eyes analysing me. 'This *new* Justin?'

'Just a friend from the toddler group,' I say without hesitation. Grandpa doesn't blink. 'Just letting me know he's ill and won't make it tomorrow,' I continue, though I can't help but break eye contact.

'Nice that you've made a new friend, Grace,' replies Grandpa eventually before quickly draining the last dregs of tea. He places the cup down gently on the coffee table and lowers Daniel onto the sofa. 'Well, I ought to be going now. So much to do.'

I don't want him to go like this, but I'm also desperate to have some headspace. I still have no idea what I'm going to do about Justin, and now Grandpa has almost caught me out in the lie. If he finds out Justin is back on the scene, he'll more than likely tell Rob and Candice, which will complicate things further. 'I guess I'll see you Sunday,' I say, forcing brightness into my voice. 'Been lovely to see you.'

'You will consider the bible reading, won't you, Grace?' he asks when he's halfway out of the door.

'I'll do it. No problem.' I don't know why I agree to the reading, maybe because of the guilt I feel for lying about Justin, though can reading a bible verse about hellfire really atone for that?

'God bless you and keep you from harm, my darling,' whispers Grandpa while placing the trilby on his balding head. 'Oh, and one more thing,' he adds as he reaches his car.

'Yes?'

'Don't allow Justin to worm his way back in, Grace darling. That one is bad news. Take it from a man who knows.'

24

GRACE
NOW

'Why did you lie to your grandpa about being back in contact with Justin?' asks Sally.

I crack my knuckles in an attempt to rid the tension from my body. As a kid, Mum used to slap the back of my hand every time she caught me doing it. 'You'll end up with arthritis, like Grandpa,' she would say. She didn't hit me hard or anything, though I still recall the sting of her sovereign ring as it caught my fingertips, especially if my hands were cold. It was the same when I was really young and she'd tan my bare backside for something or another. I'm sure my arse was forever branded with St Christopher. It seems abhorrent these days, I'd never have laid a finger on Noah, though I appreciate it was a sign of the times. 'Spare the rod, spoil the child,' Grandpa used to say.

'Grace? Can you answer the question?' There's frustration in Sally's voice now. She's started to sigh a lot in the last hour or so, as if I'm not giving her what she needs fast enough. The problem is, I don't know what she needs. All I can give her is the truth. 'We need to know absolutely everything so we can find Daniel,' she adds. 'You want him to be found, right?'

'Of course.' I dig my nails into the skin of my forearm,

further releasing the building anxiety. All I want is for Daniel to be found safe and well, I just don't know how any of this is relevant. 'Obviously, I didn't want Grandpa telling Rob and Candice that Justin was back.'

'And why was that?' she persists. 'Because you'd lied about Daniel being your son?'

I nod. 'But not just that. I knew Grandpa, Rob and Candice would disapprove of Justin being back on the scene. They'd want to confront him about why he abandoned me, and I couldn't face that. Justin broke my heart when he left, and they were all in agreement that it was the shock of that which caused the miscarriage. Well, maybe not Rob,' I add, remembering how, as a doctor, he'd explained that there was no correlation between stress and stillbirth. I vaguely recall him printing off some medical journal as proof, but cold stats and bar charts were little comfort when my heart felt as though someone had slashed it open and stuffed it with memories made of glass shards.

'Do you think it's fair to say your family weren't fond of Justin?'

'You could say that,' I snort, remembering recent family gatherings where dessert always came with a side order of Justin-bashing.

'Any idea why?'

'Well, I didn't then, but I do now.'

25

GRACE
15 DAYS EARLIER

'You want to go higher?'

Daniel squeals as I push the swing soaring into the sky. In reality, it's barely a metre from the ground but to him, it must feel like flying. I remember it well from my childhood – the whoosh of freezing-cold air as it hit my face, belly somersaulting as I swung to and fro over muddy ground where hundreds of small feet had already left their mark. Dad features in the memory, too, possibly one of the few positive ones I have of him. He was a huge man with arms as big as a bear's. He couldn't half send that swing soaring.

'Gen, gen!' shouts Daniel, kicking his legs in excitement.

There's a kiss of coldness in the air but thankfully the rain has stayed away. As it's a school day, the playground is relatively quiet, just a half-dozen, preschool children jumping all over the play equipment, their mothers jostling them up wooden steps whilst juggling beakers of juice and oversized pram bags.

'How about we have our picnic now?' I lift Daniel out of the baby swing and brace myself for the guaranteed tantrum which is certain to follow. 'We can go on again later,' I try, as he attempts to wrestle himself free of my grip. 'I have biscuits.'

His ears prick up at this and a minute later we're happily camped on a grass verge, a feast of home-made pastries, diced fruit and limp-looking jam sandwiches spread out on a picnic blanket. Candice would go spare if she knew what I fed her son when she wasn't around. I'd feel guilty if I didn't believe a diet of chia muffins and spinach bake is tantamount to child cruelty.

With Daniel appeased, I fish my mobile from the bottom of his stroller and reread the message from Justin.

Thanks for the other night. Hope I can see Daniel soon? X

I notice his bio line has changed to A Dad's Love is Eternal.

I squeeze my eyes shut. I have to tell him the truth before this goes any further. I can't imagine bonding with a child, believing them to be mine only to have them snatched away. Not only that, but Grandpa also now knows Justin's back on the scene. Didn't he make it abundantly clear when he left the house earlier? If Grandpa lets slip to Candice, there'll be hell to pay, especially if she discovers I've been using Daniel as a pawn, albeit unintentionally. No, it's best all round if I just come clean. I type, delete and retype a series of replies, unsure whether to invite him round to the house again tonight. In truth, I'm terrified of being alone with him, of what I might allow to happen if he pushes hard enough. Over the last two years, I've experienced a range of emotions towards Justin – anger, betrayal, even hatred at times – and yet, if I'm honest, my love for him never lessened. If anything, his absence only made me more desperate for him, more sure that the love we shared was the real deal. Once you've experienced real love, it's hard to live without it, no matter how much pain it might cause. Justin has been back in my life for a matter of days and already I'm drowning in thoughts of him.

I bite back tears, not wanting to cry in front of Daniel who happily stuffs his face with mushed-up banana, oblivious to the shitstorm he's caught up in. If only things were different and this beautiful baby boy was mine and Justin's, not Candice and Rob's. Rob is a doting dad, but Candice doesn't even want him, not really, he's nothing but an accessory to her.

Justin's status changes from 'last seen...' to 'online'. He's typing again.

Took a few days off work to get my head straight. Hired a car. On way over X.

I want to be sick. My fingers hover over the keypad.

I don't think...

Delete. He's still online and can see that I'm typing. Shit, Grace, just send something.

How about you come round...

No, it has to be now, not tonight. Just get it over with.

We're at High Lea Park. See you shortly x.

Hand trembling, I press send.

26

JUSTIN
15 DAYS EARLIER

The greenery reminds me of my childhood. Not the bad parts – the constant swapping of families, the sense of longing and wanting to belong, the terrifying nights when the hot, whisky breath of my dad on my pillow signalled another night of pain, torment and self-loathing. No, it reminds me of the occasional moments of freedom when nature, not the cold interiors of social services offices or sterile children's homes was my scenery.

The greenery represents softness and simplicity, harmony and happiness. When kids leave the days of play parks, they leave behind their childhood forever and enter a world of harsh, overcomplications. Or maybe that's me.

I look up at the tips of the oaks and sycamores poking at the expanse of blue. I remember the swings, the rush of wind on my face as I pushed harder, believing that if I swung high enough, I would fly over those trees, the only barriers between me and a happier land of bright colours, constant smiles and the soft touch of people who care.

Entering the park, I pass young mothers doting on their kids, genuine smiles of adoration and pride. How has my life become so messed up? Why have I not become *me*, the me I used to talk about becoming when I was with Grace in this very same park ten years ago? What happened to him?

Is it because I've let my life be moulded by others? Maybe I should have been stronger, stood up for myself. My life has constantly been in other people's hands, people that were supposed to help me. Like Jack, the foster dad I lived with from thirteen to eighteen. He knew me more than most, what I was like, but what did he make me do? Apply for the army. Would you say that's the ideal career choice for someone who doesn't like violence and confrontation, someone who'd already spent the first eight years of their life being yelled at by an abusive, alcoholic father and a negligent mother? No, me neither. Failing the army psychiatric evaluation on the grounds of 'personality disorders' didn't exactly give me the confidence boost that Jack said joining the army would.

But there is a glimmer of brightness, something that makes me pick up the pace, my eyes searching amongst the mothers and kids for that glimmer, my only glimmer. And there it is, at the far side of the roundabout and the wooden climbing frame, cuddling on a blanket on the grass at the edge of the swings, next to the oaks and the sycamores. *That* is my happy land.

Both Grace and Daniel smile as I approach. *God, I want a part of that happiness, that togetherness.* Being made to leave Grace so suddenly has been one of the many lows in my life, possibly the lowest, and there have been many, believe me. I had to leave, of course, for her sake, and mine too, though I can hardly admit that. All I can do now is look forward and hope that what happened in the past stays in the past. It's dangerous being back here in Marple, but I have no choice. Marple harbours my biggest fear. But it's also home to my only hope.

'Hi, matey.'

Daniel holds his arms out wanting me to pick him up.

Jesus! This is too much. I pick him up, plant a kiss on his soft forehead, filling my nostrils with the sweetness of clothes softener and talcum powder, the fresh smell of innocence.

'Blimey. He likes *you*,' says Grace as she stands.

'What's *not* to like, eh, little man?' I cringe. That's the first of many lies I know I'm going to have to cover up this afternoon.

I lean towards Grace, put my arm around her shoulders and kiss her on the cheek, holding the three-way embrace a little longer than is probably necessary. The feeling I get holding Daniel is like nothing I've ever felt before. I get a surge of instant feel-good, like I'm hugging myself, that he's actually physically a part of me. I want that feeling to never end, but Daniel leans into his mum. He's obviously had enough of me now even though I'm only just getting to know him, my own flesh and blood. I try to let that thought sink in.

'You look nice,' I say to Grace, trying to hide my feeling of rejection. Grace doesn't just look nice, though, she looks incredible in that powder-blue cotton dress. But she's lost even more weight in the last couple of years. I hope it's not a return to the anorexia she had before. I helped her get over it last time. I'd be horrified if I've caused it to come back in any way because of my leaving. I immediately start to self-chastise again.

'Don't look too bad yourself,' she says. It actually makes me feel awkward. I don't remember the last time somebody gave me a compliment.

We sit down on the tartan blanket. 'You've not told anybody have you?'

Grace looks confused.

'About me being back in touch, I mean?'

'No. Why?'

'Just best if we keep it quiet, you know. Keep it off social media and all that.'

'I wouldn't anyway.'

Ouch! 'Are you on Facebook, only I tried to look you up and couldn't find you?'

'I've got a profile, yes, but it's hidden, private for friends and family.'

Her comment stings. So she doesn't see me as family even though I'm the father of her son? I try not to show the hurt.

Grace is obviously less concerned about hiding her upset: 'Why don't you want me to put anything on social media, anyway? I thought you'd be proud.'

'I am. God, you don't know how proud I am, it's just... well, it's a private thing, so just keep it between me and you for now.'

She raises her eyebrows, surprised, but doesn't agree one way or the other. I have no choice but to trust her.

'So, how's he doing?' I say, trying to diffuse the tension.

She also seems happy to avoid any confrontation. 'Good. His talking is really coming on. Tell...' She pauses. 'Justin where we are.'

'Park,' barks Daniel proudly.

'Yes, park! Well done, matey. You're a bright one you are, aren't you?' I poke his belly, teasingly. *What is wrong with me? I can't stop touching him?* 'And who's this?' I point to myself.

Daniel looks blank.

'Da-ddy. I'm your Daddy, Daniel.' Just saying it out loud makes my chest swell. Daniel looks at me confused though, perfectly natural I suppose, but it still takes away some of the pleasure, knowing that he doesn't see me as such. 'And that?' I say, pointing at Grace, 'Who's that?'

Daniel looks at Grace but before he answers she points at a blackbird hopping nearby.

'Look, Daniel. A birdie. Go see if it wants to play, eh?'

I watch Daniel toddle off towards the bird. 'He's just amazing, isn't he? Do you think he gets who I am?'

Grace laughs nervously. 'No, he's no idea.'

I nod, acceptingly, but feel deflated she's not told him that he was coming to see his daddy. I need my son to understand our connection, our unbreakable bond. I need him to know I'm not just another man that makes a cameo appearance in his life then disappears again. But I can see from Grace's expression, now is not the time to push it.

'How about Candice and Rob? They doing okay? Had any kids yet?'

Grace looks away then runs a finger up and down the gold chain of her necklace.

'They seem all right. No kids though.'

'You still see them as much?'

'Not really. We're not as close as we used to be.' She suddenly shouts over to Daniel who's sitting, calmly watching the bird as it searches in the grass for food. 'Don't go any further, Daniel.' He looks over his shoulder and we both gaze in silence at him for a moment, Grace with pride in her eyes, me with a longing to pick him up, to be part of him.

'He's a great kid, a credit to you, Grace. Just wish I'd stayed around to be part of it.'

She snorts sarcastically.

'What?'

'You've still not told me the real reason why you left.'

'I told you, I panicked.'

'I've thought about it, and that's bollocks, Justin.'

I can see the smile slipping.

'What do you want me to say?' I shrug. 'I'm an arse, a coward. But I'm going to make it up to him, to you, as well.'

She says nothing, but holds my gaze, as though her eyes are scanning for lies.

'There's something I've not told you,' she says, finally.

I know what's coming. She has a boyfriend. I don't want to hear it, not now, not here on our family day out.

'This brings back some memories,' I interrupt.

Grace looks puzzled.

'The park? That tree over there, the widest oak? We carved our names on it ten years ago, remember?'

'Oh yeah. Listen, Justin...'

I stand, reach inside my denim jacket and pull out my Swiss army knife.

'Justin, I need to tell you something...'

'Sure. Give me one minute.'

'It's important. It's about... Daniel.'

But I'm already running towards the giant oak. I need to do this, to make this a day in history. I wave at Grace from the other side of the huge tree, letting her know I've found the carving, then carefully add 'Daniel' to the faded love heart on the trunk. I take a step back.

Justin + Grace + Daniel.

It feels like a birth certificate for a new family, but not like the piece of paper you get from a registry office. This is an official proclamation immortalised in nature and nobody can rescind it. Seeing all our names together for the first time gives me a surge of pride and confidence. I know I can win back Grace from whoever she's seeing now. It's my duty. It's my family.

A text message interrupts my stroll back. I haven't loaded my contacts into this new phone yet so the sender is unidentified. In the distance, I see Grace on her phone. I instinctively smile and open the text. The eight words make my blood turn icy cold. *Do you really want to ruin her life?* My heart drops like lead and I feel as if life has literally been drained out of me. How has the past caught up with me so quickly?

I need to get away, to think, to remove us all from danger. I walk back to Grace who is still talking on the phone. 'I need to go,' I mouth.

She covers the phone. 'What?'

'I've got to go. Something's come up... with Garth.'

Grace stares, speechless. What the hell must she think? I can't believe I'm doing this to her again, but she doesn't know what I know, and obviously I can't tell her. 'I'll call you,' I say, walking towards Daniel. 'See you later, matey. Daddy's got to go.' I ruffle his hair and keep walking, unable to look back. I don't want to see Grace's look of despise and disbelief as I leave.

27

GRACE
12 DAYS EARLIER

'What the hell are you playing at, Justin? You don't get to do this to me again.'

I launch the phone at the headboard and collapse back onto the bed. My eyes burn with rage, but I'll be damned if I'm going to cry over him again.

It's been three days since he left me in the park, and now he's ignoring me. I'm not strong enough to go through this again; the sleepless nights wondering where he is and if he's even alive; never being sure why he left or if he'll come back. At least when he disappeared the first time, I had Noah to keep me sane, or at least the promise of Noah. Now I have nothing.

Instinctively, I slide over to Justin's side of the bed and nuzzle into the pillow as if somehow I'll be able to smell him on the fabric, though, of course, his essence has long gone. I ache for him to be beside me again, the two of us side by side, his muscular arm around me and my head on his bare chest. Some nights, especially at the beginning of our relationship, we would remain that way until the sun came up, time forgot as we talked about our hopes and dreams, our deepest fears. I wanted to give him the whole of me and in return know all of him. One of the most heartbreaking realisations when he left was that I'd given him my soul and received only his shadow.

Reaching over to the bedside cabinet, I grab the half-drunk bottle of red by its neck and take a swig. I'd like to say it's the first bottle of the evening but in truth, there's already an empty in the recycling bin. *Three cheers for the eco-friendly alcoholic.* I've no idea when I last ate, a mouthful of Daniel's leftover sandwich at lunchtime, I think. I run a hand over my torso, disgusted by the bump of each rib – I'm nothing short of a human carcass.

My phone buzzes and a spark of hope flutters in my chest. Swiping at the screen, the hope quickly dies. It's not Justin but Grandpa, checking to see if I've found a suitable bible verse for the service. 'Shit.' With everything else that's been happening, I've forgotten all about the memorial and the stupid bloody verse.

The anxiety begins with a tingle in my fingers and toes, and a sudden feeling that I'm falling. Tears stream down my face and within seconds I'm doubled over on the bed, my mouth wide open in a silent scream. Every bad memory hurtles towards me; the coppery blood trickling from the corner of Andrew's mouth as he lay unconscious beside me; the coldness of Mum's fingertips three years later as I squeezed her hand and begged her to stay just one more minute; Noah, my miracle baby, my second chance at happiness. The memories accelerate, faster and faster, crowding together. I don't have enough room inside my head for them all – I don't want them there. I gasp for breath as the room spins, faster and faster. I curl up tight in bed, squeeze my eyes shut – *breathe, breathe.*

I reach out in the semi-darkness, grab at my mobile and hit the call button.

'Justin here. Can't pick up right now but go ahead and leave a message.'

'It's me.' My voice is thin and distant, like it's not really me, and yet it has to be. 'Please call me back I... it's Daniel.' My heart beats so fast I fear I'll pass out. I don't know what I'm saying or why. All I know is that I have to get Justin back, I can't lose another person, I just can't. 'Daniel's really poorly.' My brain screams at me to stop talking. 'You'd better come over.'

I hang up and everything turns black.

28

JUSTIN

12 DAYS EARLIER

'Erm... what's going on, Garth?'

I rub the sleep from my eyes, barely believing that my flatmate is actually cleaning, as in tidying up the apartment, and it's – I check the time on my mobile – 10pm.

'New month, new leaf, mate,' he says, grinning.

'It's still May.'

He ponders this for a while, then dismisses the fact with a 'whatever' expression and carries on scrubbing at a brown stain on the wall.

This is the third night I've spent back in the flat. Whether I want to or not, I'm resigned to the fact that life with Garth is the new normality – though there never has been anything normal where me and him are concerned.

His inability to read the situation and keep his mouth shut led to many confrontations in the children's home. Even if me or Garth weren't the ones being picked on, you could guarantee that by the end, Garth had fully involved himself whenever he saw an injustice. He was the self-appointed adjudicator of fair play, a noble quest in theory, but one that in practicality simply involved having his head shoved down a toilet rather than the kid's he was trying to defend. And inevitably, guilty by mere association, I would often have my head submerged in a porcelain bowl too.

Whether it became a habit, or genuine loyalty, he still can't break free of the protective nature he has towards me. After I told him about the warning text I received in the park he gave me a lecture about how I was being selfish and how I should stay away to do what's best for Daniel and Grace, reminding me they were happy before I appeared back in their lives and they could be happy again if I disappeared. For once he made complete sense, and I had to agree with him, despite my inner urge to be with them both. But I guess that's me all over, selfish to the point of putting them in danger. Since I ran off in the park, my phone hasn't stopped buzzing with messages and calls from Grace, but like Garth said, I need to be strong and just ignore them, even the voicemail from her that's just bleeped now.

Garth sees me looking at my phone.

'Don't,' he says, waving a dirty rag at me, threateningly. I can see it's one of my best T-shirts but decide not to bring that up right now.

'What if she's in trouble?' I ask.

'Why would she be? She never goes anywhere.'

'But what if she was?'

'Not your issue, mate. You're done with them, remember? If you start listening to messages you'll get involved, put them in danger again.'

'It's killing me.'

'Tell you what, let me listen to the message. I'll tell you if it's anything serious or just faff, okay?'

I toss the phone across the room.

He holds it to his ear for a moment. 'Nothing. Now get over

it.' He throws it back onto my bed. 'Wanna brew? I need to tell you something.'

I put my head back on the pillow and stare at the ceiling. I'm finding it hard to keep up with this new Garth. First the cleaning, now he's offering to make me a drink, and a non-alcoholic one at that. There's definitely something strange going on with him. I guess I'll find out in a few minutes.

As Garth rattles round in the kitchen, I can't help thinking about my son, that feeling of absolute joy I had when I held him in the park, better than any high I've ever felt from drink or drugs. And then Grace, her red curls on that blue dress. I was so close to being a part of that... so, so close.

I check that Garth is still occupied making a brew, turn the volume right down and press play on the voice message, my head under the sheet. It doesn't stay there for long as I focus on three words.

Daniel's really poorly.

29

GRACE
12 DAYS EARLIER

I peel open my eyes, the sound of frantic hammering pulling me from a deep sleep.

What the hell? I squint into the darkness, a groan escaping my dry lips. Dehydration claws at my throat and my head feels as though somebody has taken a baseball bat to it. I drift towards a dreamy sleep once more.

'Grace. Open the door, now!' The rapping of bare knuckles on wood jerks me fully awake. I sit bolt upright and wince as a searing pain slices through my head. It's the middle of the night and somebody is at the door, shouting my name. Who the hell is it? The police? Has something happened to Grandpa? Daniel?

Dragging myself out of bed, I stumble over to the window, my head splitting in two. How much did I even drink? The street is black and still, the only colour strains from lamp posts that illuminate a light drizzle. It's deathly silent now which makes me question if there *was* any banging and shouting or if I dreamed it. I peer harder into the darkness. 'What the...?' Frantically, I rub at the condensation with the sleeve of my pyjama top and blink the sleep from my eyes. I'm not imagining it. A figure across the road looks directly at me, his shadow melting into the blackness. I jump back.

Somebody is watching the house.

'Grace. Graaaaaayyyce!'

The shouting comes again. But it's not coming from the man in the shadows. It's Justin.

'Grace, open up now!'

I thunder down the stairs. I can't piece everything together; why is Justin here? Why is he screaming my name like a lunatic and practically smashing his fist through my front door? And if Justin is at the front door then who is watching the house?

'I'm coming. One minute.' My voice is hoarse and scratchy. Releasing the bolt, I yank open the door. 'Justin, what's the...'

'Where is he?' He pushes past me, his whole body rigid with fury. 'In hospital?' His voice breaks with emotion – anger but also something else. Is it fear?

'What...?' I'm confused. *Hospital?* What's he talking about? 'I don't...'

'Daniel. You said he was really ill.'

A hazy memory sinks my stomach. *Oh shit.* 'Justin, I...' I want to run, hide, escape, anything but attempt to fight my way out of yet another lie. Why the hell did I say Daniel was ill? 'He's fine,' I try, my voice several octaves too high.

'Where is he?'

'In bed.' *For God's sake, Grace.*

'Why the hell didn't you call me back? I've been leaving voice messages?'

Justin makes for the stairs, already halfway up by the time I register what he's going to do. *Shit, shit, double shit!*

'Justin, stop please.' I bound up the stairs after him. If he opens the nursery door, it's game over; not only will he discover that Daniel isn't there but that the room itself is a shrine to a baby that never was; *his* baby. *Oh, crap!* 'Please don't wake him up,' I plead. 'He's fine now, honestly.'

'I need to see him.' He's at the door now, pulling down on the handle.

'I said no!' Grabbing at his hoodie, I yank him back. 'You don't get to come and do this.'

He turns on me, eyes ablaze. 'He's my son, too, Grace.'

'That's rich.' I can't help myself, reverting to blame seems my only defence. I can't let him find out about Noah, not like this. 'You can't come in and out of our lives whenever it suits. Why did you disappear at the park? Why haven't you been in touch for days?'

'But...' He frowns. 'You were frantic, on the phone. Hysterical.' It isn't lost on me how he's purposefully sidestepped the question as to why he's been AWOL. I know I'm not the only one keeping secrets and although I hate the fact he's still lying to me, at least we remain on a level playing field.

'He had a temperature, that's all,' I say, trying to sound offhand. 'Was off his food.'

'What was his temperature?'

Shit. What's considered a high temperature? 'Well, initially it was like, forty...'

'Forty? Jesus Christ!' He pushes down further on the handle.

'But now it's like thirty... erm.'

'What, seven, eight?'

'Thirty-seven and a half,' I say, inwardly praying that's an acceptable temperature. 'I just overreacted.'

'Was he sick?'

'No.'

'Rash. Have you checked for a rash, Grace?'

I bring my finger to my lip, urging him to be quiet. *What an absolute bitch you are, Grace.* 'Please. He needs to rest. No rash, okay?'

'Well check again, it can come on suddenly.'

'Justin, seriously, he's fine.'

He runs a hand through his hair. 'You're absolutely sure?'

'One hundred per cent.'

He appears to consider all of this though I can tell he's still dubious. It dawns on me that what I'm witnessing is a parent's all-consuming love for their child. Weird, I know, but I feel almost envious of him. Unwittingly, I've given Justin a gift, the ability to love completely and without condition, to hold another's soul in his heart. By God, I'd have given my life for Noah had I been given the chance, a thousand times over I would have. How the hell can I take that away from Justin? Not only Daniel, but Noah too, as by confessing the truth I'll be taking not one but two children away from him.

'Grace. Please don't cry.'

It's only as Justin wraps his arms around me, his whispered words hot in my ear, that I realise I'm crying; not silently but huge wracking sobs which quickly drench his shirt with tears and guilt. I'm a bad person, the worst kind. I can't live this lie any longer but to tell the truth would surely destroy him.

'Shhh, Grace. It's okay.' I feel his hand in my hair, and then his fingers, trailing down my cheeks and to my lips, tracing their outline. No, no, no, this can't happen, no way.

'Justin, please.' I look up into his eyes, so different now to how they were just a moment ago, the anger now gone and replaced with guilt and pain. Or am I just seeing a reflection of myself?

'I messed up, Grace, there's no excuse. All I can do is spend my life making it right.'

There is something about the way he looks at me, soul laid bare, all the bad and good and every shade of grey in between begging to be freed, to have someone see him for who he really is and tell him it's okay. I know I could spend forever searching and never find another man who looks at me the way Justin does, vulnerable and yet still so mysterious. I could spend my whole life peeling back his layers only to never reach his core. 'I forgive you,' I whisper. It's true, I do. Even without knowing the truth, I forgive him for everything.

He kisses me, lightly at first, as though afraid of rejection. Every nerve in my body and mind is electrified by his touch. How can I ever reject him? I respond greedily, my mouth hard on his, tongue pushing through his teeth. In an instant it's as though we've never been apart, his touch, the feel of his skin, as familiar as my own. I stop kissing his mouth and move to his collarbone, his chest, expertly unbuttoning his shirt. His fingers lightly trail down to the nape of my neck and I respond by arching into him, feel him hardening, a groan of pleasure escaping my lips. I know what is about to happen and the thought is as terrifying as it is thrilling. If we do this, not just have sex but make love, as I'm sure we aren't capable of doing this without emotion, then I know I really will fall in love with him all over again, perhaps even more than before; a new, raw, deeper fucked-up love that is muddied in lies and betrayal.

I want to pull away but I can't, I'm incapable. I allow him to guide me through to the bedroom and lower me down onto the bed, the same bed we shared for almost a decade where his indention on the left side has patiently waited two years for his return. Pushing me down, he slips off my top and bra. I squirm under the weight of him, my now bare flesh on fire as he trails kisses from my neck down to my breasts, my stomach, his tongue circling my belly button. I pull him up towards me, remove his shirt, kiss his chest, over and over.

'Are you sure you want to do this?' he asks, his voice so genuinely sweet that I could cry.

No. I'm not sure at all but my head is no longer in charge.

'Yes,' I say. 'Yes, I'm sure.'

30

JUSTIN

11 DAYS EARLIER

There's something about watching people sleep, seeing them in their most vulnerable and natural state. No pretensions, no front, just unadulterated honesty. Back to being like a baby, I guess.

Grace lies on her side facing me, the quilt half-covering her smooth shoulders. Her hands are together under her face as if in prayer. Her lips are parted slightly, her long eyelashes resting on baby-soft cheeks. Her hair splays behind her like it's been brushed back, apart from two loose strands that draw diagonal lines across the bridge of her nose. It's a portrait that could have been painted by a master, a sleeping beauty.

Beauty and the Beast. What does she see in me? She could have anyone, yet last night, in the panting, sweaty passion, she whispered, 'I love you.' *Me*, she loves *me*! God knows why. Although I'm trying hard to banish the self-doubt, I know I'm not worthy. If Grace knew who I really am, what I'm capable of, she'd realise that too. It's only a matter of time before she finds out. Any way you look at it, there's an almighty crash coming my way again and I know I don't have the strength or the balls to go face it. But those eyes, that face, that body... *Stop kidding yourself, Justin, she's too good for you.*

It's only 5am but I gently push back the quilt, edge out of bed and get dressed, keeping my eyes on sleeping beauty all the time. I pull back the edge of the curtain and peer into the darkness. Grace asked if I had seen anybody outside last night. At the time I assumed it was because she didn't want anyone to know I was here, nosey neighbours spreading gossip and such like. But now, in the depth of the night, I wonder if it's something else. Did she think somebody was spying on her? Was she right? I scan the darkness but it's as still as a photograph and I let go of the curtain.

I creep along the landing, pausing outside Daniel's bedroom. I wonder if he's still sick and put my ear to the door, listening, hoping to hear a sound, any sound as long as it's his, but there's just silence. I look down at the door handle. The urge to see him is overwhelming. I need to touch him, my own flesh and blood, but if I go in and he wakes up, I'm going to have to confront Grace, and I am definitely not in the right state of mind for a showdown. Best to just slip away quietly.

I open the stair gate and go downstairs. This used to be my home, my sanctuary, but as I glide through now, I notice there's very little of me still left. In fact, in the living room at least, there's nothing. I feel like a ghost drifting around a previous life. Surely there's something in this house that affirms I was once part of it. What happened to all my belongings? Where's my stack of vinyl singles, my Jack Kerouac and Mark Twain paperback escapes? I need to find *something* of me.

I rummage in the sideboard drawers then the kitchen cupboards but find nothing. The cubby hole under the stairs holds more hope, but without switching on all the lights I have to rely on touch for something recognisable. There are shoes, lots of shoes, but all Grace's. There's also a pile of folded blankets. The top one has the feel of lambswool. I pull it out and hold it under the moonlight that illuminates the windowsill. I hold it to my nose. It's one of Daniel's blankets, the name stitched in large cursive lettering on one corner. Only it doesn't say Daniel, it says, *Noah*. I smile. Noah had always been Grace's first choice for a boy's name. Like many things, I guess she changed her mind.

The blue-white beams of luminescence also fall on a framed photo. It's one I hadn't noticed last time I was here. In it, Grace is laughing, pinned next to her brother, Andrew, his arms wrapped around her neck in a playful lock. How do you deal with losing someone so close, at such a young age? I think of Daniel. He has a look of Andrew, the same bright, innocent eyes. I've only known him for a few days but already there's an all-consuming bond. If anything happened to my son, I know I couldn't cope. His death would be my death. Tears fill my eyes, but the sadness is also mingled with guilt. If Grace knew what I'd done... I trace my finger over the scar on my head and try not to remember.

Part of me wants to go back upstairs. To climb in bed and cling tightly to her, to confess everything, and for her to tell me it's okay, to say 'it's all right now', the very same trinity of words I'd longed for my mum to say on so many occasions when tears dampened my pillow and blood stained the sheets.

The confluence of emotions takes me by surprise – sadness, self-disgust, regret, longing, fear, guilt – all ganging up to ambush me into a corner of despair. I back away from the window, suddenly terrified by the thought of being outside. Instead, I sit on the sofa, hugging my knees, burying my face in the blanket to stifle the cries. 'It's all right now, it's all right,' I whisper, but in the cobalt hue of moonlight my mind flashes back again and again to my life's lowlights – the neglect, the abandonment, the guilt – each adding another loathsome layer to an already repulsive canvas.

Stop remembering. Stop thinking.

My head jolts back and I open my eyes. Rubbing away the stinging sheet of sweat and tears, I notice the room is lighter than before, the first rays of sunrise now spattering the living room with speckles of pale colour. Time has disappeared again. A recurring incidence that often occurs after an overload of stress. Dissociative amnesia disorder, my doctor called it, loss of memory for random periods of time. 'A consequence of childhood trauma and abuse,' she'd said. Apparently, it's supposed to be a coping mechanism to blot out the horror of what happened when I was a boy. Typically for me, I've cocked that up too. I still remember the abuse, most of it anyway. What I don't remember is the passing of time when I'm stressed as an adult which doesn't help me cope in *any* way.

My body is heavy, drained, like I've run a marathon, but I have a sudden desperation to see Daniel. I haul myself off the sofa, put one foot on the bottom stair and look up. I need to see him, but I don't know if I can face Grace. If I wake him, I wake her. I wait for a second, hoping for the swirling fog in my mind to clear, think logically, find clarity, but none comes. I climb up the stairs as quietly as I can, flatten down my hair, and gently push open Daniel's door.

31

GRACE

'Grace, where's Daniel?'

My eyes fly wide open.

The fragments of a dream are instantly erased as I see who is towering over me.

'Justin?' My mind descends into some sort of mental free fall. What the hell is he still doing here? He left. Or did he? I was intoxicated, emotional, in need of comfort. *Oh God, I actually slept with him.*

'Grace? Where is he?' His eyes ransack the room. If he knows Daniel isn't in his cot that means he's been inside the nursery. *Shit! How does he not know?* Surely, he'd have put two and two together – there's a bloody stencil on the wall with the name Noah on it for Christ's sake!

In shock, I remain speechless. Half of my brain screams at me to tell the truth, yet the other half is already scratching around for a credible lie.

'Grace.'

'I don't know.' I sit up, realise I'm naked. *Can this actually get any worse?* Instinctively, I pull the quilt up around my chest. 'Are you sure he's not in his cot?'

'Of course I'm sure.' He rakes stiff fingers through unwashed hair. His eyes are glazed over and red-rimmed as though he hasn't slept a wink all night. 'What about the stairs? Can he get down?'

'What?'

'The stairs, Grace, the stairs. You know, those really steep things.' He heads out onto the landing, Daniel's name like shards of glass in his mouth. *What the hell am I doing to him? Last night I declared my love for him, but this isn't love, this is abuse.*

Jumping out of bed, I pull on a pair of knickers and crumpled T-shirt before sprinting down the stairs after him. 'Daniel!' I yell, my insides tightening with guilt. I don't think I've ever hated myself so much as I do right now.

The next few minutes are a blur as I follow Justin all over the house. He's shouted Daniel's name that many times his voice is hoarse and he can barely speak.

'He isn't here, Grace. Where the hell is he?'

My mind has seized up. 'It's okay, perhaps he's...' *What, Grace, perhaps he's what? Perhaps he's at home with his actual parents? Shit!* Drained, I slump onto the sofa, head in my hands. I'm going to have to come clean, I can't put Justin through this anymore. 'Justin...'

'We have to call the police.' Through my splayed fingers I catch sight of him fishing out a mobile from his jeans pocket.

'No!' Jumping up, I wrestle it from his hands. 'We can't.'

'We have to.' He makes a grab for the phone, but I hold it at arm's length.

'What the hell is the matter with you, Grace? Our son is missing.'

The wall clock chimes seven. Double shit! Candice will be here with Daniel in a matter of minutes. I can feel my blood pressure rise at the thought of Justin coming face to face with

Candice and Daniel. 'Maybe he's managed to get out the front door,' I say, the seeds of an idea sprouting straight out of my mouth. 'The police will be too long. Go look for him. The park, he might have headed there.' It's unthinkable that a sixteen-month-old would have successfully scaled his cot, descended a flight of stairs and navigated his way to a play park all by himself but, astoundingly, Justin buys it without question.

'Okay, good idea.' He pulls on his T-shirt and boots. 'What about the neighbours, shall I knock on their doors? Maybe one of them saw him?'

'No!' The reproach comes out faster than intended. 'If they'd seen him, they'd have brought him back. Just go to the park and see if he's there. If he's managed to get out the front, then that's probably where he'll have gone. I'll go check out the back.'

Justin strides to the front door. 'It's shut,' he says, stating the obvious. 'Grace, there's something...' He stops in his tracks, shakes his head. 'No.'

'What?'

'What if he's been kidnapped?'

'Why the hell would somebody kidnap him?'

'I don't know.'

It's obvious he does. 'What the hell, Justin?'

'I have to tell you...'

'Not now. Just go and look for him.' I bundle him out of the door and slam it shut before he has the chance to say anything further.

32

JUSTIN
11 DAYS EARLIER

Shit, shit, shit.

How could a sixteen-month-old open the front door and find his way to the park on his own, even if he has been there a million times already? It just doesn't make sense.

I cross the road and break into a jog. A young girl panics and steers a pram into the road as she sees me running towards her. A red post van sounds its horn and veers around her. I want to stop and tell her to be careful, but who am I to lecture, I've let my kid go missing.

I think back to last night. The questions in my mind come thick and fast as I run. If he has been taken, was it by the same person who Grace said was watching the house? When could it have happened? When I was in bed with Grace? When I was downstairs? Surely I'd have heard something?

The park seems a vastly different place from the last time I was here four days ago. I see now that the grass is muddy and strewn with litter. The swings, slides and climbing frames look tired and worn, and the great oaks have a menace about them, glowering down like bullies in a playground.

If Daniel was going to be anywhere in this park, it would be here, but the place is deserted except for a lone dog sniffing at the roundabout.

'Daniel. It's Daddy,' I shout. 'Where are you, matey?' I stand in the middle of the playground yelling in all directions. 'Daniel. Daniel!'

The dog looks up briefly and seemingly weighs up whether to join in the commotion or take flight, then does neither and continues its sniffing mission.

I know this is all because I came back after I'd been warned, and now Daniel's suffering for my mistake. It's just the latest in a long line of nuclear implosions that I've become such a master at, an artist of self-destruction. I can deal with it if it's me who pays the price for my own sins, but not my son, not now, not ever.

33

GRACE
11 DAYS EARLIER

'For God's sake, hurry up.' Trust Candice to be late today of all days. Normally she can't wait to dump her offspring on me but, of course, she chooses today to be – I check my watch – six minutes late. I've taken up surveillance at the bedroom window. I can see right to the end of the road and beyond from here, though the park remains hidden behind a barrage of woodland. Justin will be there by now, maybe even on his way back if he sprinted, which he most probably has. What the hell am I going to say if he returns and Daniel still isn't here? Or worse still, if they all turn up at the same time? It's too much. I feel like my head's going to explode. Grabbing my phone off the dresser, I fire off a message to Justin.

Any Luck?

It pings back almost immediately.

No. Should I call the police?

God no!

Not yet. Check the woodland?

Catching sight of the front end of Rob's Audi rounding the corner, I release a shaky breath. *Thank God.*

34

JUSTIN
11 DAYS EARLIER

I take out my phone and stare at the keypad. I've got to call the police, despite what Grace said. There's no choice, even though that will open a whole new can of shit when the whole reason I left in the first place comes out. I hit 999 and wait. This is it. This is where I bring this whole nightmare out into the open. This is where it starts, and this is where it ends, at least for me and Grace.

'Hello, emergency service operator. Which service do you require?'

I pause for a second: 'Police.'

'I'll connect you now.'

The phone rings once. I scan the park one more time.

'Police service. What's the address of the emergency?'

I open my mouth but no words come out.

'Hello, where are you calling from?'

I jab the call end button, then frantically stab at the keyboard again. The line goes straight to voicemail. I grit my teeth as I wait for the beep.

'It's Justin. Listen, you arsehole, I know what you're up to and it won't work. Not again. I don't give a shit what you do to me but you bring my son back right now, or I'll fucking kill you, you hear?'

I end the call, stuff the phone in my pocket and trudge back home. I'm going to have to tell Grace the truth, there's no way round it. My chest tightens as I imagine the aftermath of revealing why I really left. It'll break her, I know. And there's no way she'll let me see Daniel again. But if something happens to him, because of me, both of us might never see him again, and that will destroy her even more.

Police, Grace – either way I know I've lost any chance of making it work, of being with my family, finding that happy land. But as much as that kills me, the only thing that matters at the moment is making sure no harm comes to Daniel.

35

GRACE
11 DAYS EARLIER

'Come on, Daniel, mate.' Rob glances at me over his shoulder, his pained expression suggesting he needs assistance. 'I can't unbuckle him.'

'Where's Her Ladyship?' I gesture for Rob to step aside. Crouching down, I begin unfastening Daniel's car seat, though my hands feel as though they've been severed at the knuckle.

'You all right?' Rob places a lingering hand on my shoulder.

'Course. Just feeling a bit dizzy, that's all.' I move away from him. 'I need breakfast.' Despite feeling sick with fear, I sound relatively calm. When did I become such a proficient liar?

'Migraine.'

'What?'

'Candice. Migraine. Apparently, she's seeing stars.' He snorts. 'Nothing to do with the half bottle of gin she supped last night, of course.' He attempts a laugh, but it falls flat. It's not the first time my cousin has feigned a migraine to cover for her midweek drinking and it no doubt won't be the last. If I didn't desperately need to get Rob away from the house, I'd ask him inside for a coffee. Poor sod looks like he needs one.

Rob's always been a decent bloke, reliable and kind. When

we dated back in college, he'd often turn up at my house with roses and teddy bears. Poems too – God the poems were cringeworthy – *Roses are red, violets are blue, how you're my girlfriend, I have no clue.* Then there were the Love Hearts sweets he'd hide in my backpack, and the reams of kisses at the end of his text messages. Sweet I know, but it all made me feel a little awkward, as though he was following a How-To manual on being the perfect boyfriend. Going off to university was the excuse I needed to break things off and, although he didn't put up much of a fight at the time, he still jokes that I broke his heart. He started dating Candice around eighteen months later. It was actually me who introduced them to one another. In truth he's way too vanilla for my diva of a cousin, and she leads him a dog's life, never appreciating what he does for her. The poor man works all the hours God sends as a GP only for Candice to blow his six-figure salary on acrylic nails and handbags. Still, he seems happy enough and they've certainly stood the test of time over the nine years they've been together.

Finally managing to free Daniel, I slam the door shut with my bare foot.

'Dada!' Without warning, Daniel lunges at Rob who, startled, almost drops him.

'No, no, we haven't time.'

'Hey, what's all this about, buddy?' He pulls Daniel into a bear hug and kisses the top of his head. 'Sorry,' he says to me, throwing me a tight smile over the top of Daniel's head. 'Really clingy the last few days. I don't know what's gotten into him.'

I can hazard a guess, a random man turning up out of the blue and insisting he's his father being one. 'They go through phases. Come on, mate.' I throw a sideward glance up the street, in the direction of the park. *Oh God, no!* Panic empties my lungs of air. *Shit, shit, shit!* Justin has rounded the corner, is on his way back. 'Daniel, come on please.'

Hearing my strangled plea, Daniel wraps his arms tighter around Rob's neck. I'm scaring him. *Calm it, Grace, calm it.*

Rob physically blanches. 'Really sorry about this, Grace. Should I maybe come in for a minute?'

God no! 'Best not to. Just hand him over.' I hold out my hands, flick another glance up the road. Justin appears to be looking down at his phone though he's quickly gaining ground.

'Come on now, mate, Daddy's got to get to work.' Rob once again attempts to hand Daniel over but with no real urgency. I think a part of him is enjoying Daniel's clinginess. 'I actually think he's teething,' he says. 'I've been up and down all night with him while Her Ladyship slept soundly.' A sigh escapes his chest. 'Between me and you, I'm getting a bit fed up with it all. She...'

'I forgot, I have the pan on,' I interject. 'I was making eggs. Sorry, but I...'

'Things aren't too great at home, if you catch my drift.'

'I'm really sorry to hear that, Rob, truly.' I beckon Daniel over. 'You want chocolate, Danny? Milky Bar buttons?'

'Choc-choc.' He practically throws himself at me.

'She's talking about having another kid,' continues Rob, stuffing his hands into his trouser pockets. 'I mean she's only mildly interested in the one...'

'Maybe we can chat about it tonight,' I try. *Please, please just go.*

'Not sure what time I'll be home.' He's speaking painfully slowly, as though he's battery-operated and running out of charge. That's another reason I stopped dating him, poor sod could put Freddie Krueger to sleep.

'The clinic is ridiculously understaffed at the minute,' he drones. 'More cuts, you know? I'll try and get Candice to pick him up around five, if not I think it will be closer to seven. Either way I'll ring you and let you know.' He blows breath up into his grey, thinning hair. It's almost unthinkable that we're the same age, he looks a decade older and then some. Candice has a lot to answer for, though that one could put wrinkles on Peter Pan.

'No bother. Whenever is fine.' I take a step towards the door.

'You won't mention what I said, will you?'

'Of course not.'

'It's not that I don't love her, I just...'

'The eggs, Rob?'

'Eggs?'

'I have eggs on the hob.'

He checks his watch. 'In fairness, I haven't eaten.'

What? Seriously to God, you couldn't write this shit. 'No, you can't come in!'

'Why?' His sparse eyebrows knit together. 'Are you sure you're okay?' He looks dejected now. Taking off his glasses, he pinches the bridge of his nose. 'I saw your granddad yesterday. He said you seemed a bit off. He thought maybe Justin had made contact?' He looks at me for longer than is comfortable.

'Nope, not at all. Grandpa must have his wires crossed.' The lie tastes bitter in my mouth. In other circumstances I'd feel comfortable confiding in Rob but not about this.

'Grace, you know if he has made contact...'

'The eggs, Rob,' I say, cutting him off. 'I have to go before the pan boils over.'

'The eggs, yes.' Rob gives me a look which suggests he doesn't believe a word. 'You know you can talk to me if...'

'Yep. Thanks. We can talk tonight, all right.' Without another word, I turn and leave him stood on the pavement, slamming the door for good measure.

Taking Daniel into the living room, I ignore his pleas for chocolate, or rather 'choc-choc' and head straight for the window then watch with relief as Rob climbs into his car and fires up the engine. Justin is a hundred metres or so away now and I pray to God Rob doesn't check his rear-view mirror.

'Holy shit.' I collapse down onto the sofa, certain that if I don't sit, I'll faint.

A minute or two later, the front door slams. 'Have you found him?' Justin flies into the living room, ashen-faced. Catching sight of Daniel, he falls to his knees. 'Oh God, he's okay, thank God. I thought, I thought...' He pulls himself to standing, scoops up Daniel and squeezes him so tight I'm scared he's going to suffocate him.

'Justin, you're scaring him.'

Daniel shrieks in protest, arms and legs flaring. 'Gayce!'

'Put him down, now!'

Thankfully, Justin complies without argument. 'Sorry. Sorry, matey.' He looks over at Daniel, who is now wrapped around my leg. 'I just... I was panicking. Where was he?'

'Next door,' I say, having already planned this part of the story. 'He got into their shed. They have a cat and he likes to see it. He must have...'

Justin's brow furrows and, in an instant, I know what he's going to say. He's going to ask why Daniel has just called me Grace. I prepare myself for the lie, have the words ready in my mouth. It's okay, this one is easy. I can deal with this.

'Grace?' he says.

'Yeah?'

'How come he's fully dressed?'

36

GRACE

11 DAYS EARLIER

I look at Daniel and see, for the first time, what is so blatantly obvious. He's immaculate, as always; pressed white shirt and royal-blue shorts, chubby brown legs stuffed into knee-length pop socks and finished with baby-soft buckle shoes. How did I not realise? Even his hair is side-parted like a Victorian doll.

My gaze switches to Justin but he isn't looking at me. His eyes are darting – Daniel, the door, upstairs. 'Grace... what the...' He blinks rapidly, over and over, as though unable to understand what he's seeing. 'Why is he dressed? Why is he... what the hell, Grace?' His eyes finally settle on me, his glare like a magnifying glass, ablaze from the ball of confusion burning within. I feel myself shrivelling up. 'Justin, I...'

'What? Justin what?' His voice is mocking, an almost sneer, it's not something I've seen in him before. 'Look at him, Grace. That kid has not just got out of bed like that, do you think I'm stupid?'

I daren't speak for fear of saying the wrong thing. It's over, I know it. I just can't think... I can't... 'Daniel, come on, mate, how about you play in the garden on your slide?' My voice is flat, resolute. Taking Daniel by the hand, I lead him through to the kitchen and out into the garden. I close the door to and stand at the window, keeping an eye on him.

'You haven't answered my question, Grace?'

'It's not what you think.' I have my back to him and I know I ought to turn around, to give him that much at least, but I don't think I can. I can't witness the moment his world comes crashing down, that second in time when he realises what I have done, the monster I have become. It would be bad enough for anybody to look at me like that, but for Justin to, the man who holds my heart in his hands, it will destroy me. 'Justin, I have to tell you something.'

'There's somebody else, isn't there?'

His question throws me. 'What?' Instinctively, I turn to face him, though it's clear he's still far away, lost in a sea of pain and self-loathing. His breathing is deliberately slow. He's trying to rein himself in, for me, Daniel, himself. That alone makes me love him more.

'Is that where he was? Have you...' He clenches his fists, his eyes narrowing. 'Does he call another person Dad?'

'No!' *Shit, of course, the answer is yes, but not in the way he thinks.* 'You're being ridiculous.' *Is he?*

'Am I? I mean, is he even mine? Let's be honest, he looks nothing like me.' He's glaring at me again, his eyes an open window to his internal brokenness. 'Please, Grace.' He comes over, reaches out and grabs a tight hold of my arms, his nails digging into my bare flesh. 'Please God, tell me he's mine.'

37

JUSTIN

11 DAYS EARLIER

'Daniel is yours.' She says it slowly, deliberating on every word. 'How many times do I have to tell you?'

My face is inches from hers, her breaths shallow like hot stabs on my skin. I can't see truth, or deception. A red mist has shrouded my judgement. All I see is panic and fear. 'Why are you lying?' I yell.

Now she's shaking. Why the hell is she shaking? What's she afraid of? 'So who was he with?'

'Justin, please!'

I look up and down at this figure in front of me, this cruel, tiny figure trying to take away my very reason for living. 'Who?'

I see the whites of her eyes, her head turned away, pulled back as if she's trying to escape something. I see her arms up, defensive, straining to shield her face.

'Please, Justin, you're hurting me.'

I see the white bulges on the freckled skin of her arms where fingers squeeze deep. Then I see they're mine. *Oh God, what am I doing?* I immediately let go. 'I... I'm sorry...'

She rubs her arms, tears flowing freely. Her eyes show more hurt than her arms. 'What is wrong with you?' she blubbers.

'He's my son, Grace. I need to know. Tell me the truth.'

'Okay, the truth? Daniel didn't stay here last night. He was with Candice and Rob.'

I stare open-mouthed as I try to let the words sink in. Why would he be with Candice and Rob? But more importantly, why did Grace lie to me? My trust in her evaporates in a second. It feels like I've been winded by a sucker punch I didn't see coming.

38

GRACE
11 DAYS EARLIER

His brow creases. 'What are you talking about, he stayed at Candice and Rob's? You mean he was never here?'

'No. He wasn't.'

His pupils dilate as confusion gives way to clarity. 'So you lied to me? About him being ill?'

'Yes but... it wasn't like that.' I reach out to him, desperate to feel his touch, to have him know that none of this was ever intentional.

He bats me away. 'You're sick. You know that. Sick!'

Every word is hurled at me and I deserve it, I know I do, and yet I still don't want to hear it.

'How could you lie? How could you do that to me? Make me believe...' He backs away, hands raised. 'It doesn't matter.' He's shaking his head, as though unable to believe what I've done. 'I don't know who you are anymore.'

'I don't know why I lied, Justin, honestly. I just. I just wanted...' Sobs punctuate my words, but he doesn't come to comfort me. 'Justin, please.' I go to him once more and place a hand on either side of his face. 'Look at me, please.' I want him to see me, to look into my soul and see the remorse that lies there. 'I lied because I couldn't bear you to leave again. I love you, can't you see that?'

He glances up at me, a lost boy in a grown man's body. I see it; the years of hurt, abuse, of being lied to by people who were supposed to have loved him. And yet, looking into his eyes now is like gazing into Pandora's box, the bad stuff set free, and there, at the bottom, a flutter of hope. So what does that make me? The all-powerful, jealous God?

'You really love me?'

I trail a finger down his cheek. 'Always.'

The shadow of a smile lifts the corners of his mouth, but I can see he's still unsure. 'But I'm a mess, Grace. You don't want me, I'm bad news.'

I rest my head against his. We're so close I can feel the beating of his heart. 'Aren't we all?'

In an instant our lips are pressed together, slow and soft, a promise between us.

This is it. No going back.

'Grace?' After what feels like forever, he pulls away. 'Will you come away with me next weekend? Daniel too?'

'I...' Words leave me. I stare into his eyes, so optimistic now, so certain of our future. 'Not this weekend, right? It's Andrew's memorial this Sunday.'

'No, next. Shit, has that come round again?' There's something in the way he says it, a sneer. 'You're not expecting me to come, are you?'

'No!' I swallow down my irritation. 'Have you ever, except that first one?'

He drops his gaze. 'You know I hate churches – full of hypocrites.'

'So you always say.'

'But the weekend after?'

'I don't know yet. You know it's complicated.'

'Please. It's Caroline's birthday. I didn't know whether to go, but you know how it is with my foster dad. He just...' He shakes his head, ridding himself of whatever memory is plaguing him. 'I just want to show them that I'm not a total screw-up, Grace, now that I have you and Daniel. Please say yes.'

'Okay,' I hear myself saying, though how the hell I'm going to get Daniel away from his parents for a full weekend is anybody's guess. 'Let's do it.'

39

JUSTIN
11 DAYS EARLIER

I close the front door behind me and take a deep intake of cold, spring morning air. Save for a few solitary wisps of white, the sky is perfectly clear, unlike my head. As per usual, my mind is awash with conflicting thoughts; the ecstasy of sleeping with Grace again – not just the sex, but the intimacy, being part of her, both physically and emotionally, and the very thought that she would want me again, despite all I've put her through. But then that brightness is shaded by a dark cloud of uncertainty – how could Grace use our son like that? Do I actually know her as well as I think I do? If she can lie so easily and convincingly, what else has she told me that isn't true?

I try to steer my mind away from that doubt as I climb into the car and stare through the windscreen at the treetops swaying against the blue background. As Caroline, my foster mum, used to urge, I need to focus on the present, to find and relish those moments that bring me joy, not doubt or negativity. Being able to take *my* family to my foster parents' house is one of those moments. Perhaps, finally, they'll see I've done good, made something of myself. All right, not job-wise – fairground ride operator is not exactly a career pinnacle – but I've become a family man, a much more esteemed position than any job can provide, and one that brings with it insurmountable pride – maybe even from Jack. He can't fail to be impressed for once, can he? I feel a smile form as I picture his face when I tell him I'm a dad.

Buoyed with the thought, I start the car, check the mirrors and start to pull out. Then something catches my eye on the windscreen. I slam on the brakes, get out, and grab the piece of paper pinned under the passenger side wiper. It's a handwritten note containing one short sentence with words that bring my world crashing down around me.

40

JUSTIN
NOW

D etective Gorman's temporary absence allows me time to collect my thoughts. I need to be out there looking for Daniel, not trapped in here answering question after question. It feels like being in the care home again, my movements restricted, my basic freedoms stolen, my life in someone else's control. I've had enough of that, seriously more than enough.

'I need to go. Let me out!' I shout, hammering on the locked door. The man I recognise as the friendly desk sergeant who booked me in opens the door.

'Quit the banging, you're giving me a headache,' he says with a smile.

'I need to go, I have to find Daniel.'

The sergeant raises his hand in a calming motion. 'It's all being taken care of, we've got men out looking. You just have to be patient, let us do our thing. DC Gorman will be back in a few minutes, he's just going through some notes. Bring you another coffee?'

I shake my head and sigh. The door closes and I flop back down. I think back to the note on my windscreen. The thought does nothing to calm my anger. At the time, I had no clue who could have left that. I didn't understand why anybody would want to hurt me in that way. Now I've joined the dots, it makes complete sense, and there was only ever one person who could have written, 'He's not your child.'

(

41

JUSTIN
9 DAYS EARLIER

'He's not my kid? Who on earth would say that?' I hold the piece of paper aloft.

'His real dad?' Garth stares at me as he sips at a curly pink straw protruding from a can of extra-strong lager.

'You really don't think he looks like me? Not even a little bit?'

'Not in the slightest.'

I grab the photo and scrutinise it again. I suppose even at this age you can see that Daniel's complexion is darker than mine, his mouth wider. What if Grace is lying? She's lied before, why not now? What if Garth is right and Daniel *isn't* mine? When I was checked during the time we were trying for Daniel, my sperm count was only borderline, even though they said it was Grace who had the problem.

I get up off the sofa, grab the engagement ring from under my pillow and thrust it towards Garth. 'I was going to ask her to marry me, to be a proper family.'

Garth slurps again through the straw. 'I know.'

'I need to know if he's mine.'

'Or if he's not,' he counters, peering inside the beer can.

'I just need to know one way or the other.'

'For sure,' he repeats, unhelpfully, shaking out the last drops of lager.

'You're not being much help, mate.'

Garth lets out a loud burp, shrugs his shoulders.

'H... o... m... e... D... N... A... t... e... s... t...' I mouth as I jab at my phone.

'Mate,' says Garth, suddenly finding an interest. 'Why don't you just think about this as a lucky escape. Kids are a ball-ache, man. Stay single. That's the best advice I can give you.'

'You just don't get it, do you? I love this kid. I *want* to be his dad.'

Garth shakes his head. 'You've changed, mate. You need to have a word with yourself.'

I look down at the Buy Now button. A DNA test? Has it really come to this? Do I have to go behind Grace's back to find out if Daniel is mine? He feels like he is – the swell of love that rises when I see him, hold him, kiss him. But what if I'm imagining all that? What if he really isn't my son? I go cold at the thought. I don't want to lose him, or those feelings. Maybe it's better if I don't know. At least that way I can still feel that joy. But I know that's bullshit.

I tap my phone. 'It's done. Kit arrives tomorrow. Results in three to five days, that's... at the earliest May thirteenth, when I'm at Jack and Caroline's hopefully.'

I sit on the bed staring at the ring. Three to five days. Can I wait that long not knowing whether Daniel is mine, whether Grace is lying, whether I ask her to spend the rest of her life with me? What am I supposed to do with myself for up to five days? It feels like an eternity. Why do I have to go through this? Why does life have to be so complicated?

The more I sit and stare, the more the anger rises. There has to be a reason why I have these doubts, and for once I don't think it's down to my own paranoia. Or is it? Shit, I just don't know. Either way, the stress of not knowing is actually making me feel like puking and I can't go three days feeling like this from today until the thirteenth. Surely I'll be able to tell from Grace's reaction if I just ask her directly, no bullshit, just straight to the point. I need to ask her now, face to face. Then it hits me. I jump to my feet. 'It's definitely the tenth today, right?'

'Aha.' He nods.

Shit. May twelfth. Andrew's memorial. Grace will be at church. I can't have it out with her there – not in front of *him*. Or can I? But he can't know I'm back on the scene. But I can't not know, either. Sod it. I grab my jacket and head out the door.

'Where you going?' asks Garth.

'Church.'

'Cool. Throw one up for me... and one for yourself,' he adds as I slam the door. 'You're gonna need a bit of help from the big man if you get back involved with Grace.'

42

GRACE
9 DAYS EARLIER

'Let the little children come to me, and do not hinder them, for the kingdom of heaven... erm, sorry... the kingdom...' I frantically search for my place in the scripture. My hands are shaking so much the words are jumping all over. Why do bible pages have to be so bloody thin and the text so small? It's ironic really, given that the core audience is octogenarians who are generally as blind as Bartimaeus. 'Belongs to...' From the pulpit, I glance up at a sea of sombre faces. Most are Black Caribbean, some Black South African. Grandpa has always run his church inclusive to all races and nationalities but, as with most congregations, the numbers have grown from word of mouth within already close-knit communities. I've always felt like the black sheep of the flock, or rather the white sheep. It's an unfounded emotion really. Not once have I been made to feel different for being mixed race, not by my family nor the church; I guess it's just an insecurity I've fashioned for myself.

I spot Candice in the gathering. 'You're doing great,' she mouths. She's dressed like some sort of bride in a pure-white off-the-shoulder dress and kitten heels. Beside her, Rob wrestles with a hyperactive Daniel who's desperate to escape his clutches. 'Dum!' he squeals, pointing up at the stage. 'Bam, bam!'

'Belongs to such as these,' I finish moments later, breathing a heavy sigh of relief as I close the bible. I look up at my brother's image on the projector screen. I know I'm likely biased, but he really was the most beautiful-looking boy – angelically so, with eyes the colour of rich earth and cheekbones any female would die for. There's no doubt he'd have been a seriously handsome man had he have survived the crash – a heartbreaker you might say – though Andrew wouldn't have broken hearts, he'd have healed them. He was a lot like Mum in that way, blessed with empathy. He felt others' pain acutely, though I'm not sure that's so much of a blessing as a curse. What would the twenty-nine-year-old version of Andrew make of all of this today?

'Well done, cuz.' Candice squeezes my hand lightly as I take my seat beside her. 'You okay?'

I nod, though in truth I'm not sure I am. Thoughts of Andrew always leave me feeling peculiar – not sad as such as it's been sixteen years since he died, just out of sorts.

'Rob said Grandpa had been talking about you the other day.'

'Oh.' I suddenly feel too hot. I use the order of service to fan myself down. 'What was he saying?'

Candice leans in. 'Said he thought Justin might be back in contact?' Her breath is hot in my ear. 'Is it true?'

I shake my head. 'Not at all.' My voice is little more than a squeak. 'It was just a friend, that's all.'

'Yeah, a guy from playgroup apparently. Come off it, Grace, you don't even go to playgroup with Daniel.'

It's true, I don't. I did consider going along in the early days of childminding, but I knew all the other adults there would likely be mothers. I couldn't face that, being the odd one out. To this day I still envy other mums, Candice included. Some of them just don't appreciate what they have or how lucky they are.

'Is everything all right?' asks Candice, leaning her head against my shoulder. 'You can tell me anything, you know.'

I'm saved from answering as the six-piece worship band break into an exuberant rendition of 'Amazing Grace'.

I glance over at Rob who's singing with gusto; somewhat of a farce seeing as though he's a self-proclaimed agnostic. That's Rob all over though, a people-pleaser. He catches me looking and turns a healthy shade of pink.

'You fancy a drink one night this week?' says Candice, straightening up. 'There's something I need to discuss with you actually, about Rob.' Her voice drops to a whisper. 'He's hiding something, Grace.'

I raise an eyebrow, both surprised and intrigued. 'Hiding something how?'

'I'll tell you when we go out.' She throws daggers over at Rob, but he doesn't appear to notice. 'So you're up for it then?' she asks, turning back to me.

'Sure, how about Wednesday?' It's perfect timing actually as I need to speak to her, too, about taking Daniel away for the weekend, though what excuse I'm going to give is anybody's guess.

The band finishes playing and, on Grandpa's instruction, we take our seats.

'My sheep hear my voice, and I know them,' begins Grandpa, his wise eyes sweeping over the congregation. Grandpa is what you'd call an evangelist – winning hearts for Jesus with his God-given charm. Christians travel far and wide to hear him preach, though usually I find myself drifting off during his sermons.

Candice is now swiping away on her mobile that she has

concealed behind her handbag. 'Oh my God, have you seen Kylie Jenner's dress?' She flashes me the phone. 'Lush.'

I smirk, then feel guilty as I know Grandpa is now talking about Andrew and, as his sister, I ought to be paying attention. I force myself to tune in to promises of eternal life and paradise but within minutes I'm daydreaming about next weekend with Justin; the three of us feeding baby goats at the petting farm close to his foster parents' house, then the two of us drinking red wine on the cobbled courtyard while Daniel sleeps. 'We must forgive the person who took this precious boy.' Grandpa's words puncture my fantasy. I stare at him, aghast. In what world does he expect me to forgive the coward who not only stole my brother's life, but never came forward to atone? 'As Christians we must do as Christ did,' he continues. 'Forgiveness is...' He stops dead, surprise or shock stealing his words. 'Forgiveness is...' he repeats, sweat now gathering on his upper lip.

I look over my shoulder to try and decipher what's bothering him.

Christ no!

Justin catches my eye and frowns. He looks from me to Candice and Rob, and back again. I gesture for him to step outside and glance over at Candice who's now engrossed in some TikTok video. Rob is bouncing Daniel on his knee and blowing raspberries on his cheeks. I have to get Justin away from them. If Rob and Candice see him, then I'm done for.

Somehow, I manage to stand. 'Going for a pee,' I whisper to Candice, and pray she doesn't turn around as I head up the aisle.

'What the hell are you doing here?' I seethe, once Justin and I are safely in the car park. 'I haven't even told Grandpa you're back.'

'Well, I sensed *that* from the daggers he gave me,' says Justin, practically spitting the words at me. 'Almost seems as though you're ashamed of me.'

'Don't be ridiculous. You know when you left, people weren't happy. I need time to tell them, that's all.'

'Them?'

'Grandpa. Rob and Candice.'

'Thought you said you hardly saw them? That a lie too?' He leans back against the railings and crosses his arms.

'I'm not arguing with you here.' I look behind me to check nobody has followed us out.

'God, you really are determined to keep me a dirty secret, aren't you,' he mocks, though when I turn back to face him I see the pain in his eyes.

'What's got into you?'

He pulls a folded-up piece of paper from his jeans pocket and hands it to me. 'Look at this and tell me the truth.'

I read the words scrawled in black marker. 'What the hell? Who sent you this?'

'Your hands are shaking.' Justin snatches the note from me and stuffs it back into his pocket. 'Something you need to confess?'

I know this is the perfect moment to end the lunacy once and for all. I steel myself, knowing that once the words are spoken, they can't be taken back. 'Justin, I...'

'If Daniel isn't my son, it'll kill me,' he says. 'I love him, Grace. He's my only real flesh and blood.'

I see so much pain in his eyes that I want to cry. 'He *is* your son,' I lie. 'Honestly.'

He cups my face in his hands and looks me deep in the eyes. 'Promise?'

'I do,' I whisper, all the while looking over his shoulder to make sure Candice or Rob aren't heading our way. 'I wouldn't lie to you, Justin.'

43

GRACE
6 DAYS EARLIER

'So, you said you needed to tell me something, about Rob?'

Candice plucks an olive from its cocktail stick with her teeth. It's her fifth drink of the night and she's beginning to look bleary-eyed.

'Don't look now but the guys to the left are seriously checking me out.' She smirks behind the frosted rim of a Martini glass. 'One of them is half decent too.'

I sneak a glance over at the fresh-faced 'suits' propping up the bar, two blood-red Cosmopolitans the only colour in their otherwise dull appearance. The whole rooftop bar is, in fact, an exhibition of my worst nightmare; gleaming, white, high-top tables and chairs, secluded booths upholstered in gaudy pink velvet, and all set to a soundtrack of canned-laughter and plastic R&B. 'They all look the same these days. Half-mast trousers and no chest hair in sight. Give me a real man any day.'

'Give me *any* man any day,' says Candice slurping the last dregs of alcohol. She flashes them a coy smile; all pouty lips and wide, made-up eyes.

'Stop it!' I playfully kick her under the table. 'Think you ought to make that your last. And anyway, stop avoiding the question. You said Rob was hiding something on Sunday, that's why you wanted to talk to me.'

'Oh, I don't know, Grace, I'm not sure I want to talk about it now.' I'm taken aback when tears spring into her eyes.

'Shit, you all right?'

She fans her face, her sharp acrylics dangerously close to taking an eye out. 'I'm fine. Bloody hay fever.' A quick touch up of her lower lashes and it's as though the moment never happened. I'm left wondering what the hell just happened as she clicks her fingers at a passing waiter. 'Dos más, babe.'

'Deece, I know they serve tapas but...'

'And a couple of Jägerbomb chasers, yeah.'

Inwardly I cry. 'Don't you think it's time we got going? It's a school night.'

'Come off it,' she snorts, fanning her long dark hair over one shoulder. 'It's only eleven. If it was Thursday, I'd have said yeah because Friday I have Mrs Salmon in for a pedicure.' She heaves. 'Feet like Frodo Baggins. Anyway, it's not like you work.'

I laugh, incredulous. 'Apart from the ten-hour days looking after your son.'

'Well, he's hardly work is he,' she says, deadpan. 'Just stick him in front of *Peppa Pig* and he's happy as a pig in... oh, ha! See what I did there.'

'You're a comedy genius. But seriously, I've got to be up...'

'Zip.' She trails a finger across glossy red lips. 'You're out for my birthday, which means you don't get to go home without at least seeing double.'

Under the table, I pop the clasp on my handbag and check my mobile. My heart sinks. There's still no message from Justin. Although I did my best on Sunday to reassure him that the note he received meant nothing, I can't shake the feeling that he's still suspicious. And who the hell actually sent the note in the first place? I've racked my brain for days, but nobody is springing to mind. Perhaps Justin wrote the note himself? A way to try and trip me up. But if he did do that, it's because he already has his doubts.

'Here.' Dropping the mobile back into the bag, I pull out the reason I've endured three hours of drunken small talk. 'A present for you.'

Candice squeals. 'Really? A present. For me?' She takes the envelope and rips it open like she's a five-year-old expecting there to be a two-pound coin taped inside. 'But didn't you buy me that...' She looks at me, wide-eyed. 'Baby brain, Grace. I'm so sorry.'

'The candle holder,' I interject, though the blank stare remains intact.

'God yeah. Loved it.' She fashions a love heart with her hands. 'Best gift ever.'

The waiter returns with our drinks, saving me from having to watch the moment she opens the envelope. Inside, my nerves are shot. The gift is a serious gamble and could easily be a week's wages up the swanny.

'What?' She unfolds the printed confirmation and holds it to the lantern which centres the table. 'A spa weekend? Oh my God! Hale Country Club? That's like the bomb!' She leans over and pecks my cheek. 'I'm actually psyched. It's been ages since we spent proper time together.'

I almost spit out my drink. 'It's not for me and you, you idiot, it's for you and Rob. This weekend.'

'God no!' She drops the printout as though it's just caught fire. 'Rob all slimy in body butter and paper underpants, no thank you.'

I suppress a laugh, the vision not the best accompaniment to a belly full of Martini. 'Come on, Deece, it'll do you good. I'll have Danny boy.'

'Oh no, Grace, seriously.' She holds a hand to her mouth and takes a slow breath as though settling reflux. 'I'm not sure I could stomach it. Can't *you* just come, and Rob can have Daniel?'

'No, I can't. I mean I'm honoured, like.' I force a smile but inside the panic is mounting. If she doesn't go to the spa with Rob and let me look after Daniel, I can't go to Justin's foster parents and then he'll want to know why. Besides, there's a part of me desperate to go, to be a family, the three of us, if only for a weekend. Then afterwards, I'll tell him the truth. I have to. 'I bought it so the two of *you* can have some quality time.'

'Well, I don't want to go with him.' She drops the shot of Jäger into the glass of Red Bull and necks it back.

'Aren't you meant to wait for me? Like cheers or something.'

'I hate him, Grace,' she snaps, now teary-eyed again. 'He's a twat.'

'Why? Come on, what's he done? Tell me.'

'Nothing. It doesn't matter.' She proceeds to click at thin air. 'Waiter!'

'Candice, I'm not having another shot. Here.' I slide the second Jägerbomb across the table. 'Knock yourself out.'

'He's having an affair with someone, I'm sure,' she blurts out, at the exact moment the second liquor crashes into the amber liquid. She knocks it back in one. 'He doesn't even love me anymore. I'm going to be left with nothing, Grace, absolutely sod all.' Slamming the glass down onto the table, she scowls, though her eyes are no longer working in tandem.

'What? That doesn't make sense. Rob loves you. He said you were talking about having another baby. That it was your idea.'

'Oh yeah, I said that all right. More child maintenance.' She winks and rubs her finger and thumb together. 'Then when I've dropped this next sprog, I'll tell him I know about his affair and kick him out. He can go get fucked, Grace. Literally!'

I'm speechless. I just can't imagine Rob would ever do something like that, but I suppose you can never be sure. 'I don't know what to say, Deece, I...' I hold my hands up in defeat. 'Are you certain?'

She shrugs. 'Out till all hours, really cagey with his phone. He's hiding something.' She swallows down what appears to be another influx of tears. 'No, sod it!' She bangs her hand on the table, poker face restored. 'I'll take him on this spa weekend and get to the bottom of it once and for all. But I'll tell you something,' she slurs, her finger jabbing at my chest. 'If I do find out he's knobbing someone else, his crack hair won't be all he'll be returning without.'

44

JUSTIN
3 DAYS EARLIER

'I've missed this place,' says Grace.

I gaze through the windscreen at the tall electric gates. Beyond them, a red gravel driveway curves out of sight some two-hundred yards along two opposing banks of dense hedgerow.

It's the most relaxed I've seen her since we reconnected. I get out of the car and push a button on the stone wall. After a few seconds the ironwork slowly sweeps open and we inch through the entranceway.

We drive in silence for a minute, taking in the grandiose surroundings. 'When was the last time you saw them?' I ask.

'I haven't, not since you left.'

I steal a glance to see if there's any animosity behind her words, but her eyes are focused on the stone fountain centrepiece we steer round in front of an ivy-clad facade.

'And you?' she asks.

'Same. Last time was with you, Caroline's sixtieth. That was a helluva party, remember?'

She laughs. 'I do. Especially those stables.'

'Oh, yeah. Forgot about that. Had a hay rash on my backside for weeks.'

My happiest years were spent in this house, not just the stables I hasten to add, though admittedly the bar for 'happy' was set pretty low from my time in care homes.

I know I was lucky in that respect at least. There aren't many who can say they spent their teens in a twelve-bedroom Georgian mansion on forty acres of land. Jack and Caroline did well for themselves, that's for sure. I wish I could say the same for myself. I turn and look at Daniel in the back seat. I've always wanted to make Jack proud. With this surprise, surely I can now.

Jack and Caroline stand in the doorway waving. Even in their sixties they look like the perfect happy couple. I learnt a lot from them about give and take in a relationship. In theirs it was mainly Caroline giving Jack shit and him taking it, but it was a good lesson in letting things go over your head. But it also taught me to stand up for myself more than he ever did. She has a loving heart, but man could she be a bitch to him sometimes.

While I release Daniel from the car seat, Grace rushes to give them a hug.

'It's been sooo long,' says Caroline. 'We thought you must have fallen out with us.'

'Nah, never,' said Grace. 'You'll always be my favourite in-laws.'

'How've you been, love,' says Jack. I can hear the sincerity in his voice. He always did like Grace, sometimes a bit too much I suspected. He gives her a peck on the cheek.

'Get your bags later, Justin,' he shouts over. 'Come and have a drink first.'

'You go in,' I shout over my shoulder. 'Whisky for me.'

'Okay, we'll be in the kitchen.'

I wait till they disappear inside before I lift Daniel out. 'What do you think, matey?' I say, pointing at the house and gardens. 'This is where Daddy used to live. You'll have a house like this when you're older.' I carry him through the door into the cavernous entrance hall. 'Just do what Daddy says, not what he does, eh?'

The house is exactly as I remember. Classical and elegant, but with enough personality in the scattering of faces smiling from professional, studio-shot, framed photos to avoid feeling cold and impersonal. With each loud footstep on polished marble I recollect more memories; kicking a ball down long bedroom corridors; bounding four steps at a time down the carpeted staircase that fans out onto the reception area like a peacock's tail; skidding Jack's car round and round the fountain in my early teens. I could actually drive by the time I was sixteen, just never took my test until much later. I guess I was never sober enough.

Daniel gazes up at the crystal chandelier dangling from the high ceiling as we stride towards the laughs echoing from a room on the far side of the hallway. We pass two sturdy, panelled doors – one a never-used drawing room and the other, Jack's study, the scene of many a lecture. The kitchen door is open. I feel a knot in my stomach. This is my moment.

Grace and Jack stand at the breakfast island with their backs to me, his hand on the small of her back. Caroline leans on the Aga cooker at the far side, a huge glass of red swishing in her hand as she commands the conversation. She sees me enter and her mouth drops open.

'What the...'

'Jack, Caroline...' I announce. Jack and Grace both wheel round. 'This is Daniel. My son.' I give him a squeeze. Right on cue he smiles the sweetest smile.

Jack's eyes widen. 'Good heavens!' He gazes from me to Grace – and addresses her: 'Well done... congratulations.'

And me? I need him to look at me, to recognise me, my achievement. He gives her a hug.

'How old is he?' barks Caroline. It's a strange first question, but then again, she can be a strange person.

'Sixteen months,' I say quietly.

'And you didn't think to tell us till now?' Her cheeks are flushed, a combination of wine and irritation, always a dangerous combination for Caroline. If history is anything to go by, the only way to avoid an argument with her is to make a hasty exit.

Grace knows this too. She seems to sense my deflation and jumps in. 'It's a bit complicated, Caroline,' she says with a smile. 'We'll tell you all about it at dinner, eh?' She walks over and winks as she takes Daniel from my arms. 'Come on, let's go get the bags and unpack.'

45

GRACE
3 DAYS EARLIER

'Dickheads.'

Justin slams the bedroom door and slumps down onto the chesterfield chaise longue. Behind him, a sash window is partially open.

'Be quiet. What if they're in the garden?' I place Daniel onto a king-size bed neatly made up with an array of white-gold pillows and matching throw. It all looks like it cost the earth, as is standard in the Astley residence. 'God, Justin, I wish we hadn't given Daniel all that chocolate now, what if he chucks up on these sheets? They're probably Egyptian cotton or something.'

'I don't give a shit,' he snaps. 'And I don't care if they can hear me either. They weren't interested that I'd had a kid. Don't even know why we bothered coming.'

'They did care.' Hauling the suitcase onto the bed, I busy myself with the unpacking. 'It was a shock, that's all, you can hardly blame them.' I pull out Justin's suit and look for a place to hang it. I see that it's made of cheap cotton and has gone bobbly from over-washing. I imagine the rest of the guests at Caroline's party tomorrow will be wearing cashmere and silk. I've packed a few high-street dresses that I found buried at the back of the wardrobe. We're going to look like a right pair of paupers. 'Did you even bring a tie?' I ask, now rummaging in the depths of the case. I pull out a dozen pairs of balled-up socks and toss them onto the bed. 'Who brings this many pairs of socks for two nights, Justin?'

'I just thought Jack at least would have shown a bit more interest.' The anger has extinguished now, leaving only sadness.

So this is about Jack, not Caroline. I thought as much. I've lost count of the amount of times over the years Justin has tried, and, in his mind at least, failed, to gain Jack's approval. I don't think Jack does anything wrong per se, apart from continually failing to live up to Justin's father/son fantasies. I choose my next words carefully, knowing if I don't talk Justin down now the whole weekend will be ruined. 'I saw the pride in Jack's eyes, even if you didn't. He was absolutely made up. Just give him time to get his head round it.'

Justin sighs. 'Don't know what I expected anyway, really. I disappear for two years then turn up with a kid I've only known a few weeks. Fucking loser.'

'Language!' I raise my eyebrows over at Daniel who's busy launching Justin's socks at the velvet headboard.

'Shit, sorry... I mean...'

'Crumbs?' I offer, concealing a grin. 'Or sugar? Either's fine.' I quickly feign interest in the remaining unpacked items. 'You've brought tea bags too.' I hold up the unopened box of PG Tips. 'You're a nutter, you know that?'

'Can't be drinking that Earl Grey shite.' He blanches. 'I mean rubbish.' He joins Daniel on the bed and scoops him up onto his knee. 'Anyway, forget about them. This is my first full weekend with you, and I can't wait.' He tickles Daniel's belly and he squeals with delight.

My stomach sinks. How is Justin going to cope when he realises Daniel isn't his child? Not only that but his actual son died before he ever had the chance to live?

I imagine a few choice swear words are going to be the least of my worries.

46

GRACE
3 DAYS EARLIER

'Jack, carve this before it gets cold.'

Caroline places a wooden platter of pork roast between the polished silver goblets, cutlery and vegetable tureens decorating the solid oak dining table. It looks like a medieval banquet. 'I'm sorry we don't have a high chair, obviously if we'd have known the child existed...' The jibe is directed at me, the latest in a long line since we arrived.

'Don't worry.'

'Oh, I'm not.' She places a napkin on her lap and smooths it out. 'Help yourself to parsnips. Looks like you need filling out a bit.'

I feel my cheeks burn. I don't remember Caroline being quite so hostile, though I always knew she wasn't one to mince her words. Justin and I found it hilarious, the way she'd call a spade a spade and Jack a pissed-up pervert when he'd talk to my chest after getting sloshed on brandy. She might act all prim and proper, swanning around her stately home like the Queen of Sheba in petticoats and pearls, but at heart, she'll always be the working-class daughter of an Irish docker. I imagine it was her own upbringing that enabled her to foster children such as

Justin, to see their worth and potential despite the hand they were dealt with. Caroline's never divulged why she and Jack never had children of their own and I've never asked, though I assume they'd have loved to had God permitted.

'I am sorry about not telling you earlier,' I say, feeling suddenly dejected. I don't want Caroline to hate me; she was good to me when Justin and I first got together, always ready to lend an ear when I wanted to offload about Mum and Andrew.

After Justin first disappeared Caroline and I were in regular phone contact but, for reasons unclear to me, I never plucked up the courage to tell her I was pregnant. I guess in a way I always believed that Justin would return, and then we could break the news to Caroline and Jack together as he'd have wanted. When Noah died, I severed all ties, unable to admit that not only had I kept my pregnancy a secret for months, but that I was too useless to even carry him to term.

'What's done is done, Grace,' she says through a sigh. There's no heat in her voice now, which I think is worse. Being the brunt of a person's anger is one thing but knowing you're responsible for their hurt – that's something else entirely. 'It wasn't just your fault was it though?' She frowns at Justin who stares down at his lap, his top lip clamped between his teeth.

'Caroline.' Jack fixes her with a stare but she's not for backing down.

'These things need to be said, Jack. It's not right.' She clatters a spoonful of home-made apple sauce onto her plate.

'Look, Danny, carrots,' I say, far too enthusiastically. 'That's what Bing Bunny eats.' I jostle him from one knee to the other in an attempt to get comfy. The high-back chairs, upholstered in suede and the colour of old gold are about as comfortable as Jack's drunken innuendos.

The whole dining room is, in fact, like being on the set of *Downton Abbey*; a gold runner centres the long table with twin silver candelabras housing tall, white candlesticks that will likely never drip wax. It's a far cry from my dining room, which is really just an IKEA table shoved into the corner of the living room and heaped full of Daniel's books, magazines and overdue bills.

'Looks lovely, this,' forces Justin, helping himself to roast potatoes. I wish I felt comfortable enough to eat because it all looks and smells incredible. Caroline can certainly cook I'll give her that.

'Don't know when I last had a nosh-up like this,' adds Justin.

'Hmm.' Caroline purses her lips as though sucking on a lemon. Clearly, she isn't finished. 'Still cooking him all that processed rubbish, Grace?'

'I haven't actually been cooking him anything at all, have I, Caroline, seeing as though he walked out on me for two years?' I quip, done with walking on eggshells.

'But that's all in the past now,' says Justin, almost pleading for Caroline to drop it. He squeezes hold of my hand under the table. I squeeze it back and make a conscious effort to put my conscience to one side, if only for a weekend. We deserve this much, I tell myself, one weekend as a family, the way it always should have been.

'Everything that happened was my fault,' Justin continues, gazing at Daniel. His eyes are lost in wonder and love. I shuffle uncomfortably in my chair. 'Like I explained on the phone the other night. None of what's happened is Grace's fault so please don't blame her.'

'I blame you both,' counters Caroline, not missing a beat.

Jack's hand hovers over the wooden carving board. 'One slice or two, love?' he asks me after an uncomfortably long silence. His almond-shaped head glistens with sweat from carving. It's actually a good job Justin isn't Jack's biological son, I'm not superficial by any means but I'm not sure I ever could have swum in that gene pool.

'Just a small one, please.'

Jack glances up at me, his dark eyes twinkling under the light of the crystal chandelier. 'Always had you down for liking your meat nice and succulent, Grace.'

'If that was the case, she'd not be asking you to dish it up,' quips Caroline. She smirks at me, leaving Jack as pink as the pork's belly.

I grin back and, just like that, we've made an unspoken truce.

'Does Daniel like all vegetables, lovey?' asks Caroline a moment later, scooping a shiny ladle into a medley of veg. 'If he's anything like Justin, he'll think a parsnip is tantamount to poison.' She flashes a wide smile over at Justin who laughs out loud, clearly relieved in the change of atmosphere. 'I used to have to tell him broccoli was dinosaur trees, wouldn't mind, but he was about fourteen at the time.'

'Good job you pair came along when you did – I'd have developed scurvy,' jokes Justin.

'Remember that dog we used to have, lad?' says Jack, transferring a forkful of pork onto my plate without comment. 'You named him SuperTed and used to sneak him all the green stuff when *she* wasn't looking.' He points his fork at Caroline.

'Oh yeah, SuperTed.' Justin looks off into the distance for a second, lost in happy memories. 'Good times. I hope I can make similar memories for Daniel.' He leans over and ruffles his hair. 'Not hope, will.'

'Well, you've all the time in the world now, haven't you, lad?' says Jack, pride shining from his eyes. 'You're a good kid, Jus, always were. Just no messing it up again, eh?'

'I promise I won't, Dad,' he replies, sincerely.

Underneath the table, I place my hand on his thigh and squeeze it tight. Calling Jack 'Dad' is such a monumental thing for Justin and not something he feels able to do often, only in truly heartfelt moments. Is this one of those moments? The rejoining of a family, the blessing of an added member? And all of it a big, fat lie? I pick up my knife and fork and begin cutting Daniel's potatoes and vegetables into tiny pieces, scraping the cutlery on the bone china.

'Careful, Grace, that's my best crockery. I'd like to keep the pattern on it if that's okay with you,' says Caroline smiling, though I can hear the strain in her voice. She's not as easily fooled as Jack and I'm sure she senses something isn't quite right.

Jack finally sits, having completed his meat-serving duties. 'Let's just put the past behind us now, eh, and enjoy the evening. I, for one, am made up I have a grandson. Better late than never I say.' He pours a hefty glass of red for himself and then tops up the rest. 'To new beginnings,' he toasts. 'Remember, we'll always be here for you, both of you, whatever you need.'

He turns and winks at me. I hate Jack's leching when he's drunk. Justin misses it, he always does, or at least pretends to.

'Whatever you want, you only have to ask,' he continues.

'To new beginnings,' says Justin, now beaming from ear to ear. 'Nothing is going to come in the way of our family ever again.'

At first, I think a glass has smashed, but then I realise somebody is hammering at the window.

47

JUSTIN
3 DAYS EARLIER

'What the hell is that?' Jack's head turns in all directions, his impressive intake of Rioja nullifying his ability to pinpoint from which of the six windows in the dining hall the banging emanates.

Caroline screams as a face presses against the glass pane closest to her. 'Jack! Get your gun.'

Despite the dark, and the glass-contorted features, I know exactly who it is and race over to open the window. 'It's okay, it's Garth, my mate.'

Garth clambers through, dusts himself off, then grins and nods at each of us as though it's a perfectly normal entrance. 'What you all having?' he says calmly, pointing at the half-finished plates. The blood dripping from his hand raises more imperative questions.

'What the hell happened to you?' I ask.

'I, erm... had a little falling out with something.'

Grace comes over and starts dabbing at his hand with her napkin.

'Excuse me, that's French linen!' shouts Caroline.

Jack sits with an inane smile on his face and a bulbous glass of red cradled in his hand. 'I'm curious, Gareth, how did you get through the gates?'

'It's Garth. Without the E. Had to give those up years ago.' He laughs loudly until he realises nobody else gets it.

'Caroline, have you got any bandages? These cuts are quite deep,' says Grace, still nursing Garth's hand wounds.

'You want me to fetch a first-aid kit for the burglar?'

Garth holds his hands up in protest. 'No, really, I'm okay. I just need to have a word with Justin, that's all, then I'll be gone.'

'Not at all,' says Jack. 'You're a friend of Justin's, so you're a friend of ours,' he slurs. 'Come, sit.' He pats an imaginary chair beside him.

'Oh, for God's sake,' shouts Caroline throwing her napkin on the table as she gets up.

'Very kind. Don't mind if I do,' says Garth. 'Only had a bag of Wotsits all day.'

I throw him an angry glance. 'What the hell are you doing here?'

He winks conspiratorially. 'You forgot something.'

48

JUSTIN

I lie on the bed and watch Grace as she sits in her underwear removing make-up in front of a dressing-table mirror. A thick black bobble holds the hair off her face. With her slim physique and makeshift headband she looks like a gym teacher.

I can't help but feel admiration for someone who's near entire life is taken over by an infant, yet she still finds time to both glam up, and then spend just as long at night-time to glam down again. It shows a self-pride, something that still remains elusive in my life.

It's not that I'm a complete down-and-out when it comes to looks, but my own physical attractiveness has never been a priority. I guess with the scar and my blunt features I've resigned myself to the fact that I'm never going to turn heads for the right reason, no matter how much work I put in with my appearance. Hopefully, Daniel will develop more of Grace's physicality.

I reach into my back pocket and pull out the small photo that Caroline gave to me earlier. It's one of the very few pictures I've seen of me as a toddler. I glance down at Daniel who sleeps peacefully in a travel cot beside the bed.

'He looks like me when he's asleep, doesn't he?' I ask Grace quietly.

She tugs off the bobble, letting her hair tumble over her bare shoulders. 'Hmm,' she says, uncommitting.

'Sleeping with his mouth open like that,' I persist.

She begins to brush her hair with one of Caroline's antique, pearl-handled hairbrushes, then looks over her shoulder at Daniel. 'Yeah, I suppose so,' she says casually. She turns back to the mirror.

Propping myself up with one elbow, I continue comparing Daniel's face to my own in the photograph. 'He's got your eyes, but my nose though, hasn't he?'

Grace doesn't bother turning around this time. 'Nah. Not sure who he got those eyes from to be honest.'

I study again, determined to find a resemblance, but Grace is right. Apart from sleeping with his mouth open, there really is no definitive similarity. My doubts surface again, and the inevitable inquisition begins. Who *did* he get those eyes from if it's not me and it's not Grace? How could somebody as beautiful as Grace not get accosted by men falling over themselves to climb in bed with her, and why would she not be tempted, especially when we were going through such a difficult time trying to conceive?

Officially, it was her anorexia that was determined to be the cause of infertility, but that didn't lessen the impact of me still believing I was less of a man for not providing us with a family. Habit of a lifetime, I suppose, the feeling that it was my fault whatever the problem had been instilled in me from an early age.

Thankfully, the image of another man sleeping with Grace doesn't have time to form in my mind as Daniel stirs from his sleep with a small groan. Instinctively, Grace springs into action, even though I'm sure she couldn't possibly have heard him.

I put my hand up and swing my legs off the bed. 'It's okay, I'll see to him.'

She pauses, fighting her maternal instinct.

'I want to,' I insist, lifting Daniel gently from his cot. 'Come here, matey. I've got you. Shh, shh...' I rock him gently on my lap, staring at his perfect sleepy face, feeling the warmth of his snug body. How can he not be mine? I can just feel it, the connection, the love, the staring into each other's eyes – whoever's they resemble. As quickly as he wakes, his delicate little eyelids droop and he falls asleep again.

Grace glances in the mirror. 'Put him back down,' she whispers.

I'm hesitant. I want this moment to last. Father and son, a holy unity – and Grace makes up the Trinity, it's the way it's meant to be. In my mind she is almost holy, such is my absolute love for her. *Christ! This boy is making me feel religious now.* How can such a small being have such an overwhelming impact? I lower him down and stroke his hair gently. This *has* to be my son, he just has to be. And Grace has to be mine. I need her for me to feel whole.

I lie back down, discreetly reach beneath the pillow and pull out the engagement ring box, slipping it out of sight under my leg.

I check to see if Grace noticed. If she has, she's not letting on.

In my mind I run through the two proposal options. I've narrowed it down to the 'traditional route', down on one knee at her side of the bed, or the more intimate way, pulling it from under the pillow after we've made love. In reality I know I should wait until the paternity test results have come through, but right now in this romantic setting, I have so much love and I need to show it, but the moment needs to be perfect. My hand rests on the box as I ponder. Sod it. I can't wait. The thought excites me. I'll just ask her now anyway.

'Grace?'

She doesn't hear me. 'Grace,' I say again louder.

She turns and puts a finger to her lips, her face coated in a mask of white cream. 'Shhh,' she says sternly. 'You'll wake him again. I'm knackered, that's the last thing I want.'

She's tired, edgy, I can sense it, but I can't miss this moment. I continue gazing at her for a minute, happy to be the one who can lie here and watch her get ready for bed. Nobody else gets to do that right here and now, just me. I'm the chosen one, despite royally screwing it up before.

I sit up again. This is it. It's time. My heart pounds as I step towards her. She looks at me in the mirror, forces a quick smile. I place a hand on her bare shoulder. She offers no more than a sideways glance as her fingers smooth her craned neck.

'Grace,' I whisper.

'Hmm?' She turns, looks quizzical at first, her eyebrows wrinkled as to why I'm kneeling. Then her gaze slides to the small black box open in my palm. She stops rubbing. Her mouth drops open.

I swallow hard. 'Grace, will you marry me?'

Her eyes move to mine, but silence remains. It cuts deep.

I hear myself babbling, backing off. I lower my hand. 'I know, sorry, it was a stupid thing to do, how can I expect you to say...'

'Yes.' She says it softly.

I can see her eyes are welling up. *Is she saying it through sympathy, because she can't say no?* 'Really? Are you sure?'

I slide the ring onto her finger, put my arms round her and pull her close. I'm going to be a husband. And a father. A family man. I don't know what to do with the surge of happiness bursting through my body. I want to express it, to shout so loud that it echoes through the hallways of Jack's mansion and out into the streets so everyone can hear it. But I can't. I don't know how. Instead, I say, 'I will never, ever hurt you again, Grace, I promise you, on my life.'

She dabs her eyes with the back of her hand and wipes cream off my cheek. 'I know,' she says. 'I believe you.'

I stay kneeling as we stare into each other's eyes, holding hands. This really does feel like a life shift, like I've turned a corner. Her eyes search mine. I see trust, like she believes me, but I can't help feeling there's a sense of sadness too. I need her to stop feeling sorry for me. But for that, I need to stop feeling sorry for myself. I need to be a man – a strong, confident man who can take care of his family. In my mind I make a vow that this is exactly who I will be from now on.

49

GRACE

2 DAYS EARLIER

Caroline shoves an enormous fry-up in front of me. 'Here you go, lovey. Get some meat on them bones, you're as thin as a rake.'

'You got a bit of the old Tommy K, Caz?' asks Garth, his mouth stuffed full of mushed-up sausage.

I fight the urge to vomit. 'Give it a rest, will you?'

'What?' He crams in another forkful, his cheeks still bulging from the first. 'Don't be such a princess, all comes out the same hole in the end.' He belches loudly.

'You're gross.' I attempt a sip of sugary tea but my stomach lurches in protest. I never intended to drink so much last night but, once Daniel had fallen asleep, it was all too easy to bury my conscience at the bottom of a bottle. Now, my head is throbbing, a combination of dehydration and stress. I wrongly assumed that this weekend would provide some clarity, a way through all the mess; though I'd be lying if I said a part of me didn't want to indulge in the fantasy of the three of us being a family. I guess the problem with fantasies is that they're forever at the mercy of the truth.

Justin skulks into the kitchen wearing an oversized T-shirt

and a pair of checked pyjama bottoms, Jack's I imagine. He squints at Daniel who pushes a model steam train along the marble floor. 'Cute. I'll take you on a proper train soon, mate.' His voice is gruff, as though his vocal cords have been wrapped in sandpaper. 'How much did we even drink last night?' He sits down on the stool beside me and pilfers a slice of toast from Garth's plate.

'How should I know? I was pissed when I arrived.' Garth proceeds to squirt a half bottle of ketchup onto the side of his plate. 'Cheers, Caz, you're a legend.'

'It's Caroline, Gareth.'

'Garth.'

She rolls her eyes. 'Morning, Justin, love.' She pecks him on the cheek. 'Sleep well?'

'Like a king.' He wraps an arm around me and pulls me into him. 'Things couldn't be better, hey Grace?' He winks at me conspiringly. 'Shall we tell them?' He whispers into my ear, the excitement emanating from him.

'Not yet.' I place a hand on his thigh and give it a squeeze. 'Let me get my head around it first, yeah?'

Justin nods but his eyes cloud over.

'Maybe tonight,' I add, not wanting to hurt him.

Christ! I've agreed to marry him. Why don't I just ask him if he'd like Daniel to be our pageboy and Candice the maid of honour to really screw everything up.

'Something wrong with that breakfast, Grace?' quips Caroline. She leans across me and hands Justin a mug of coffee. 'Black and sweet, that's right, isn't it?'

'Yep. And we're not just talking about coffee,' says Garth.

'Shut up, you dickhead.' Justin's jaw clenches.

'Language.' Caroline playfully clouts him around the back of the head. 'Child present.'

I glance down at the now cold, greasy rashers of bacon and

the fried egg congealed in thick oil. Nausea claws at my throat. 'There's nothing wrong with the breakfast, honestly I just feel a bit queasy. You know how much of a lightweight I am.' I attempt a laugh but it's not convincing. 'Oh and happy birthday by the way, it completely slipped my mind till now.'

'Oh, don't worry, love,' says Caroline, now back at the Aga where another half-dozen eggs sizzle and spit. She doesn't look her usual prim self this morning. Void of make-up, the masses of crow's feet around her bloodshot eyes add an extra decade onto her now sixty-four years. 'Let's be honest, you're only here for the party,' she quips. 'Why the hell would you remember it's my birthday?'

My face burns. 'Honest to God I...'

'I'm joking, Grace.' She shakes her head. 'Heavens, when did you become so uptight?'

'Sorry.' I sink my fork into a blood-red tomato. 'So what's the plan for this morning?' I nudge Justin in the ribs. 'Take it you'll be wanting to get back home, Garth? I don't mind dropping you at the train station once I've had a shower.'

'Nah, you're all right. Might as well stick around for the shindig, eh, Jus?' He mops up the remainder of his bean juice with his last hunk of toast.

I sigh loudly but Garth seems to neither notice nor care. Him being here is ruining everything. This weekend was meant to be *our* time as a family; Justin, me and Daniel – not a pissing school reunion with the class clown.

'Excuse me, I think I'm going to puke.' Scraping back the stool, I grab my mobile from the breakfast bar and head to the downstairs loo. Locking myself in, I slump onto the toilet seat and hold my head in my hands. Why am I even here? What did I hope to achieve? All I've done is complicate things further, involved more innocent people in my madness. Absentmindedly, I swipe in the pattern to unlock my phone and see a message from Candice.

Danny boy Ok? Hotel is lush x

It was sent last night, around the same time that Garth came quite literally crashing into our lives. I fire off a reply, glad that at least one of us is enjoying the weekend.

All good here. Are you reconnecting with Rob? X

The reply is almost immediate.

He's gone for a sauna. I've got his phone. Let's see what he's hiding. X

50

GRACE
NOW

'So did Candice discover something on her husband's phone?'

'She did.' I fidget in my seat, looking everywhere but at Sally. I'm not comfortable with this line of questioning.

'What did she discover, Grace?'

'It was ...' Anger churns inside of me but I fight to keep my expression neutral. 'Look, you need to ask Rob. It isn't for me to say.'

'We're questioning him as well, Grace, but it's important we get your side too.'

I glance at my solicitor for instruction, who unhelpfully shrugs. I bite the inside of my cheek, unsure whether to tell the truth or not. Obviously, *anything* that will help to find Daniel is worth confessing but surely what Candice found on Rob's phone has no connection to Daniel's disappearance.

Or does it?

51

JUSTIN

2 DAYS EARLIER

Garth leans over the breakfast table, a dollop of tomato sauce on his chin. 'Get your nuts in last night, then?'

'Keep your voice down!' I gesture over at Caroline who's now buttering toast.

Garth pulls a 'whatever' face before pilfering my last half sausage. 'Starving, I am. Hey, Jus, bring back memories?' He performs some weird sex act on the sausage. 'For an old house, the walls aren't half thin here.' He winks conspiratorially.

'Stop being a dick!' I wait for him to stop laughing before I continue. 'Listen, I've got something to tell you.' I drop my voice to a whisper. 'I proposed last night.'

Garth visibly pales. 'Why the hell would you do that? You got the DNA back then?'

The reminder that Daniel might not actually be my son causes a lump to lodge in my throat. 'No, but it doesn't matter, I trust her.' Even as I protest this out loud, I wonder if I'm really being truthful. Do I trust Grace implicitly? She didn't exactly jump for joy when I proposed last night, did she? Then, of course, there was the note on my car, which said blatantly that I wasn't Daniel's father. One of Jack's many sayings is 'there's no smoke without fire', and I can't help but feel these alarm bells signal a raging inferno.

'Well, that's good then. S'pose she said yes, so congrats and all that.' Garth hides his expression behind a mug of tea, but I see the disappointment in his eyes.

'It won't change anything between me and you, mate.'

'Yeah, whatever.' He slurps the tea noisily. 'But rather you than me, bro.'

Here we go. Garth has never been able to keep his opinions to himself for more than a nanosecond. 'And why's that?'

He shrugs. 'She's hiding something. Can see it in her eyes. Shifty as hell.'

I don't immediately answer. That I can't bring myself to leap to Grace's defence says a lot. 'He's my kid,' I mutter eventually. 'I can feel it.'

Garth slams down his mug and scrapes back the chair. 'Your funeral, mate. I'm going for a smoke.' He saunters out through the patio doors and into the garden.

'What was all that about?' Caroline dumps a plate of toast down beside me and takes the empty mugs. I don't answer until she's busy filling the dishwasher.

'Nothing, just Garth being Garth.' I debate whether to confide in Caroline about my suspicions surrounding Daniel's paternity, but think better of it. Yesterday, Caroline was furious with Grace for keeping Daniel a secret and I don't want to rock the boat anymore. I also want to announce our engagement this evening and want Caroline and Jack to be pleased.

'Gareth's jealous,' remarks Caroline matter-of-factly. 'He doesn't like to see you happy. Wants to keep you miserable and reliant on him. He'll cause trouble for you, mark my words.'

Although I know she speaks sense, and that Garth *is* likely jealous, I also know him better than her, better than anyone, in fact. Garth is as good as a brother. There's no way he'd intentionally cause trouble for me. Though I can't deny he's done nothing but cast doubt in my mind since the moment I told him about Daniel. A worrying thought catches me off guard. What if Garth wrote the note on my windscreen? Could he really stoop that low to keep me away from Grace?

My mobile vibrates on the breakfast table, a message from a number I don't recognise.

I know everything. I'm going to the police.

I feel my face flush. Without hesitation, I bash out a reply.

No, don't, I'll…

What? I'll do what? Tell Grace what I did? There's no way I can do that. If I tell her the truth now, she'll never agree to marry me and I can kiss goodbye to my son. I hold my finger on the backspace button and watch the words disappear, my thoughts racing; who is the message from? Are they bluffing about the police? I think I know the answer to both, but I can't be sure.

'Hey, fancy sharing a shower?'

Grace's hot breath in my ear makes me jump. I drop the phone onto the table.

'What you so uptight about?'

I glance down at the upturned phone, the message still on display. If Grace reads it over my shoulder, I'm done for.

'Nothing. You made me jump. Is Danny all right?'

I attempt to steer her attention over to Daniel who's tottering around the kitchen waving a wooden spatula in the air.

'He's fine.' She barely looks at him. 'Shall we go to the pub for lunch this afternoon? Just me, you and Danny?'

'Sounds good,' I say, my brain now working overtime. I'm going to have to ask Jack for money, a lot of money. I need to get

Grace and Daniel away from here for good, before everything blows up and I lose everything.

'What you lovebirds whispering about?' Garth moseys past us, reeking of stale smoke. 'Congratulations by the way,' he says loudly to Grace. 'He's a keeper. Don't fuck it up, yeah?'

He stuffs his mobile back into his jeans pocket and smirks.

52

GRACE

2 DAYS EARLIER

Shoehorning Daniel into the cramped, leather-clad booth at the Fox & Hound, I clock the ice bucket on the adjacent table, the neck of a white wine bottle poking seductively out of the top. 'I guess it's too early for alcohol, right?'

'Trust me, it's never too early for alcohol.' Justin pulls out his mobile and jabs angrily at the screen. 'Sorry, just Garth,' he mumbles. 'Wants to know if he can borrow a pair of my boxers or should he ask Jack.' He shakes his head.

I study the wine list – though I haven't the first clue what I'm looking at; *Semillon, Chardonnay, Riesling.*

'What will it be then?' snaps Justin. 'We haven't got long.'

I shoot him a look. 'What's got into you?'

'Nothing,' he counters. 'You're just taking forever.'

'I'm actually not.' I toss the wine list across the table. 'Whatever then, you choose.'

'Look, sorry,' he says, breathing out. 'Just got a lot on my plate.'

'Haven't we all.'

'You know I can only handle Jack and Caroline for short bursts.'

When I don't reply he leans in and cups my face in his hands, forcing me to look up at him. 'I'm sorry, okay, I'm a dickhead.'

I roll my eyes. 'That's hardly news.'

Justin smirks before averting his gaze to Daniel. 'What do you fancy then, Danny boy? Chef's crockpot lamb stew and dumplings or rustic beef caldo, whatever the hell that is.'

'I think that's a tad disturbing to be fair,' I joke. 'Lamb and beef on the menu when the view from the bay window is fields of cows and sheep.'

Justin feigns a laugh but I sense he's still uptight. Surely Jack and Caroline haven't rattled him *that* much? I can't think of a single thing they've done other than accommodate us. Which begs the question, what is Justin *really* worried about?

'Right,' he says, now scanning the drinks menu. 'A couple of white wines and a Coke for Danny, yeah?'

'He's *one*, Justin. Coke will have him bouncing off the walls and rot his teeth. Water or orange.' I don't mean to sound offhand but his mood is clearly rubbing off on me.

'Right. Course, sorry. Shit at this dad lark, aren't I?' For a minute I think he might cry.

My stomach sinks. 'Course not. It's new to you, that's all. Look, I'm sorry, let's start again, hey? We're meant to be celebrating.'

'And you're sure you want to marry me?' he asks abruptly.

I frown. 'Of course.'

'Are you sure? Only you didn't exactly jump at it last night.'

Guilt burns my cheeks. 'It was a shock, that's all. I want to marry you, now stop stressing. Look, Danny, sheep.' I lift Daniel onto my knee and point to a flock of sheep in the field opposite. 'Can you say baa?'

Thankfully, Justin takes the hint that the conversation is over and goes in pursuit of alcohol. If I wasn't responsible for Daniel, I'm pretty sure I'd drink the pub dry.

I didn't want to confess the truth about Daniel this weekend, but what choice do I have? If we announce the engagement tonight at Caroline's party then it'll only dig the hole deeper.

I spend the next few minutes people-watching in an attempt to distract myself from the shitshow I'm starring in.

There's the typical assortment of country folk; locals enjoying an afternoon pint of some strangely named ale: families like us, though not like us at all really – real families, void of lies and deceit, a husband, wife and kids – though who knows really. Perhaps they're all just as bad, hiding things, pretending to be something they're not. Even the pub itself is play-acting with its clean-cut logs neatly positioned on a pristine fireplace and faux-brass horseshoes hung at measured distances above the bar.

With Justin heading back, I quickly check my phone for messages. I've heard nothing from Candice since this morning and I'm intrigued to hear what, if anything, she's discovered on Rob's phone. I can't for a second imagine there'll be anything untoward going on, Rob's not the type to play away.

'Grace. Give us a hand, will you?' Justin towers over me juggling a round of drinks, a miniature pack of crayons and a kid's menu the size of Great Britain. Relieving him of the drinks, I settle Daniel down with the crayons and menu. 'He's got a really good pincer grip, hasn't he?' he continues, now much happier.

'Pincer grip. Where the hell did you learn that?'

'I've been swatting up. On toddler milestones. He's advanced for his age, you know, Grace. You've done an amazing job with him.'

I spend far too long staring at Daniel colouring, deciding on the best way to respond. What do I even say to that? Ironically, I have done well with Daniel. Every day, or at least Monday to Friday, I've put my all into his development, have done way more than Rob and Candice ever have, so why shouldn't I take the credit? 'Thanks, Justin. And you're amazing with him too. I'm proud of you, really I am.'

'Look,' he says, taking a deep breath. 'I have an idea.' I catch something flash beneath the surface of his casual expression – nerves? 'I didn't know if to say anything. Because well, I wasn't sure whether you'd go for it but I suppose I... Okay, listen, just don't dismiss it straight away.'

'Just spit it out.' I take a large gulp of wine.

'I think we should start afresh. The three of us.'

I open my mouth to protest but there's something about the way he looks at me, so full of hope, that makes the words die in my throat.

'Don't dismiss it, please. I just want you to think about it. Jack said last night he would help us in any way he can and I think he'd be good for the cash we'll need for a clean break. We can move somewhere, Tenerife maybe, you always liked it there when we went on holiday?'

'Tenerife?' I almost spit out my drink. 'What about the house? What about Daniel's friends, his life?' My voice no longer sounds like my own. 'Justin! I can't just take Daniel and leave.'

'Just say you'll think about it?' His voice breaks into an almost plea. Why does he need to get away? Or rather *who* does he need to get away from? What the hell is Justin hiding?

'Please, Grace,' he whispers, his eyes now burning into me. 'I need you to say you'll think about it.'

'Okay,' I relent, knowing the lie which will inevitably force its way out of my mouth even though all I want to do is tell the truth. 'I'll give it some thought. Now hurry up and order because it's already midday and Jack said to be back for two at the latest to take you shooting.'

'That's when I'll ask him for the money,' he says, now beaming. 'That's what we need, Grace, I know it. A fresh start, the three of us, a real family at last.'

53

JUSTIN
2 DAYS EARLIER

'How far is it?' I heave the three gun cases further onto my shoulder. How've I got landed with carrying all the shotguns like a manservant while these two stroll in front of me as if they're lifelong buddies? Jack and I have so much in common, so much history, yet it's Garth he chooses to befriend and converse with on this interminably long march to the shooting area.

It irks me how someone who doesn't give a shit what they say or how they behave can form an instant connection with somebody, while I'm constantly modifying my manner to appease and fit in.

'Are we there yet?' mocks Garth over his shoulder. 'You sound like a fucking child.'

I actually feel the petulance of a child right now, scuffing borrowed wellies through gorse while Garth, my dope-smoking, no-verbal-filter drifter has his arm draped around the shoulders of Jack, the well-to-do, mansion-dwelling, steel exporter who I consider to be *my* dad, not his, and from whom I need reassurance, and help.

'Keep up, lad,' jokes Jack. They both laugh.

I'm envious of them; Jack for his wealth, even though partly inherited, and the consequential stability of knowing any kind of expenditure is never an issue; and Garth for his ability to not give a shit what anybody thinks of him, happy in who he is, not needing the approval or acceptance of anyone else. Right now, I'd give anything for that freedom, to not have this incessant itch of insecurity that I'm not good enough, the manacles of appeasement marshalling every word and action in front of others.

'These are heavy,' I complain.

'Stop whinging, you poof,' says Garth.

I realise that I pass my words and actions through this border control with everybody, but none more so than with Jack. The urge to hear and feel Jack's approval is almost primal, like I can't help it. It's a fix, a need, one that occupies an unhealthy amount of my thoughts when in his company. How has it got to the stage where my sense of self-worth is in the hands of another man? How can it be self-worth when it can only be assigned by someone else?

I focus on slowing my heart rate, trying to convince myself that it's the exertion of carrying these damn guns rather than anxiety causing the banging in my chest. *I need to ask him now! I need to know that my life isn't going to fall apart.*

I step up the pace to get beside my foster dad. 'Jack?'

He stops in his tracks.

'You know you said if I needed anything...'

He puts a finger to his lips. 'Shush. We're here.'

I distribute the gun cases in silence. It's the first time I've held a weapon since trying to join the army. I stare down at this manufacturer of misery in my hands – the breach, the trigger, the barrel, the stock – all designed with one thing in mind – ending a life. My heart quickens further.

Jack is showing Garth how to load two shells into the barrel.

Neither of them has realised Garth's shotgun is pointing at me, that's how invisible I am to Jack right now.

'Garth, point that thing away, you idiot!'

This lack of caring reminds me how far apart Jack and I have grown since I first pulled up outside his ivy-cloaked heaven in a social worker's car, aged thirteen: 'You've struck lucky here, Justin. Don't fuck it up,' were the social worker's departing words as I stood gaping at the mansion wondering who in their right mind could see *me*, out of all the care home misfits, settling into such salubrious surroundings.

Nobody was more surprised than I was when I was still part of the good life twelve months later, towing the line for fear of losing it all. I guess complacency had a lot to do with the subsequent troubles once the varnish of living a rich kid's life rubbed off after that first year. Both Jack and Caroline were brilliant, but even their love and encouragement wasn't enough to patch up the damage that had already been done in my childhood.

My intrinsic need to destroy anything good manifested itself first in petty crimes like shoplifting and smoking weed, before progressing to stealing cars and selling class-A drugs. It was only Jack's influence in high places that kept me out of prison for so long, but inevitably even that wasn't enough in the end. Naturally, the older and more delinquent I grew, the more their patience thinned, and I knew that my time with them was coming to an end.

Even though I brought it about myself, the pain of being told to leave the house in my late teens was the catalyst that propelled me down the rabbit hole of depression that I'm still now trying to claw my way out of.

Years of counselling have made me aware that to gain the respect of others, like Jack, I first need to have the respect of myself, and it's for this reason that so far, I've never approached him for financial help, despite the homelessness and the poverty-stricken life I've created for myself.

I'm trapped in a fury of emotions – jealousy, insecurity, helplessness – coupled with the awareness that I'm impotent in being able to protect the ones I treasure, in fact, I'm the opposite, a burden on both their financial and physical well-being.

Deep in my heart I know that what I want is the opposite of what they must have. In short, I'm bad news for everyone. Including myself.

Suddenly the answer is obvious, a pain-free future staring at me right there in my own hands, loaded. How easy would it be to solve all problems with one squeeze on a curl of metal, like a genie clicking his finger, granting every wish come true.

54

GRACE

2 DAYS EARLIER

Caroline's bedroom is just as lavish as the rest of the estate; a flourish of bows tie the velvet drapes back as elegantly as Harrods gift wrapping, while a crystal chandelier rains shimmering sparkles onto the bedspread like a glorified disco ball.

'I look like a flaming undercooked turkey!' says Caroline with a grimace, a blush-pink feather dress the object of her revulsion. 'It looked lovely on that Cheryl Cole as well.'

I suppress a grin. 'It looks lovely on you too, Caroline.'

'You're a good liar, Grace.' She turns sidewards in the full-length mirror and sucks in her stomach. 'No, I best not. Jack might mistake me for one of those coots and shoot me.' She throws me a wry smile. 'Back to the drawing board. Do us a favour and unzip me at the back.'

I roll my eyes before wrestling with the zip. Caroline's hardly overweight, but I think a size twelve was pushing it. 'I need to go and call my cousin in a minute. You remember Candice?' Even saying her name out loud causes my heart rate to spike.

'Vaguely.' Caroline pulls the feather dress over her head and tosses it onto the bed beside me. 'Might as well chuck that right in the bloody bin. What's so urgent you need to speak to her about, anyway?'

'Oh, nothing. She's having some marital problems, that's all.'

'Aren't we all.' Caroline reappears from her dressing area with another half-dozen designer dresses, half of which still have labels on. The price tag on one is more than my week's wage. 'I want to throttle Jack ninety per cent of the time, the lecherous old goat.' She laughs out loud before catching my eye in the mirror. 'I'm glad Justin saw sense and came back to you, you know, Grace.'

I'm taken aback by the sudden shift in conversation. Although Caroline's still smiling, I now see sadness in her eyes.

'You know he never had it easy,' she says, the smile melting into a frown. 'I don't know how anyone can treat their own flesh the way he was treated. You know what he went through in his early years, don't you?'

'Some, yeah.'

There's a beat of silence as we both consider the horrors Justin endured in his childhood. I think I've only scratched the surface of the abuse he suffered, not only at the hands of his biological parents but also in the children's home. It makes me feel guilty to think about it. I may have had my fair share of heartbreak and lacked self-esteem, but in contrast my childhood was heaven compared to his.

'It still haunts me to think of that accident, you know.'

My heart rate instantly picks up. 'What accident?'

Caroline pauses, her cheeks flushing pink. 'Oh. You know, the...' She blows out a shaky breath. 'God, Grace, I thought he'd told you. It's where he got the scar from.'

I shake my head, confused. 'You mean when he fell out of the tree?'

Caroline shoos off the subject with a wave of the hand. 'Best we keep all that in the past now.' She turns away and makes a show of inspecting herself in the latest dress, but I can tell her heart is no longer in it.

'He didn't get the scar from falling out of a tree then?'

Caroline considers me before answering. 'He was a mess back then, Grace, that's all you need to know. You know he suffered blackouts as a child?'

I nod.

'He'd go into these awful rages. It was terrifying.' She looks off into the distance. 'He used to say some horrible things, lash out at Jack. He couldn't remember doing it afterward. It was like he'd suddenly snap back to being the placid little boy who still sucked his thumb and cried at films when he didn't think we were looking. Bloody *Bambi* got him every time.' She laughs sadly before plastering a smile back onto her face. 'But it's come good for him in the end. That boy in there will be the making of him, you mark my words.' She gestures next door to the guest bedroom where Daniel is sleeping. 'Hey, luvvie, what's wrong?'

I'm not even aware of the tears dripping down my face until I feel Caroline's heaviness on the mattress. She wraps her arms around me and instinctively I place my head on her chest.

'Come on, Grace, it can't be that bad.' She strokes my hair, just like Mum used to do when I was a little girl. It only makes me cry harder. 'Sweetheart,' she continues, her voice soft in my ear. 'I didn't want to say anything, you know... about your weight, it's none of my business. But are you having those problems again?'

She doesn't need to specify. We both know she's referring to my battle with anorexia.

'I don't know. Not intentionally.' I study my reflection and am horrified at the contrast between us; Caroline is naturally attractive, though not in a classical way. She's far from slim, but somehow her curves only accentuate her natural beauty. The map of wrinkles on her forehead and around her eyes tells, not of an ageing woman but of a life lived and enjoyed. She's genuine in her fullness. In contrast, I'm little more than a ghost.

'Tell me what's bothering you, Grace. Is it all this Justin stuff?'

'No. It isn't him. Caroline...' I look up at her. 'I did a bad thing. I've lied... to Justin, to you all.'

'If this is about you not telling me you were pregnant, it's okay. It was a shock at first, of course it was, but I bet you'll have had your reasons. There's no hard feelings, love. I'm sorry if I made it seem that way. You know how I can be.'

I pull away from her, self-hatred burning deep in my heart. The only way to ease the burden of guilt is to confess everything. 'It's not that. It's...' I break eye contact, unable to find the right words. How can I tell her what I've done? That I've betrayed her, Justin and Jack. How can I admit that I've dug a hole as deep as a grave, and that I deserve nothing more than to be thrown in it?

'Bloody hell, luvvie, you've got mascara all down this dress now. It was the front runner an' all.' Caroline's interruption steals the confession from my lips. 'Look, Grace,' she continues, now back in front of the mirror scrutinising herself. 'Whatever it is, it won't be as bad as you think. Justin is back in your life and you're blessed to have such a beautiful little boy.' She unfastens the gown and allows it to drop to the floor. 'As long as you have those two by your side, then there's nothing that can't be fixed. Am I right?' She clicks her fingers at a velvety, pink ball gown on the top of the pile.

'You're right,' I say, handing it to her. 'And I'll do whatever it takes to keep us all together.'

'That's my girl.' She slips the gown over her head. 'Oh, look at this one,' she says, twirling around with the agility of a woman half her age. 'I think we have a winner.'

55

JUSTIN
2 DAYS EARLIER

'For God's sake, lad. Have I taught you nothing?' Jack's hands are on the barrel, guiding its aim away from my face. His eyes linger on mine – not angry or annoyed, just knowing – *not here, not now* – then he walks away – blind to the mist that muddles my thoughts, turning his back on my suffering.

I fumble with the safety catch and tilt my head down to avoid them noticing. *Stop crying! Get a grip.* As Jack would drum into me constantly, '*You rarely find the right thing to do on the path of least resistance.*' I have to find another way to stop these trembling hands, this hammering heartbeat, the profuse sweat mingling with the tears.

The right thing to do. What *is* the right thing to do? *Do something, anything.*

'Jack, I need to borrow some money,' I suddenly blurt out like a random thought.

He lowers his gun, unhinges the barrel, and turns back to me. A swirl of smoke spirals from the smoking breech. Garth is oblivious and carries on blasting at imaginary foul with alarming regularity.

'What for?'

I want to say, *Does it matter what for? I'm asking for your help.*
'To start a new life with Grace and Daniel.'

'And do what, exactly?' He raises his eyebrows.

'Just set us up... house, car, the usual stuff.'

'And you have no money of your own? Even though you've
started a family? Did you not think about that first?'

Come on, Jack, don't put me through this. 'I got into a bit of a
mess, and now with Grace and Daniel and everything, I need to
get us out of it.'

'I see. You know, you rarely find the right thing to do along
the path of...'

'I know, I know... the path of least resistance and all that,' I
interrupt dismissively. 'So you keep telling me.'

'But what would you learn if I just gave you the money, just
like that?'

I try hard to control the anger bubbling inside. I fail. 'I'm not
asking for a fucking life lesson, I'm asking for your help.' Jack's
expression darkens, and I immediately regret the tone.

His voice is cold and distant now. 'There's no need for that.'

'I'm sorry.'

'When are you going to learn to stand on your own two feet,
be a man for once?' He sighs.

A pain like an electric shock makes me physically jump, like
an exposed nerve poked and prodded. 'So will you help me or
not?' I say it loud to be heard above the constant high-pitched
ringing in my ears.

'It's not that simple.'

'It is. Yes or no?'

'No.'

My body jolts again. 'You said you'd help. *Anything*, you
said... just last night!'

'Listen, Justin. I can't keep cleaning up your mess. You're a
father now, act like one.'

His words smother me like a hand across my mouth, stealing my breath. 'You're my dad. You're *meant* to help me.'

'I've done more than enough for you, lad. Loved you like a son.' Jack shakes his head, his disappointment palpable. 'But when all's said and done, you're not even my flesh and blood.'

Not his flesh and blood? It's the first time I've heard this, the first time I've felt it. It's a blow I didn't see coming. I feel myself sinking lower as if underwater, further and further from the surface where survival lies.

Jack is still blathering in the background, '... everything I've done is to *help* you, to make you a better man...'

Garth has moved closer, his gun still pointing skywards, chasing clouds. 'Justin. What's up, bro?'

'Fuck off!' I back away, lose my footing and hit the ground.

I can't see, like I've gone blind. Muffled sounds mingle with the high-pitched screams of a young boy, and voices, so many voices, each chant the same question: *What have you done, Justin? What have you done?* I stagger to my feet, the ground spiralling below as a narrow line of vision returns. I swipe at a hand that grips my arm and run for my life into the dense woodland.

56

GRACE

2 DAYS EARLIER

Caroline marches over to where I'm playing with Daniel on the preened lawn, a murderous expression on her made-up face. 'Where the hell are they? I'm going to kill Jack, I promise.' An angry red rash has snaked its way up from her chest to her neck, a yardstick for her inner fury. It clashes with the winning dusky-pink gown.

It's now close to 5.30pm and an army of frazzled caterers are still rushing around with platters of sea creatures and meaty salvers. The centrepiece, a spit-roasted pig complete with hairy snout, is doing nothing for my lingering hangover. What's wrong with cheese on sticks and a good old tuna vol-au-vent?

'I have no idea where they are, honestly.' I look over Caroline's shoulder in the direction of the wrought-iron gates which are now open to allow access to guests. There's still no sign of Jack, Justin and Garth, despite them being under strict instructions to be back by 4.30 at the very latest. Well, Jack and Justin at least, Garth is welcome to stay out until Jesus returns. 'I bet it's something to do with Garth, probably shot himself in the foot.'

Caroline doesn't react. I'm not even sure she's heard me. I

follow her gaze to a middle-aged couple who are busy scrutinising a draped table of fancy cheeses and bloated bread baskets. Behind them, a backdrop of white fairy lights cascades over a grove of fir trees, quite magical if they weren't pulsating like at some sort of teen rave.

'Good Lord, Grace, this is turning into a disaster.'

I place a hand on Caroline's shoulder and give it a gentle squeeze. 'I mean I suppose it could be a good thing. It's probably best all the guests are tanked up before Garth makes an appearance.'

This at least raises a smile, though I can tell she's still mithered. 'Go and see if Mr and Mrs Mogg need a top-up will you, love. I'll nip back inside and ring Jack again.'

Although I feel self-conscious sauntering up to a couple I've never met, I know it's what Caroline needs of me right now. When I was a child I'd hide behind Mum whenever I was faced with a new situation or fresh faces, using her as a physical shield between me and them. Later, as a teenager, I did the same thing with Candice, no longer physically hiding as I had with Mum but always keeping her close.

I keep one eye on Daniel as I make my way over to Mr and Mrs Mogg. They're the second couple to arrive in the last ten minutes, the 'early birds' Mum used to joke. 'Do they not know when you say seven you mean eight,' she'd say. Though this only seemed true of the White British folk; eight o'clock to many of our South African friends meant somewhere before midnight.

The first to arrive tonight was Jack's sister and brother-in-law; he's the aristocratic type, all tweed jackets and curly moustache. Jack's sister, if I remember correctly, likes a good knees-up and can get more lairy than Caroline. I check they're well topped-up but they seem happy enough over by the marquee, scoffing some sort of folded fish hors d'oeuvres from a waiter who looks about as comfortable as I feel. The ruffled skater dress and kitten heels make me look less Elizabeth Taylor and more Avril Lavigne.

The Moggs, in comparison, are dressed for the occasion, though on closer inspection it's clear that Mrs Mogg is much older than her expensively dyed hair and figure-flattering silk dress would have you believe.

'Hiya, I'm Grace, nice to meet you.' I consider whether it's customary to shake hands or lean in and kiss... But what? His cheek? Her cheek? Should I curtsey?

'Are you staff?' Mrs Mogg wrinkles her nose before linking arms with her husband and pulling him close. They even smell expensive.

'Caroline asked me to see if you'd like a top-up.'

'A top-up, yes. About time.' Mrs Mogg hands me her champagne glass and like an idiot, I thank her for it. 'Something a tad more vintage if it's not too much trouble. I'm not sure my palate can take another Blanc de Blancs.' She snorts out a laugh. 'Vintage, dear.' She places a manicured hand on my arm. 'It means the grapes were all harvested in a single year. Something from the sixties would suffice.'

'Okay, I'll...'

'Just ask Caroline, she'll understand,' she says, shooing me away.

'Okay. Sure.' Face burning, I hurry back over to the drinks table, both embarrassed and annoyed. I should have told Mr and Mrs Snob to get their own bloody drinks; Justin would have. Even Garth, for all his misgivings, and there are plenty, would have told them where to go. Indignantly, I slosh a half-drank bottle of cava into the two glasses.

'Chateau Mouton,' I declare a moment later, grateful for Google. 'Though Caroline said not to broadcast it.'

'Got it.' Mrs Snob taps the side of her nose. 'Mum's the word.'

'All good?' I ask, watching her take a sip.

'Like an old friend.'

'Just what I thought.' I suppress a smile. 'If you'll excuse me.' Head held high, I saunter back to Daniel and scoop him up. 'Don't ever grow up thinking anybody's better than you, mate.' Positioning him on my hip, I make my way over to Caroline who is now fussing around the latest set of guests. 'No news?'

'Still ringing out.' I can see she's now close to the edge. 'Did you sort the Moggs out?' she asks while tickling Daniel under the arm. 'He really is a bonny baby. Justin's a lucky man.'

'Moggs all taken care of,' I say, ignoring the comment about Justin. The less I think about that situation the better. 'How do you even know them?'

'Oh, Alistair Mogg is Jack's golfing buddy.' She rolls her eyes. 'I know, I know. They're... hard work, shall we say.'

'Complete and utter toffs if you ask me.'

She laughs out loud. 'I remember why I like you now, Gracie.'

Her words dislodge feelings I didn't even realise were jammed: relief, joy, but also guilt and sadness. Caroline's approval means the world, though I know it's born out of lies and deceit. 'Listen,' I say, keen to be on my own to process everything. 'You go do what you do best. Make everyone feel at home. I'll go and ring Justin again.'

'Okay, and tell him if they're not here in the next ten minutes I'm going to stick those rifles where the sun don't shine.'

'Where the hell are you?' I seethe, Justin's answer machine the catalyst for my suppressed emotions. 'Caroline is going nuts. Hurry up for God's sake!' I hang up, though I'm conscious to keep the phone at hand in case he rings back. 'I'll tell you what, Danny boy, your daddy has a lot to...' I stop dead, my heart sinking. When did I start to believe my lies? 'Coming here wasn't a good idea was it, buddy?'

The phone vibrates. 'Justin, about bloody...'

'Justin?' Candice's voice stops me in my tracks.

Shit! 'Candice, it's not what...'

'I need to speak to you, Grace,' she interrupts, her voice breathy as though she's trying to stifle tears.

'What's the matter?' My pulse thunders in my ears – Justin, Daniel – does she know?

'There's something I have to tell you,' she whispers, her voice now breaking into quiet sobs. 'I'm coming to yours now. Keep Danny safe till I get there. I'm scared, Grace.'

'What do you mean keep Danny safe? Is he in danger?'

But she's already hung up.

57

JUSTIN
2 DAYS EARLIER

I vault over a fallen tree then flop to the ground, feeling the coarse bark against my neck and back. The undergrowth is dense, a blend of dark shadows mottled with spots of light from the fading rays that stab through the canopy above. My chest heaves up and down, desperate for air as I try to figure out where I am, why I'm here, why I'm out of breath, and why there's a gun in my hands? My entire body is tense, every muscle contracted, ready to fight. But why? Who or what am I fighting?

I can see by the angles of sunlight that daylight is ending. *What happened today? Why am I out of breath?* I try to recollect the last few hours but it's a complete blank, like my day started here, behind this tree trunk, my amnesia disorder kicking in again.

I consciously slow my breathing and piece by piece it all comes back to me, not the physical act of getting here, that's gone forever, but the reasons why I got stressed – the text message this morning, Garth's insistence that Grace can't be trusted, and Jack's words, *not his flesh and blood*. Each one plays a part in the dismantling of a dream, or more succinctly, the dismantling of my life.

I lie thinking about my past, my present and my future. Life started off shit, has turned to shit, and looks like it will end shit. I guess it was destined to be. Perhaps it was too much to expect that starting from such a low baseline of abuse and abandonment that any kind of happiness, or even just contentment, was possible. It feels like I've been kidding myself all along, chasing something that would forever be out of my reach. Which, in reality, makes my whole life a farce. It was never going to end well. I should have known that from the start. Why have I constantly been trying to kid myself?

The universe keeps throwing me signs of what I deserve in life, like the accident. Perhaps fate intended *me* to die screaming that day, but then decided that the crueller punishment would be to have me live, to replay the horror night after night, and to be branded with a deep scar, a physical reminder that I was the one responsible.

The sound of a woodpecker tapping like distant machine-gun fire makes my ears tune in to the surroundings. A breeze stirs the treetops, causing the shadows and patches of light to swap places back and forth, back and forth. A light rain begins to fall. Branches crunch behind me. Footsteps? An animal? Falling twigs? I hold my breath as I listen intently.

A beep from my mobile makes me jump. There are over a dozen missed calls and texts. This latest is a message from Grace saying she's had to leave Jack and Caroline's, an emergency apparently. Maybe she knows about what I did and can't face me. I look down at the gun on my lap. Maybe she won't need to ever again. But is that the coward's way? Am I a coward, or just a realist?

What's to gain from staying alive? I have no future with Grace now, the truth *will* come to light and then she'll hate me forever. It will destroy my heart when she takes Daniel away from me, and inevitably she will. I've lost everything, the sense of belonging, of being a family. And Jack and Caroline, I've lost them too, now.

So where do I go from here? I'm bad news for everyone, including myself. The answer is obvious. A pain-free future for those around me lies right there in my own hands, loaded.

Only it's not that easy. Yes, it would get rid of the gut-wrenching guilt of having messed everything up. It'll banish forever the futile hope that one day I'll be a useful and fully functioning part of someone's life. But it's just so... so final. Deep down, I know I'm defeated, but do I really still want to give in?

I check through the missed messages in the vain hope that one, just one, has something positive for me to hold on to. None do. One message does stand out though. I squint as I read it in the half light. It's solved my dilemma about whether to carry on.

You're leaving me with no choice. Meet me in the next hour or I'll tell Grace everything.

It was sent over three hours ago from the same number as this morning. I let the phone slip from my fingers onto the damp moss and lichen, and gaze down at the cold, steel antidote to an imperfect life. One squeeze, two barrels, three wishes granted. Suddenly I'm staring into the dark chambers of 12-gauge salvation.

58

GRACE
2 DAYS EARLIER

My phone rings in the central well of the car, its sound muffled by the fat drops of rain that hammer against the windscreen. I daren't take my eyes off the road to check the caller ID, though I assume it's either Justin or Candice. After she hung up a half hour ago, I've been ringing her repeatedly but it goes straight to voicemail. Justin, too, still isn't answering so I've left him a message explaining that Candice is distressed and I need to be with her. I just hope to God he doesn't follow me.

Leaning forward so my nose is virtually pressed against the windscreen, I focus on the winding country road ahead. Even with my full beam on I can barely see beyond the bonnet and my wipers are no match for the weather. I can't help but feel sorry for Caroline. A storm wasn't forecast and the garden party will be ruined.

'You all right, Danny boy?' I check on him in the rear-view mirror. Strapped into his car seat, he's sucking furiously on a dummy, his eyes drooping with sleep. At gone 6.15pm it's now his bedtime. 'You go to sleep, buddy, we'll be home soon.'

Without warning, a gush of wind buffets the car across the

road making me lose my grip on the wheel. My stomach lurches. 'Shit!' I manage to regain control but if I'm not careful, we're going to have an accident. The thought steals my breath away.

I stop the car and rest my head on the steering wheel, desperately trying to get my breathing under control. I really ought to turn back but what would I tell Candice? I'm a nervous driver at the best of times, likely due to the accident I was involved in as a child, the one in which Andrew was killed. That, too, happened on a country road in the black of night. The memory is sketchy, like a fading dream, though the panic prior to the crash is what I remember most vividly, how adrenaline had flooded my system as Mum swerved the car, my eyes blinded by oncoming headlights.

Time passes in a blur as I think of that night – five minutes, ten, twenty. I check on Daniel and am relieved to see he's fallen asleep. Rain continues to fall as though desperate to wash everything away. I wish it could erase the lies, the deceit. In truth, I wish it would erase me.

The police never caught the driver who smashed into us. The car was stolen and no fingerprints were ever found. Over the years I've thought about the perpetrator, if he, or she, is still haunted by the life they took. As a Christian, Mum worked hard at forgiveness but I'm certain she never truly managed it, neither for the driver or herself.

My phone pings, snapping me back to reality. It's Caroline, asking whether I've heard from Justin. So he still isn't back? What the hell has happened to him? Starting the engine, I cautiously push down on the accelerator and continue towards home.

Finally taking the slip road onto the M63, I breathe a sigh of relief. It's relatively quiet so I veer into the middle lane and pick up speed. If Candice is already at the house, how the hell am I going to explain being out with Daniel at this time? Though judging by how distressed she sounded on the phone, I doubt she'll even register the time. What was it she said again? Keep Danny safe until I get there? Why would she be worried about Daniel's safety? One thing's for sure – she was petrified, but of what? Or rather who? Surely not Rob. I'm certain there's no way he would ever harm Daniel, or anybody come to that. But if she isn't afraid of Rob, then who?

Taking the exit, I head in the direction of home. 'Crap!' My heart rate picks up as I see Candice's silver Honda outside the house. She must have left the spa soon after speaking to me on the phone. What does she need to tell me that's so important? I prepare my story; Daniel was restless so I took him for a drive in order to get him to sleep. I know I need to keep my cool, especially if she's found out about Justin. Parking my car behind hers, I unclip Daniel's safety harness and scoop him up. Asleep, he's like a dead weight and doesn't even stir when I hoist him over my shoulder. I feel a stab of guilt. Poor soul should be tucked up in bed.

I hear it first, the pounding of heavy feet on wet concrete. I glance up just as a figure rounds the corner, disappearing out of sight. A man, I'm certain. The same man who was watching the house last week? Or am I being paranoid? I hurry towards Candice's car but, seeing that she isn't inside, head towards the house. The front gate has been left wide open, not usually a cause for concern, but something doesn't feel right. I fiddle around in my handbag for the house key which proves difficult while holding Daniel.

'Deece, you there?' It's pitch black, though thankfully an adjacent street lamp casts a soft glow onto the garden path allowing slight visibility. Finally locating the house key, I look up.

My words die in my mouth. I stand paralysed, mind in free fall. Candice is lying face down on the path, surrounded by a halo of blood. 'Candice!' I half-sprint down the path towards her trying not to wake Daniel on my shoulder. I kneel down beside her, grab her by the arm and shake her. 'Deece.' She doesn't move. 'Candice! Wake up!' I check her wrist. There's no pulse.

59

GRACE
2 DAYS EARLIER

'I've already told you everything I know. Please, I have to go and be with my cousin.'

The more senior of the two officers, a silver-haired DI, reclines back into the sofa cushion and crosses his arms. His dark eyebrows furrow into a frown. 'So, you have absolutely no idea who might want to hurt your cousin?'

'No. There is nobody.' Instinctively I glance up at the wall clock. It's now over an hour since the ambulance rushed Candice to hospital and I still haven't been updated on her condition. I'm desperate to go and be with her but until Grandpa arrives to take care of Daniel, I've no choice but to stay put.

'Grace, we know you're in shock but time really is of the essence.' The inspector's voice is gentle and yet it still oozes authority. Under different circumstances I'd feel pleased that the police are taking the assault so seriously but I can't help panicking over what else this competent DI will unearth. Have I been committing a crime in purposely lying to Justin? Would it be classed as fraud? Deception?

'I honestly don't know what to tell you.' I hold out my hands, a gesture of openness, but I see that they're shaking and I know the officer has clocked it too. Why am I feeling so guilt-ridden?

'Is there something you aren't telling us, Grace?'

My mind flashes back to the phone call; Candice's fraught words playing on a loop. *Keep Daniel safe. I'm scared, Grace.* I know I ought to tell them about the call as well as Candice and Rob's marital problems but what good would that do? I've considered over and over whether Rob could have done it but there's just no way, he wouldn't, he couldn't. If anything he's too soft, a gentleman, some might even say a pushover. If Rob becomes the focus of the investigation, then the real perpetrator will get away scot-free. But if it wasn't Rob, then who? And why isn't Rob picking up his phone?

'Your cousin has been brutally attacked, Grace,' continues the DI, harder now. 'Our job is to find out who's responsible.'

Tears instinctively spring to my eyes. I can't lose Candice too. Aside from Grandpa and Daniel she's my last living relative that I have anything to do with. Perhaps I have no choice but to tell the truth; what if Rob *was* having an affair? Is it possible a jealous mistress is to blame? I open my mouth then close it again, the confession stuck in my conscience.

'Grace?'

'Okay,' I say, conceding I have little choice but to tell them everything I know. 'She was distressed, on the phone,' I confess, my face burning hot with shame.

The officer's eyebrows shoot up, but he doesn't utter a word.

'She said something about keeping Daniel safe,' I continue, averting eye contact. 'Said she was scared.'

'And you didn't think this was important information to share an hour ago?' He shakes his head, voice hardening. 'We could ultimately be looking at a murder investigation here so do us all a favour and stop withholding information. That, too, is also a criminal offence by the way.'

I place my head in my hands and let the tears flow. This is all my fault. I packed Candice off to the spa, even paid for it. Now she's likely dead. Gone. She must be. Or at the very least alone and frightened. She needs me and I'm not there. I want to be with her. To hold her hand. To say I'm sorry. I can't let her die alone. I can't. And Daniel. He can't lose his mother. Shit! A sudden thought steals my breath away. What if the officers discover my lie and suspect I was behind the assault? That I wanted Candice dead and Rob in prison so I could keep Daniel for myself. Would they jump to such a conclusion? My whole body begins to tremble.

'Look, I know it's difficult...'

'I suffer panic attacks,' I interrupt. 'I think I'm having one right now.' My voice is thin and distant – I'm losing myself.

'Take a deep breath. It's important you relay word for word what your cousin said on the phone,' interjects the second officer who up until now has remained silent. I look over at him, but his face is blurred. The thoughts keep on accelerating. Faster and faster. Candice. Bleeding out. Alone. Andrew. His hand cold. Mum, ashen. Noah... The room is spinning. I squeeze my eyes shut. I need it to stop. I start to gasp. I can't breathe. I'm going to die. Please God, make it stop.

'Grace? Breathe, it's okay.' The officer's voice is muffled but I know it's the more senior one. I feel his hand on my shoulder, squeezing gently. 'Just breathe,' he urges. I prise open my eyes, see a flash of gold on his ring finger. Somehow it helps to calm me a little.

'I'm sorry.' I force myself to breathe deeply through my nose.

'Who do you think she was scared of, Grace?' he asks. 'Please. Do this for your cousin.'

'Rob,' I whisper, barely believing the words which are forming in my mouth. 'She found something on his phone. You need to find Rob.'

60

JUSTIN
2 DAYS EARLIER

I hear the footsteps again. Are they getting closer? I cock my head, hold my breath. The bitter smell of spent gunpowder under my nose refocuses my attention to more pressing matters. I tighten my finger around the trigger, the small arc of metal pressuring into bone. Questions flash through my mind in milliseconds. How much finger pressure is needed before the explosion? Will I see the flash before I feel it? Will death be black and calm? I close my eyes.

'Justin.'

The voice is distant, recognisable. Is it real, imagined, or did I already pull the trigger, and this is part of being dead?

'Justin!'

It's louder this time. The cracking of feet on fallen twigs closer. I open my eyes and spot Garth twenty yards away, clambering towards me.

He stumbles over a fallen branch. 'Fucking hell, mate,' he says, a white, rain-sodden Nirvana T-shirt translucent on his skinny chest. 'Don't you think we're a bit old for hide-and-seek?' As he rights himself he notices the shotgun pointing at my face and stops in his tracks. 'Whoa.'

He holds out a hand as if to say stop. We lock eyes, a calm self-hatred in mine, panic in his.

'What you doing, Jus?' He takes a step forward.

'Don't...'

He stops, holds both hands out in front of him. The shrouded moon casts a strained pallor over the trees, the undergrowth and Garth's face, like a vintage black-and-white horror film.

'Think about it, man. Think about what you're doing, what you're leaving behind,' he says.

My voice is calm, quiet, low. 'Nothing. I'm leaving nothing behind.'

'You're leaving *me*,' he says.

'You don't need me, mate, nobody does.'

Garth lowers himself into a half-crouch readying himself for a gunshot, his hands outstretched still trying to instil some kind of calm. 'I do, mate. You don't realise how much.'

My eyes flick from his hands back to his eyes. They look sorrowful. For a flickering moment I feel pity for him having to witness this. The image of me blowing my brains out will stay with him forever. *Poor sod, as if he's not messed up enough already.*

'Mate, please...' He points to the gun and makes a lowering motion with his hand. 'You can't do this. Think about Grace and Daniel. They need you too.'

I take my finger off the trigger and pull the barrel away from my face, partly to spare him the vision, and partly because I know he's right. I can't leave Daniel now, not when he likely *is* my son. 'Grace has gone,' I say flatly. 'I think she knows. You know, about the reason I left.'

'Shit,' says Garth, mirroring my tone. 'But whatever happens with Grace, you still got Danny. He's your kid, mate, for sure, it's obvious.' Traces of breath wisp in the air as the temperature starts to fall quickly. They remind me of the smoking gun barrels from this afternoon before the world was turned upside down.

I frown. 'You've always been adamant he isn't.'

'Well... I just said that, didn't I... I didn't want you to leave me in the shit...' He screws his face into an expression that's half apologetic, and half regretful.

My eyes narrow. 'Caroline was right all along, wasn't she? You wanted to screw my life up. Make me as miserable as you!'

'Now come on, Jus, no need for melodramatics.'

A heat rises from my stomach, passes through my arms, rises into my neck, my throat, my head. My whole life I've stood by this man, classed him as a brother, and now... 'You're no mate to me. You're nothing but a parasite.'

For the first time in a while I feel like moving, leaping at this idiot pathetically gawping at me. Instead, I grab the gun and point it at Garth.

'Mate... wait...' Vapour clouds form and dissipate with each utterance. Like his words, they have no strength.

He starts to back away as I slowly stand, my jaw clenched tight, eyes burning with rage.

'Jus, stop! You're not thinking straight. Put the fucking gun down!' His hands are higher now, shielding his petrified face, waving in fear.

I glare down the barrel at this stupid, miserable idiot who has put me through hell my whole life. I tug the wooden stock tighter into my shoulder ready to absorb the recoil impact.

61

GRACE
2 DAYS EARLIER

'Your cousin's husband is meeting us at the police station,' says the DI as he comes back into the living room with two more mugs of tea. 'He's still in Hale at the moment.'

I breathe a sigh of relief. If Rob is still at the spa then surely it can't have been him that attacked Candice – but if not him, then who?

'I need to call Grandpa again, he isn't picking up,' I say, keen to get to the hospital to see how Candice is. 'Have you any updates on how she is?'

'An officer is at the hospital now,' replies the younger of the two policemen, a PC Mason. 'If there's any development, we'll let you know.'

'I just need to take some more details,' adds the DI, flipping open his notepad and pen. 'You said you were at a family gathering with Candice's son, Daniel, this evening – I'll need the address of this gathering.' He looks at me expectantly, pen poised.

My stomach flips. 'Why do you need to know that? The party has nothing to do with what happened to Candice.'

He shrugs. 'Just protocol. Where was it?'

'Cheshire, a place called Astley House.'

'And what time did you leave?'

'Just after I got the call from Candice. Ten, fifteen minutes later, I guess.' I sip at the tea but it burns my lips.

'And what time exactly did you get home?'

'Haven't you already asked me this?'

'Just need it once more – for the record.'

The officer is eyeing me suspiciously. What does he think I'm hiding?

I rack my brain for a time but everything is a blur. Time seemed to slow down when I saw Candice lying there, out cold. Then the last few hours have been like living in a nightmare, one where time ceases to exist. 'I honestly don't know. Just before I called the ambulance.'

'The call came into the station at 7.45pm,' says Mason. 'When did you leave the Astley residence?'

'I don't know. Close to six maybe. I left soon after Candice called.'

'Can we check the call log on your phone? Just for our enquiries?'

'Am I under obligation?' I suddenly feel out of my depth, like I am the one being accused.

'No,' says the DI. 'Not yet.' There's a threat to his voice I haven't heard before.

'Sure.' I hand over the phone – my heart pounding at what messages they might find on there. Will they read the thread with Justin? The one where I make out Daniel is our son.

'You received the call at 5.50pm, and you say you left the property ten minutes later. Does it take almost two hours to drive back from their house?'

It's a loaded question, and the officer knows it. 'I think it's normally about forty minutes but...'

'But what?'

'There was a storm. I'm a nervous driver. We hit a bend in the road and I nearly lost control. It shook me up. I sat in the car for a while, getting my bearings.'

'A while?'

'An hour, maybe a little less. I told you, I suffer from anxiety. I couldn't get myself relaxed enough to drive.'

'And then you took the motorway?'

'I did.'

'Don't worry then,' says the officer. 'We can see if you were picked up on any of the cameras. It'll be timestamped.' He smiles reassuringly, though knowing I definitely returned home after the attack does little to quench the nerves.

'And you didn't see anything suspicious when you arrived home?'

I suddenly remember the shadowy figure disappearing around the corner as I got out of the car. Was this the perpetrator fleeing the scene or just coincidence?

'I think I saw somebody,' I admit. 'A man. It happened so quick.'

'A man?' The DI looks at me expectantly. 'I need more than that? What was he doing? Wearing?'

'I... I can't remember,' I say, now stuttering. 'I didn't see much. Just the shadow of someone rounding the corner. And the sound of him running.'

'Running?' The DI's eyebrows shoot up into his forehead. 'Why didn't you mention this earlier?'

Heat burns my cheeks. 'I only just remembered. The shock I suppose. But I honestly didn't see what he was wearing. It was dark.'

'We'll check the cameras in the surrounding area,' he says, more to himself, I think. 'And it was your boyfriend's mother's party you say?' he continues. 'Can I take the occupants' full names?'

'Caroline and Jack Astley.' This is all getting out of control. If the police speak to Caroline and Jack, they'll likely mention Daniel. Then another thought. What if they want to interview Justin?

'And your partner's name too,' says the DI, as if reading my mind. 'Is he still at the residence?'

'Justin Roberts.' I can barely breathe. 'They're his foster parents,' I add, feeling the need to explain the different surnames.

'You okay?'

'Just worried about my cousin,' I garble. 'I'm not sure if Justin is still there. He went out early afternoon shooting with Jack, that's his foster dad, and Garth, his friend, Justin's friend not Jack's.' I'm aware how much I'm waffling. 'He hadn't returned by the time Candice called and I couldn't get in contact with him, so I sent him a voicemail explaining that I had to come back.'

The phone rings in the officer's hand. 'Caroline,' he reads – handing it over. The implication is for me to answer.

'Hi, Caroline.' My voice is shaking.

'Grace, hi darling. Is your cousin all right? I do hope it was nothing too serious.'

My face crumples.

'Grace... what's wrong?'

'She was attacked,' I say, barely able to get my words out. 'Has gone in an ambulance. The police are here now.'

I hear the sharp intake of breath on the other end of the line. 'Good Lord, who would do a thing like that?'

The officer mouths for me to put the phone on speaker. I blindly do as he asks.

'The police are here now,' I say, 'I think they need to take statements from you all.'

'What the bloody hell has it got to do with us?' says Caroline sternly. 'How could we be of help, we're miles away?'

'Mrs Astley, this is Detective Inspector Thompson,' says the officer. 'I'll be sending someone up there to take some statements this evening. Nothing to worry about. Can I get your full address?'

Caroline relays her address though I can tell she's far from happy. 'I bloody never should have had this party, knew it would be doomed from the get-go... the bloody storm, you having to take off, and now Jack has come back with his tail between his legs.'

'Only Jack?' I ask, 'You mean Justin and Garth are on their way here?' I imagine, having received the voice message, they've headed back to provide support. *Oh God, it's all going to come out.*

'No, Grace,' she says. 'At least not that I know of. Justin is insured on Jack's car so I'd assume he'd have taken that if he's followed. He has his keys still so it's possible.' I clock the officer's face. He's looking at me with suspicion.

'When was Justin last seen?' interrupts the officer.

'Jack said he disappeared at just gone two,' says Caroline without any trace of issue. 'He was angry after Jack refused him money to do a runner with you and Daniel, apparently.' She sighs lightly though there's a trace of humour. 'That lad must think we're made of money. They were looking for him for hours but he's completely AWOL.'

My eyes fix on the officers – the implication is clear.

62

JUSTIN
NOW

'Sugar?'

DC Gorman tosses a couple of white sachets onto the table and thanks his junior for the plastic cups. The coffee tastes exactly like you'd expect any vending machine product to taste like – insipid and artificial – shit, in other words. But it provides a welcome break from the questions. The detective stands upright against the off-white wall. His shirt matches the off-white paint, beer belly threatening to pop the buttons as he stretches his back. It makes me wonder if he's married. If he had a wife, would she let him wear such old shirts to work? Wouldn't she keep him supplied with new, pristine workwear? Isn't that how marriages are supposed to work, each looking out for the other, a duo of mutual care and concern?

'I want to know more about your relationship with Garth,' says the detective, resuming the formalities. He twists his head from side to side. I can hear the pop of cracking bones from where I sit.

I feel my eyes starting to well up. The last thing I want to do right now is show weakness, but he's touched a raw nerve as guilt and regret, my loyal life companions, surface yet again. I lean forward, forearms on my thighs, looking down into the murky brown liquid to hide my eyes.

'Would you say you were best friends?' he continues.

I nod, Garth's petrified eyes flashing in my mind. *Stop crying. Get a grip.*

'Do you believe Garth is in any way involved with Daniel's disappearance?'

I shake my head.

'Was he aware that you'd taken Daniel against the will of his mother?'

Thankfully I'm spared from answering. There's a knock on the door. The coffee-carrier passes DC Gorman a note and whispers something. I hear the name 'Garth'. They both look over at me.

Finally, I find strength in my voice. 'It's Garth, isn't it? He's dead, isn't he?'

63

JUSTIN
2 DAYS EARLIER

'You need to know why,' shrieks Garth, panic in his voice. He holds his hands above his head like he's in one of the cowboy films his glassy eyes fixate on throughout the night.

'It makes no difference why,' I answer. His face is perfectly lined up with the small brass bead halfway down the barrel. 'I thought you were my mate.'

On top of being petrified, Garth looks genuinely hurt. 'I didn't want to lose you again. You're always leaving me... after the kids' home, when you first met Grace, now again... everybody leaves me. You don't know how that feels. It hurts, man, it really hurts.' He clutches his head with both hands and lets out a cry.

'Stop being fucking dramatic. You've dragged me down all my life.'

'Aaargh.' Garth screams again. 'Shoot me. Just shoot me.'

The need to cause him pain is intense. I grit my teeth.

He screams again then drops to his knees, still holding his head.

I take a step forward and press the barrel into his downturned head. He looks up at me, eyes glistening and whispers, 'Do it. Please, please, please… just do it now.' He grabs the end of the barrel and holds it to his temple. My breathing quickens until the air rushing from my nostrils is audible, like a bull readying to charge.

But I can't. I can't end his poor pathetic life, just like I couldn't end my own. As much as I believe Grace and Daniel are my world, this whimpering figure at my feet is my family. The irony is I want him to feel pain, like I do, but on the other hand, I owe him. Until now, he's always been my protector.

I lie the shotgun on the ground and clasp his head into me, squeezing with a mixture of both anger and love. Garth's shoulders rise and fall. It's the first time I've seen him cry, and he's endured much more shit than this throughout his life.

'Okay, okay,' I say, embracing his head. 'I'm here, I'm not going to leave you.'

Garth pulls away, wipes his eyes and nose on his sleeve. 'I love you, Jus, always have, right from the minute you walked into the kids' home, you and that shitty Ninja Turtles backpack.' He laughs through his tears. 'I know I'm a dickhead, mate, a loser. But when I'm with you… you make me think I'm all right, you know, like I *am* somebody.'

'When one limps, we both limp, remember.' I lean over and wipe a tear from his cheek. 'I love you, too, mate. Never forget that.'

Garth play-punches me on the arm. 'Yeah, all right. But no need to get all puffy on me, yeah.'

I'm relieved to see the grin back in place.

'Were you really going to off me?' he asks.

I'm saved from answering by Garth's phone, a tinny 'Birdie Song' ringtone violating the silence of the forest. He holds it to his ear. 'Yeah, I'm with him now… yeah, he's okay, he's fine.' There's a gap as he listens, then he looks up startled. 'Grace's cousin has been attacked. The police have been onto Caroline. They're on their way to the house now to speak to everyone.'

Everyone? They mean me! I reach into my pocket for my phone and pull out Jack's car keys. The police are going to think I used Jack's car to drive to Grace's house, that it was me who attacked Candice. Not only that, my hand is covered in blood. I try to remember what happened between the time I was out with Jack and Garth, and coming round in the forest, but no matter how hard I dig inside my memory, nothing surfaces. It's as if I was asleep or unconscious. I have no idea if the blood is mine, or someone else's.

'Come on, get up.' I haul Garth to his feet. 'We've got to get out of here.'

Garth looks confused. 'Why?'

I show him the latest of dozens of messages and missed calls that have popped up on my phone.

Garth cranes his neck, running his finger under each word as he reads aloud:

'Justin, if you hadn't gathered yet, it's Candice. I've just rang Grace. She has a right to know.'

'Shit!'

'The police are going to see that's one of the last messages sent from her phone before she was attacked,' I explain.

'Shit,' repeats Garth.

I pick the gun up and brush the leaves off Garth's shins. 'We need to go, now.'

64

GRACE
2 DAYS EARLIER

'Justin, where the hell are you? And why in God's name haven't you been answering?'

'What's happened to Candice?' he snaps. 'And more to the point why the hell are the police coming here?'

'There's no need to speak to me like...'

'No, I'm sorry, I'm just...' He takes a sharp intake of breath. In the background, I can make out the whisper of leaves in the gusty wind and the dying trickles of rain. He must still be in the woods. God, how long has he been missing now? All I've done since the police left is watch the clock, each tick like a timer on a bomb, dragging me forward to the moment of the explosion. It's coming, I know it.

Ten, nine...

There's no way of stopping it now, too many people are involved; Jack and Caroline, the police, whoever left the note on Justin's car outing my lies. A deluge of icy fear grips me around the throat as realisation hits. It's all related – the note, the man watching the house, Candice's attacker and Justin's disappearance two years ago.

Eight, seven...

Surely it has to be linked – but how?

Justin has started to jog. I can hear his raspy breaths and the trample of twigs and dead leaves underfoot. Why did he run from Jack and Garth? Why is he still running now? 'Grace, I'm going to drive back to yours now, I'll take Jack's car.' He's panting and snivelling. The yearning to reach down the phone and hold him close is almost primal; I *need* to love him, to fix him, to rid him of whatever is plaguing him but I can't. The realisation is like shards of glass in my gut. How can I heal him of the past only to cut him to the core with the present? How can I rob him of the future he so desperately craves?

'Pack a bag for you and Daniel,' he barks.

Six, five...

There's still so much I don't know about his past, about the incident that left him maimed. He said he'd fallen from a tree. Why would he lie to me about that? How well do I really know Justin? 'Justin, I can't run away. I need to see Candice and...'

'No, you fucking can't!' I flinch at his spite before realising his words are no longer directed at me. 'Don't you think you've done enough damage?'

'Justin, who's that? Who're you talking to? Is that Garth?'

'Just get your stuff packed. I'm not asking, Grace.'

'But I can't just...'

Four, three...

'You can and you will! I'm not losing you and Daniel. I won't!' His words rip through me; so raw, like an open wound. 'I *will* not lose that child, Grace, you hear me? Over my dead body. I won't let them win.'

'Them? Justin, who are you talking about?'

Two...

'Not now, okay. I have to go. I can see the police.'

One.

65

GRACE
1 DAY EARLIER

I wake suddenly, cold and clammy. My neck is stiff with sleep and every sense is on high alert. I quickly realise I'm at home, slumped on the sofa. The dress I wore to Caroline's party last night is twisted around me and drenched in sweat. I didn't mean to drift off. How did sleep manage to find me when Candice is fighting for her life? What kind of person does that make me? I press my face into the cushion and allow the tears to flow. The events of last night come hard and fast; Candice, splayed out on the hard wet ground, her lifeless body framed in dark blood; the blurred blue lights of the ambulance as it tore through the rain-washed streets; Rob's secrets; Justin's lies. I can't make sense of it all – the pieces are falling too fast, piling on top of one another, like a game of Tetris. No matter how hard I try I can't make them fit together.

I sit up and gaze out of the window. My tears turn the rainy morning into a blur of yellow and grey and the headlights from the first flurry of traffic into smudged stars. I'm so sad, so confused. My life is falling apart and there can be no happy ending.

Sighing, I switch on the lamp and take my mobile from the

coffee table and check it for messages or calls. My heart sinks. Hovering over Justin's name, I consider calling him then think better of it. Last night he told me to pack my bags, to have Daniel ready to leave. I can't run away with him, there's just no way.

Where is he now? Why didn't he come last night like he said he would? Have the police caught up with him, arrested him for Candice's assault? Why would Justin be a suspect? What was Candice coming to tell me? Something about Justin? Did she discover something about him on Rob's phone?

The sound of creaking floorboards above sends adrenaline surging through me. I strain my ears, hear it again – heavy footsteps, slow and deliberate.

The realisation is immediate. Somebody is in the house.

Shit, Daniel! How the hell did I forget that Daniel is asleep upstairs? I'm on my feet in seconds, a hand gripped on the lounge door handle.

Keep Daniel safe. I'm scared, Grace. Candice's words are like a knife in the gut. I freeze, fear suddenly bolting my feet to the floor. Is this it? The moment of truth. I will myself to move, to call out, to thunder up the stairs and protect the child who I love as my own. Only protect him from what? From who? The panic is mounting, the air strangling me. A bang, a clatter. I cower.

Be strong, Grace, darling. Mum's words, spoken from the grave, somehow propel me through to the kitchen. I head towards the knife rack, the tips of the sharp blades like a cluster of stars in the night sky. My hand encircles the largest, six inches of cold steel. I squeeze it tight.

In the hallway, I take the stairs, treading carefully. My laboured breaths come hard and fast. How can he not hear? I hold out the knife in front of me, wonder if I'll be ballsy enough to use it should I need to. I imagine it sliding through flesh, another person's blood trickling through my fingers. A life ebbing away.

As I reach the top of the stairs, I see light seeping out from underneath Noah's closed door, illuminating the landing. The bathroom door is open, and I catch my reflection in the mirror; a haunted figure, little more than a ghost, and the knife – gleaming in the half-light – awaiting its first kill.

I step forward, press my ear against the bedroom door and listen. The breathing inside is heavy, laborious, a man's. He's opening and closing drawers.

Fear crawls within me at the sound of him. Every part of me wants to run, to hide, but I can't turn back – not now. What if it were Noah? Would I still be standing here, deliberating my next move, trembling like a coward? I think of him, hear his voice that never was – *Mama, mama. Help me!*

I fling open the door and strike.

66

GRACE
1 DAY EARLIER

The emancipated figure cowers before me, withered brown hands raised in surrender. 'Grace, it's me. Stop!'

I stumble backwards, mumbling incoherently. I can hear my voice bouncing off the nursery walls but my mind can't process what I'm saying. The knife slips from my grip and hits the floor.

'Oh shit. Grandpa! No, God no...' The blade's edge is dripping crimson, the cream carpet now ingesting the overspill. Grandpa stumbles backwards, his eyes wide and his sallow skin palling grey. I lunge forward, hold him up before he falls. It's like holding up a bag of loose bones. 'Grandpa? Talk to me.' His coat sleeve is torn but I can't see any wound. 'Oh God!'

'No, Grace, no.' He pushes me off with surprising strength. 'It's not me, it's you, your hand Grace, your hand.'

I look down at my open palm where blood is gushing from ripped flesh. I open my mouth, stunned, searing hot pain now shooting up my arm. The blade must have somehow sliced through my hand when I lashed out at Grandpa. 'I think I'm going to...' My voice trails behind me, my stomach turning to a black hole.

'It's all right.' Grandpa's face is now inches away from mine.

I'm on the floor, my head propped up against the wall. 'I've got you. It's all right.'

Grandpa wraps my hand in a cotton cloth – I see that it's one of Noah's muslins. It's never been used and now the fresh, white cotton is soaked in blood.

I'm sorry, baby boy, Mummy is so sorry.

I cradle him in my arms, the white muslin that should have mopped up his milky dribbles, now a shroud. The blood is already drying on the cotton, patches of brown that no amount of scrubbing will erase.

I'm so sorry I couldn't protect you, Noah. Mummy is so very sorry.

'Grace!' Grandpa shakes me awake. 'You're losing quite a lot of blood. We have to call an ambulance.'

'No!' I attempt to stand but it's no use, my legs feel severed at the knee. 'What the hell are you doing here? Why break into my house?' I look beyond him to Noah who is reaching over the bars of the cot, crying, his arms wide open to me. 'Help me get up. My baby needs me.'

'You were asleep,' stutters Grandpa, not attempting to take my arm. 'I didn't want to wake you. I hardly broke in. Here, child.' He goes to Noah and scoops him up. 'It's okay, Grandpa has you.'

I squeeze the muslin tighter around my hand, gasping at the pain. 'Give him to me, please. Give me my son.'

Grandpa frowns. 'Grace, I think we need to call...'

'No!' I manage to heave myself up, the dizziness starting to clear. 'Just tell me why you're here?'

'Rob has a key,' he says quickly. 'Shh, Daniel, it's all right, boy.'

'But why not just knock?' I reach out for Daniel, but Grandpa takes a step away from me. 'What are you doing? He wants me. What's the matter with you?' I hold out my arms to Daniel.

'Who is this, Grace?' he asks, pointing at Daniel. I'm confused by the question and I'm sure it shows. 'Who am I holding right now?' he clarifies. Having the question repeated doesn't make it any less bizarre.

'Erm, Daniel,' I say, now concerned for Grandpa's state of mind. I scan him again for any signs of injury.

He nods, seemingly satisfied with the answer. 'I think you were a tad confused that's all. Are you feeling all right now?' He lowers Daniel who runs straight over to me.

'I can't pick you up, mate, I have a bit of a poorly hand. Look, why don't you play with those teddy bears over there?' I guide Daniel in the direction of his toy basket. 'So Rob's been released then?' I ask.

'This morning. That's why he gave me the key because he wanted me to...' He stops dead.

'What? He wanted you to what?' I push out the question through clenched teeth, my hand now throbbing. Carefully I peel back the cloth and take a look. It's definitely going to need stitches, but I can't go to A & E. I have to protect Daniel, though from what, I still have no idea. From Grandpa? Surely not. 'Please, Grandpa, just tell me what's going on. Why did you break into my house?'

'I told you, I had a key. You were asleep. The other good news is that Candice has regained consciousness.'

'What?' At once the news of my cousin being well overrides the pain in my hand. 'Thank God! So she's told the police who attacked her? That it wasn't Rob?'

Grandpa shakes his head. 'I don't know. Rob only told me that the police released him without charge and that Candice has woken up.' His eyes suddenly glaze over. 'Why did you point the finger at Rob, Grace, after everything he's done for you?'

Grandpa's words awaken a memory I've tried my whole adult life to erase.

It was a long time ago, shortly after Mum died. I'd hit rock bottom, saw nothing ahead of me but darkness. Grandpa tried hard to help me, to make me see that there was still a life worth living, despite the pain of losing his daughter. Only I couldn't escape the darkness no matter how hard I tried, it followed me everywhere, a black shadow. The pills were my saviour, a way out, a one-way journey to oblivion. I took them all – swallowed them down with Mum's leftover brandy.

Rob saved me – not just physically, but mentally too. I don't remember ringing him, begging for help. I must have done, though, because the next thing I knew he was beside me in the back of an ambulance. Afterwards, when I'd healed, physically at least, he secured me a job as a receptionist at the practice where he was training as a GP. Over the coming months he never once left my side; he cooked for me, ran errands, listened to me night after night as I battled through the depression. In my heart I knew Rob wanted more than to be my saviour, to heal me. Only I couldn't, not with Rob, no matter how much I knew he wanted it. I couldn't love him in that way.

A few years later he married Candice and I guess the rest is history.

'You know Rob has always loved you, Grace,' says Grandpa now. 'From the moment the two of you courted back in college. You telling the police that you suspected him of hurting Candice has hurt him badly, more than I think you realise.'

I swallow down a lump of shame. 'I'll phone him later, apologise.'

'Forgiveness is a wonderful thing, Grace,' says Grandpa, the light now back in his eyes. 'I hope he can find it in his heart to forgive you.' He gestures at the cloth around my hand. 'Can I take a look?'

Once again I peel back the muslin. 'Seems to have stopped.'

'I still think it'll need stitches.'

'I'll go later. Come on, Danny.' I hold out my free hand and guide Daniel out of the bedroom and down the stairs, leaving Grandpa to trail behind.

'Why didn't you come last night anyway?' I ask, slumping down onto the sofa, the muslin replaced with a dose of TCP and a badly wrapped bandage. I'm struggling to process what has just happened, how close I came to hurting my grandfather, how easily I could have taken his life. I force myself to blot it out, to push it far from my mind and concentrate instead on getting to the truth.

'I didn't get your message until this morning,' he says, his dark eyes not meeting mine. He's holding back something, I'm certain. 'Came as quite a shock when Rob called round this morning.'

I check the time – 7am. 'He came straight to you after being released?'

Grandpa shrugs. 'As I said, he wanted me to collect Daniel. Didn't want to face you after what you'd said to the police, so he gave me the key.'

His story doesn't ring true. Why would Rob give him a key? If Rob knew that Daniel was with me then he'd also know I'd be home, so why give him the key?

I'm about to demand answers when Grandpa pulls his mobile from his trouser pocket. He studies the screen.

'Who is it? Grandpa, tell me,' I demand when he doesn't immediately answer. 'Is something wrong?'

He flinches. 'Sorry. Nothing of importance.' He jabs at the screen before returning the mobile to his pocket.

There's a breath of silence before Grandpa expels a heavy sigh. 'Grace.' His gaze falls down to his lap. 'There's something you should know. But you have to know I did this for you.'

My stomach sinks. 'What?'

He squeezes his eyes shut and breathes in deeply. 'Okay,

don't be mad. When I visited you a few weeks ago I saw the message on your phone.' He smiles sadly. 'Despite what you said I knew Justin was back on the scene.'

I feel my jaw clench. 'Go on.'

'I asked Rob to watch the house, just to be sure.'

So I wasn't imagining it, the shadow of a man, that uneasy feeling of being watched. It was Rob the whole time. 'But why? I don't understand.'

'Grace, you're not going to like this, but you have to believe me. That man, Justin,' he spits out his name, 'he's bad news. I just wanted to protect you. Rob too, that's all we wanted.'

'Bad news how?' I'm on my feet now, pacing, my mind pulling in opposite directions. I know Justin better than anyone and he's a good man, has a pure heart, I'm certain of it. And yet – he left me, a pregnant, vulnerable woman. There's also the fact that he's never told me the real reason why he left. And now, so desperate to get away, to run and hide. From what? From who? 'What about Candice?' I ask, shock giving way to anger. 'Did she know too? Were you all in on it?'

Grandpa shakes his head. 'She doesn't know.'

'But what has Justin done?' I ask again, my voice a desperate plea. 'Why do I need protecting?' Whatever it is, however bad, I have to know.

'That's something you're going to have to ask him,' says Grandpa, now making for the door. 'I really can't tell you that.' He takes out his car keys and swings them around his finger as if everything is right in the world, as if I haven't nearly stabbed him to death. 'Right, best I go see Candice in the hospital. I'll phone you later. Please do go and get that hand checked out, though, Grace. And if Justin comes here, ask him the real reason he left. It's time you knew the truth.'

'And you can't just tell me?'

He shakes his head. 'This has to come from him. It's the very least he can do.'

'Okay, I'll ask him,' I say, my head now a tangle of thoughts. 'I'll go and visit Candice later, too, and phone Rob.' I don't understand any of this but there's nothing else for it but to speak with Justin. 'What a bloody mess.'

Grandpa leans in and kisses me lightly on the cheek. 'It'll all sort itself out in the end, Grace. These things always do.'

It's only as Grandpa climbs into his car that I realise he hasn't taken Daniel with him as Rob has asked.

67

JUSTIN

1 DAY EARLIER

I try not to look as I pass the park where I picnicked with Grace and Daniel. It could have been such a great day, should have been – Daniel's hugs, his playfulness, Grace's effortless beauty, that all-embracing feeling of family. And then the reminder. Simple words on a screen that put me back in my place, back where I belong. Every silver lining always has a dark cloud, I guess.

As I round the corner towards Grace's house, I slow the car to a halt. If the police are here, I'm done, but surprisingly there's no sign, yet. I kerb-crawl on to Grace's house, my foot hovering over the accelerator, ready to make a hasty departure if necessary, but all seems calm. A neighbour, two doors along, is already hosing his car. *For God's sake, man! It's 8am on a Sunday. Get a life.*

I incorporate my anger into the hammering on Grace's front door. She opens the door, surprise all over her face. Shocked I'm here, or shocked at the ferocity of my knocking? I don't know and don't care.

'We've got to go,' I announce, striding past her into the hallway. 'Pack a bag.'

'Excuse me?' She slams the door behind me. 'Where the hell have you been?'

'Where's Daniel?' I demand, ignoring the question.

'Would you mind telling me what's going on?'

'Pack a bag, quick. I've told you.'

Grace grabs my arm with a bandaged hand as I head down the hallway. 'Stop. Justin. Tell me where you've been. What are you hiding?'

'What have you done to your hand?' I ask, ignoring her questions.

'Oh... uhm... nothing, cut it on a corned-beef tin. Never mind that, tell me what's going on.'

'Where is he?'

'In the kitchen. Tell me what you're doing.'

Grace follows me into the kitchen. Daniel is sat in a high chair shoving beans and toast into his mouth. He smiles as he sees me, kicks his legs in excitement.

I wipe his bib over the orange stains on his chin, cheeks and nose, and scoop him up. 'Hi, matey. You ready to come with Daddy?'

Grace tries to grab Daniel from my arms. 'Whoa. What are you doing?' she shrieks.

I push her away. 'Leave him.'

'And why have you got scratches all over your arms?'

'I'll tell you in the car. Come on! You need to pack.'

'Justin, I'm not doing anything until you tell me what's going on.'

'I'm not going down for attacking Candice.'

'What do you mean? Why would the police think *you* attacked Candice?'

'I had Jack's car keys. I'd disappeared during the time she was attacked.'

'So?'

'So trust me, that's enough. This was planned to frame me.'

Grace's brow wrinkles. 'You're being ridiculous. The police have no reason to suspect you.' She holds out her arms. 'Give me Daniel. Now!'

Daniel's eyes widen and his lips start to tremble. He reaches out to Grace.

'It's okay, matey. Mummy will be with you in a minute. Daddy's got you now.'

'Justin!' Her voice grows cold, aggressive.

'I'm not going down for something I didn't do, Grace. Now pack a bag.'

'Listen, Grandpa's gone to the hospital to see Candice. She's woken up. She'll tell the police who it was.'

'Trust me, she won't, your grandpa will make sure of it.'

'Grandpa has just been trying to protect me... both him *and* Rob.'

'Protect you?' I shout. 'Grandad and Rob? Can't you see? It's me who's trying to protect you. Me, Grace!' I carry Daniel to the doorway but Grace gets there first and blocks the way.

'You're not taking Daniel.' Her fists are clenched, ready for a fight.

'I am. And you're coming too.'

She suddenly changes tack, her voice softening, like a kidnap victim trying to befriend her captor. She puts a hand on my arm. 'Are you okay? You're acting weird. Sit down for a minute...'

'Jesus!' The clock in my mind ticks louder. 'We're in danger, Grace. *He* was watching the house, and obviously put the note on my windscreen... if we don't go *right* now, I'll lose everything, he made damn sure I knew that.'

'You have to calm down and tell me what's going on. Put Daniel down and I'll make us a brew.'

'A brew? For God's sake, Grace. You don't get it.' I grab hold of her arm and pull her with me as I push past. 'There's stuff you don't know.'

'Justin. Get off. You're scaring me.'

'We're going... now... and that's it.' I keep Daniel away from her, knowing she'll have to follow if I take him.

'Okay, okay. But let go of my arm. You're hurting me.' She snatches coats for her and Daniel and closes the door behind her. I quickly check up and down the road then hurry Grace into the car.

'Car seat,' she says and tries to get out.

I pass Daniel to her in the back. 'We haven't got time. You'll have to hold him.'

In the rear-view mirror, Grace hugs Daniel tight. They both look terrified. 'Where are we going?' she asks quietly.

A car appears in the mirror. I put my foot down, ignoring the question. The wheels spin and screech as I pull away. *Shit. Am I too late already?*

68

GRACE

1 DAY EARLIER

Houses and parked cars pass in a blur as Justin's car picks up speed, the tyres hissing as they skim pools of rainwater. 'Justin, you need to stop the car, now! It's not safe having Daniel on my knee, what if there's an accident?'

He glares at me in the rear-view mirror. 'I'm a careful driver.'

Fumbling around with the seat belt, I secure it tightly around myself and wedge an arm under Daniel's ribcage. He writhes on my lap and cries.

'It's okay, mate, I've got you.' I kiss the top of his head and hold him close. If anything happens to him, I'll never forgive myself... or Justin. 'Justin, you're scaring him.'

Justin's jaw clenches. 'I'm not scaring him, Grace, you are! Stop carrying on, for God's sake.' His voice is measured and void of emotion, as though a switch has tripped in his head.

I change tack, forcing myself to sound calm. 'Come on, Danny boy, shall we look for Minis out the window? I used to play that game with...'

'Mini pinch! 2 – 1.'

'Ow, that hurt. Mum. Muuuuuuum! Grace pinched me really hard.'

'*No I didn't, stop being a baby.*'

'*Muuuuum!*'

'*Stop squabbling you two. Brothers and sisters should look after one another, not fight like cat and dog.*'

'Grace, why are you crying? Stop crying please.'

'Sorry.' I bite my lip tightly in an attempt to stop the whimper in my throat escaping. Crying isn't going to help. It won't calm Justin down – it won't bring back Andrew. I so wish I could go back, if only to let Andrew win the game. Why did I have to pinch him so bloody hard?

'Justin, you need to listen to me, okay.' I lean over the back of the headrest, place my hand on his shoulder and squeeze it lightly. 'We should talk, me and you. Get things out in the open once and for all. Let me call Rob, he'll pick Dan...'

The car suddenly loses control, swerving over to the left side of the road. Justin grips hold of the steering wheel, his knuckles mottled white. 'Fuck! You're ringing nobody.' He breaks hard, flinging Daniel and me forward. I start screaming; at Justin, at myself, at Mum for not swerving quickly enough.

'*Mum? Andrew?*'

It was silent bar the sound of rain hammering on metal. Why weren't they screaming? Shouting out? 'Mum... help me.'

I couldn't move, was pinned down by the collapsing roof, the pain the only thing keeping me from slipping away. Blue lights flickered at the corner of my vision followed by a sound, a wailing siren. 'Andrew?' I was fading fast. Losing myself. I opened my mouth, tasted the warm, coppery blood on my tongue. 'I'm sorry, Andrew...'

'I should have let you win.'

'What are you talking about? Grace?' Justin's voice pulls me from the darkness. I see we're on the motorway, gaining speed – 80, 85, 90. I wrap both arms around Daniel and whisper shushing noises into his ear. 'It's all right, baby boy. You're safe now.'

'Daniel, it's okay, matey, it's okay,' reiterates Justin. 'Daddy will make it all right.'

A scream bubbles up in the pit of my stomach. *You're not his dad! I lied, Justin. Our child is dead, he died, in my arms, and where were you? Nowhere. No-fucking-where!*

'Grace! It'll be all right.' He taps his fingers rhythmically on the steering wheel. 'Trust me. Please just don't ring anybody, okay? I just need to get us away. I can't lose my son, I can't...' Without warning, he veers into the fast lane causing the car behind to brake sharply. Horns blast in quick succession.

'You idiot!' The fear of a moment ago curdles to anger. How dare he put us in danger like this. Whatever he's running from, whatever he thinks he knows, it doesn't warrant this. I feel a sudden urge to hurt him, to make him pay for everything. 'Do you realise how irresponsible you're being?' I scream, spit showering the back of the headrest. 'Maybe you were right all along, Justin. You're not cut out to be a father. You're the worst.'

For a moment my words fall around the car like snow, each one a cold reminder of the decision Justin made two years ago. Then he fixes his eyes onto me, the snow freezing to hail.

'Look, I didn't mean that, I...'

'You bitch!' The heat in his voice is pain disguised, I know it, yet it doesn't make it any easier to hear. 'But yeah, you're right. I am,' he says, self-loathing punctuating every word. 'I'm a useless. Fucking. Waste of space.' He slows the car to an almost stop. I eye the door handle, contemplate making a run for it. Only I can't leave him, not like this. 'I should have killed myself when I had the chance,' he mumbles, to himself. I'm sure I wasn't meant to hear it.

A fistful of tablets lay scattered on the nightstand. Surely that would be enough to end it all. Mum's brandy glowed in the semi-darkness, a beacon of light to a better place. The pad and pen lay untouched; pristine white pages yet to be spoiled by black confessions.

All I wanted was to go and be with them, to feel Mum's arms holding me tight, to play hopscotch with Andrew on the path, our fingers chalky, our white shoelaces double-knotted like Mum had taught us. 'You want to play a game, brother? I have a feeling you'll win this time.'

'Grace, I need you to know I did it for you. I did it for Daniel.'

'I have to get Daniel home,' I say, all of my fight now gone. 'Please, Justin, just let us out of the car and I'll ring Rob to pick us up. You don't...'

He bangs his fists hard against the steering wheel. 'Have you not been listening to a single word I've said? You might think I'm a useless dad, but I will not allow *them* to take my child. I won't allow them to have me put me away for something I haven't done.'

'Who are 'them'? Rob and Candice? I don't understand.'

He closes his eyes, takes a deep breath then opens them again. 'Candice sent me a message. She sent it just before she was attacked. Wanted to meet me at the house. She... discovered something.'

'What? Discovered what?' The frustration of being kept in the dark is too much. If he doesn't tell me soon, I think I'm going to explode. 'Tell me, Justin! Whatever it is, just tell me.'

'Maybe it wasn't even her that sent it,' he says, smirking to himself. 'Maybe she was already cold on the ground and the message was sent to point the finger at me.'

'Justin.' My voice is shaking but I can no longer control it. I'm not even sure I want to. 'You said yourself, you lose time. That you're not always responsible for your actions. That they wouldn't let you in the army because of it.'

He fixes me with a glare. 'What are you saying, Grace?'

I swallow down the fear, clutch Daniel tighter. Do I believe what I am about to say? 'What if it was you who hurt Candice? What if you did it and can't remember?'

He laughs out loud, shakes his head, his eyes a vacant window. 'And what if I did, Grace? What if it *was* me who attacked Candice?'

69

GRACE
1 DAY EARLIER

'I didn't attack Candice,' says Justin, when we're safely hidden in the B & B. 'I can't even believe you'd think that.'

'I don't,' I relent, too exhausted to argue. 'But you have to realise how strange you're acting.'

'God, this place is shit!'

Justin jabs angrily at the buttons of a small television set on a badly whitewashed set of drawers. 'I think they've superglued them so we have to pay for the remote. Cheapskates!'

'Calm down.'

In fairness he has a point, the room is well past its best-by date; everything from the brown-and-amber Paisley curtains to the sagging mattresses are in desperate need of the bin. 'Please, let's just go back home,' I try. 'I'll call Candice and she'll take Daniel for the night and we can talk properly.'

'Don't ring her, please.' Justin slumps down onto the edge of the bed and buries his head in his hands.

I eye my mobile on the dresser and see there are now a half dozen missed calls. 'I have to…'

'I said no!'

Daniel instinctively puts his arms out to me. I scoop him up and hold him close. 'It's all right, Justin didn't mean to shout.'

Justin glares at me through splayed fingers. 'I'm *Dad* to him, not Justin.'

I don't respond.

'Mama,' whimpers Daniel, burying his head in my chest.

'It's okay, go to sleep.' I lay him on the bed beside me and pacify him with a dummy. 'I'll phone Mama, okay,' I whisper into his ear. 'She'll come soon.'

'We just need to stay here a few nights,' says Justin, calmer now. 'Until I figure something more permanent out.'

'More permanent how? I can't just...'

His mobile rings, cutting me dead. 'It's Jack.' He swipes the phone off the bed. 'What should I do?'

'Well, I think you ought to speak to him, don't you? Perhaps the police have been in touch.' I pray he answers the phone, knowing that if anybody can talk sense into Justin, it's Jack.

Justin hesitates. 'I want to speak to him privately,' he says, swallowing down what I take to be fear. 'I'm going outside.' He heads for the door and then stops and looks back at my phone.

'I won't ring Candice back,' I promise.

He eyes me suspiciously. 'I'll be back in a minute.'

I keep one eye glued to my mobile for a good five minutes after Justin leaves the room. It's positioned on the edge of the dresser in the right-hand corner. I know that if I decide to make the call, I have to put the phone back in the exact same place or he'll notice. Justin is meticulous like that, has had it drilled into him from his care home days.

I know that growing up in care did strange things to him; we'd often joke about his little quirks; the way he'd stash chocolate bars at the back of the fridge and lay out his clothes on the dresser for the next morning. He'd cherish every little thing too – a throwaway birthday card to me would be a prized possession to him. He'd slide it under his mattress to reread over and over, the message an affirmation that someone loved him, that there were people in the world who cared enough to remember the day he entered the world.

That's what has always baffled me. Two years ago, he had it all, a partner who loved him and a child on the way. Why would he throw it all away? What was so bad that he *had* to leave?

'You just stay there a minute, mate.' I take out a handful of leaflets from a dog-eared presentation folder courtesy of the B & B and hand them to Daniel.

I glance over at the phone and consider leaving it untouched.

'Mama.' Daniel twiddles my hair between his thumb and forefinger. 'Mama.' He starts to whimper.

I stroke the small of his back, his baby-blue cotton vest soft to the touch. 'I love you, Noah.'

'Mama,' he repeats, more urgently now. 'Mama back.'

His words, spoken so innocently, turn my stomach. What have I become? I never should have allowed Daniel to become caught up in my grief. I shouldn't be using him as a replacement for Noah. 'Okay Danny, let Grace ring Mummy for you.'

My hand hovers over the phone. I recoil as my fingers brush the screen, as though it's a grenade ready to detonate. I tap in the passcode and the screen flashes with missed calls and WhatsApp messages.

Candice: *Where R U? X*
Sent: 11.02am.

Rob: *I'm picking up Candice, she's discharging herself. Told her she shouldn't but you know what she's like. Coming to collect Daniel.*
Sent 12.34pm.

Candice: *Just tried ringing. Where u at? X*
Sent 2.05pm.

Grandpa: *Grace, Candice and Rob are out of their minds with worry. Please answer.*
Sent 3.30pm.

Rob: *Are you with HIM Grace? You have no idea what he's capable of. You're leaving me with no option but to call the police.*
Sent 4.18pm.

Candice: *RING ME BACK!!!*
Sent 5.03pm.

Candice: *Police called. They got your location. U know it's kidnap rite?*
Sent 5.45pm.

70

JUSTIN

1 DAY EARLIER

'Jesus, Justin!'

I can picture Jack on the other end of the line, angry, slowly shaking his head in disapproval, disappointed in me yet again.

'You owe her the truth, do you hear me?'

'I know,' I murmur. 'I never attacked Candice though. You believe me, don't you?'

'I do, lad.' There's a pause before Jack speaks again. He's softer now, a father patiently imparting wisdom to his son. 'Look, tell Grace the truth, if not for yourself then for her and Daniel. He's your priority now. You need to do this for him.'

I'm taken aback by his change of tack. I expected another stern lecture reminding me how I still have a lot to learn, how I can't keep making the same mistakes again, that I'm useless, basically.

'Okay,' I say quietly, ready to put the phone down, but he hasn't finished.

'Listen, having a son is the most precious thing a man can have. Remember that. You... are *my* son. *You*, Justin, are the most precious thing *I* have.'

I swallow, trying to contain the lump in my throat.

'I should have told you I loved you more often. Old school, I guess. Don't make that same mistake with Daniel, eh? You'll be a great dad to him. I can already see that. But tell her everything, the truth. It's the only way forward.' He ends the call.

You, Justin, are the most precious thing I have. Jack's words keep replaying on a loop. I stop pacing, stand on the tiny grass lawn for a moment, awash in a warm wave of peace and contentment for the first time in ages. *The most precious thing I have.* It's true. I feel at one with Jack, fathers united in knowing what's best for their sons. It's time to come clean, for Daniel's sake. I have to tell Grace the painful truth about why I left.

Grace sits at the edge of the bed, stroking Daniel's hair. His long eyelashes flicker over half-shut eyes, sleep beckoning him to a cosy world free of stress and confusion. How I envy him. I'm reluctant to step away from the embrace of Jack's words, but truths have to be told.

I sit down opposite Grace and take her hand, the nerves and uncertainty returning. *Do you really want to do this, Justin?* I take a deep breath. 'It's time I told you why I left that day.' I fix my eyes on hers. As I open my mouth to speak again, she brushes a finger across the scar on my face.

'Caroline let slip that you didn't get this from falling out of a tree,' she says softly. 'Tell me what happened.'

Her sudden deflection throws me. Does she not want to know? Is she afraid of what I might say? I'd built myself up to tell her about the day I left, not about the guilt over Andrew that has torn me apart for so many years. But it's a time of truth, and that one has to be faced too.

I can't bear to look her in the eye as I begin to tell her what happened. 'I'll tell you,' I say to the floor. 'But you have to promise not to hate me.'

'Go on.'

'You know I was a mess when I was rejected by the army.'

'I know.'

'My head was screwed. I was angry, confused, still young, in my teens... didn't know what I was doing. I used to drink and drive all the time. One afternoon I'd had a blazing row with Jack, like through-the-roof blazing. I wasn't thinking, must have taken Jack's car, and driven through the woods, too fast, too drunk, can't remember any of it... only how it ended.' I glance up. She looks terrified at what I'm about to tell her.

'I must have lost control coming out of the trees,' I continue, 'Clipped a kerb or something, I don't know, like I said, it's a blank. All I remember is suddenly being aware that I'm behind the wheel of a car that's sliding out of control. I see a young boy, on a bike, staring, nearer, nearer, and then... there was a bang, Grace. He was gone.' I look up again, try to catch my breath, try to check the tears that have already started rolling down my cheeks. She moves her hand away, puts it over her mouth, the separation between us never more apparent.

'I was confused, shocked, thought I'd killed him. I tried to run, but a man saw it happen, grabbed me, wouldn't let me go. He must have smelled the booze on my breath. His wife was screaming, kneeling over this young, lifeless body in the road.' I look up again. Grace is slowly shaking her head, trying to take it all in.

'He was thirteen, Grace, thirteen years old.' I pause, reliving the shock, unable to step out of the memory.

Grace drops her hands to her lap then speaks at last, her lips quivering. 'Why have you never told me?'

'I couldn't. He was the same age as Andrew. I honestly thought I'd killed him. He wasn't moving, had to be rushed to hospital.' I stand and wander to the window, unable to sit and look Grace in the eye. 'It never went to court. Jack had to pay the parents thousands to stop them pressing charges, and I had to have seven stitches from when I hit the windscreen. And then they disowned me, said they wanted nothing else to do with me. I was alone, in shock, ashamed. If I'd told you, you'd have had the same hate for me as you have for that drunk driver who killed Andrew and got away with it. I was no better, just luckier I guess, as he didn't die.'

'So as usual, you pretended it never happened.' A look of disgust touches Grace's eyes, and I know I've ruined everything.

The silence that follows is quickly swallowed up by an alert from my mobile that lies on the bed. I glance at the screen and my stomach flips.

Grace also sees it and reads aloud: 'Paternity DNA results.' She looks up. 'Justin, what the...'

I grab the phone. 'I had to know.' A look of panic flashes in Grace's eyes.

'Justin, no, don't read that email!'

'Why? What will it say?' I suddenly feel breathless, dread coursing through me.

'You can't read it.' Grace snatches the phone and holds it at arm's length. 'You don't understand.' Her voice has changed, it's shriller. She's scared, I realise. Completely terrified.

'I have to know.' I wrestle the phone from her grip, anger taking over. If Daniel isn't my son, what's left for me to live for?

'Justin, I'm begging you. Let me explain!'

'Explain what? Why are you scared?' I spit the question at her, now more certain than ever that Garth was right all along. I frantically jab in the passcode. It fails, which allows Grace another attempt to prise the phone out of my hand.

'Listen to me, Justin.' Tears well in her eyes. 'It's not what you think.'

I grab her hand and peel away her fingers. She's no match for my strength. 'So he isn't mine, is he?' My heart pounds as I attempt the passcode again. The phone unlocks. 'He isn't my son. You lied to me. You cheated. Whose is he?'

Grace holds her head in her hands and cries. 'It's not what you think,' she repeats. 'I wanted to tell you, Justin. I didn't mean to...'

I tune out as I scan the email, looking for the crucial information.

My breath catches in my throat as I read the result.

'Shit!' I read it again, barely believing, and look over at Grace who is bawling her eyes out. 'Grace, it's okay. Stop crying.' I reach over and pull her towards me. 'Daniel *is* mine. He's *my* son, Grace.'

71

GRACE
1 DAY EARLIER

'I'm sorry I went behind your back, I just had to be sure.' Justin holds his head in his hands and breathes relief. 'Of course, he's mine, I could feel it. Shit, what an idiot I've been.'

I try to comprehend what's just happened. A moment ago, I was certain my lies were about to be exposed and now... there *has* to be a mistake.

'Let me see.'

Justin hands me the phone sheepishly.

I skim-read the email, bypassing percentages and medical jargon in search of its conclusion.

```
Based on our analysis, it is practically
proven that Mr Justin Roberts is the
biological father of Child A.
```

'What did you send off?' I demand. 'Daniel's hair, saliva?'

'What does it matter?'

'It matters!' I fight to keep the tremor out of my voice, but it's no use. Why the hell has the test concluded that Justin is

Daniel's father? He isn't, obviously, as Daniel isn't my son. He's Candice and…

I feel the blood drain from my face.

'Grace? What's the matter? It was just hair, hair from his brush.'

I force myself to look down at Daniel, my stomach turning to icy water at the realisation. How did I not see it before? Daniel has Justin's ski-slope nose; the same heart-shaped face and downturned lips.

I open my mouth, but the words are lodged like there's a plug in my throat.

'Look, I don't know why you were so worried. If there was somebody else, I mean, shit, that hurts, but we can talk about that later,' I hear Justin say, though his voice is way off, as though bubble-wrapped. 'It's all right, though, I forgive you. It was a shit time for both of us back then.' He pulls me into a hug, shushes me. I remain there, suffocating in his betrayal.

Daniel is nestling into me now, weaving his fingers through my hair, and Justin is telling me to calm down, that I'm frightening *our* son. I cry more, huge, retching sobs until I'm choking.

'Grace! What's up?'

I throw him off of me. 'Just get out.' I wipe the tears out of my eyes and force myself to breathe. 'Just get the hell away from me.'

Justin falls silent, his eyes wide and bewildered.

Right on cue, my mobile rings, and Candice's sickeningly attractive face beams up at me from the call display.

'Don't answer it!' Justin grabs the phone and stabs at the end call button.

'Why, what are you hiding?' I ask with an eerie sense of déjà vu.

Justin's eyes flash with fear and for a moment I think he

might have worked it out. 'I told you, they're trying to ruin me. They want me to go down for the assault on Candice.'

Quickly he discards my phone on the dresser so it's out of reach.

Questions crowd in on me, all of them without answers. Did Justin know Candice was pregnant when he left? Does Candice even know that Daniel is Justin's son? And what about Rob, does he know he's been bringing up another man's child? I need to demand answers, but I'm terrified to hear them.

'Grace, it's okay, if you had an affair, I mean. We don't have to deal with that now.'

I bet we don't! Anger curdles to hatred. I've been so stupid, so naïve.

Headlights suddenly swish across the curtains. Both Justin and I look over at the window and then a message pings on my mobile.

Justin grabs it from the dresser. *We're here. Where are you?* he reads, his skin paling. 'Fuck, Grace! You told her where we were.'

I don't respond.

'We need to leave.' Before I can stop him, Justin has grabbed Daniel and is heading for the door.

'No, don't...' I go after them, but Justin's already unbolting the B & B's front door by the time I reach the stairs. The owner appears from a side door and demands we keep the noise down, but I barely acknowledge her.

Somehow, I make it outside; everything is happening too quickly, and I can't grab hold of a single thought, as though I'm falling through my own mind. Justin and Candice, Daniel and Noah. How has everything got so screwed up?

It's dark now, and the wind blows my hair into my eyes so I can barely see. The sound of boots on gravel up ahead suggests Justin's heading for the car. 'Justin, get back. Bring Daniel back!'

'Grace. Stop!' I spin around as I hear Rob's voice. He's

marching towards me, a murderous expression on his face. Candice is behind him, slumped against the car.

'Do not let him go anywhere with Daniel, Grace,' barks Rob, now almost level with me. 'I'll kill him!'

'What the hell is he talking about?' Justin appears out of the darkness. He has Daniel slung over his shoulder and Rob makes a lunge for him.

'Stop!' I shoot my arm out, obstructing Rob. 'You'll scare Danny.'

Justin presses his face close to Rob's, his eyes narrowing. 'This is fuck all to do with you, piss off!'

Daniel turns and holds out his arms towards Rob. 'Dada!'

Justin freezes.

I brace myself, knowing that this is the moment of truth.

Justin shoots me a look. 'Grace? Why is Danny calling him Dad?'

I look from Justin to Rob and back again. 'Because he is.' My voice has a detached, muffled quality. 'Daniel is Rob and Candice's son.'

Justin steps back, his eyes flitting from me to Rob. 'What? He isn't your son?'

I shake my head.

'But I'm his dad. The DNA test, it said...'

I watch in horror as the penny drops.

72

JUSTIN

'Grace, I... Shit!'

'Yeah, bit of a shock for me, too,' says Grace dryly. She can't bring herself to look at me. 'But it's true, right? You had an affair. With *her*.' She gestures at Candice who strides towards us, arms outstretched.

I tighten my grip around Daniel, hitch him further up my chest and angle my body instinctively to protect him. He's my son, my *only* blood relative. I'm not about to let Candice and that arsehole take him away from me. 'It wasn't an affair. It was a stupid, one-off mistake,' I plead to Grace, but I know it's irrelevant. Whether it was once, twice or a hundred times, I was a dick. I betrayed her and then fled like a coward. 'Grace... please.' I reach out my hand, but she bats it away.

'How could you do that to me?' Every word stabs at my heart, the pain in Grace's voice raw. 'With Candice, *my* cousin, Justin!' Her eyes swell with tears, ready to burst.

I have no words, no excuses. What I did was unforgivable. It was stupid, selfish, weak. It was one moment, one single action that has caused so much damage. And not just to Grace, but to me as well. But I can also tell there's something else. Grace is holding back, I sense it.

'Why did you lie to me about Daniel?' I blurt out. 'Why did you say he was yours? You were pregnant. Or was that a lie too?'

The deluge of tears begins, and I know instantly I've got it wrong.

'He died... stillborn. *Our* child died, Justin. Our Noah died.'

I need to go to her, to kiss away her pain and heal the scars of grief that I've inflicted, but I can't. I'm frozen by guilt. If I hadn't walked away, our baby, Noah, might still be alive. The shock of me leaving must have caused this to happen.

Rob, forever Grace's saviour, wraps his arms around her. *Prick!* She buries her face into his chest, and he whispers something to her. Anger rises but I fight back the urge to react.

Candice stands next to Grace but ignores her sobs. 'Justin, give me Danny.' She has her hood pulled low and appears unsteady. Was it me who hurt her yesterday? Did I have a blackout? I remember her messaging me, threatening to tell Grace. Is it possible that I drove to meet her and then... it's all a blur, the memories from leaving Jack and Garth at the shooting range veiled in a dark mist. I edge backwards, shake my head.

'I've been trying to track you down all this time,' she continues, smiling. *Why is she smiling?*

'I wanted to tell you about Daniel.'

Grace shoots her a look, and Candice mumbles a half-hearted apology before diverting her attention back to me. 'But we can be a family now, Justin, the three of us. We can be together, like we always wanted.'

I hear the laugh escape my lips. 'You're out of your tiny mind!' Fury quickly replaces the disbelief. 'I've *never* wanted to be with you. You stalked me, wouldn't leave me alone!'

Now it's Candice who laughs, her smile distorting to a sneer.

She nods at Daniel. 'He wouldn't have happened if you didn't want to be with me.'

'You're evil,' I hiss.

'Well, if you *don't* want me, you don't get Danny either. We come as a pair. Give him to me.'

My heart pounds. Nobody is taking my boy! I edge back further, clutching Daniel until I bump into the car door. I have to get away, I can't handle this, the lies and deceit, the threats.

'Justin, what the hell are you doing?'

Rob marches towards me as I bundle my son into the back of the car and jump in the driver's seat.

'Give me my son, now!' he rants.

I lock the doors just as Rob grabs the handle.

'He isn't your son,' I shout through the passenger window.

'He is on paper.'

So he knew all along! *Prick.*

Rob bangs his fists on the glass. 'I'll make sure you never see him again you lying, cheating fucker!'

'Rob, stop!' Grace is pulling on Rob's arm. 'Justin, they've called the police. Let Daniel out.'

'Justin, please, I'm on your side.' Candice pushes Rob out of the way and peers through the window. Despite her pleading tone, I notice her eyes are bone dry. 'I messaged you yesterday as soon as I realised what Rob was up to. I saw the photos of you on his phone going in and out of Grace's house, and I saw the message warning you what would happen if you went back to Grace.'

I put the key in the ignition.

'I figured it out, Justin,' continues Candice. 'Rob knew all along about the affair and that Daniel was yours. It's blackmail.'

I start the engine.

'Pleeease. I'll tell the police that, and we can be together, but you have to let Daniel out.'

'What the hell is she on about?' Grace looks from me to Rob. 'Rob, what did you do?'

Rob shoots me a warning look. It's a half plea, half threat.

I curl my fingers tight around the steering wheel, fury rising as the truth hits. It all makes sense now. 'You intended to bring my child up as your own all along, you bastard. You knew she was pregnant and that it was mine and you couldn't bear the thought of me wanting to be involved. That's why you blackmailed me, isn't it?'

'Rob, what's he talking about?' asks Grace.

The colour drains from Rob's face. He squeezes his eyes shut. 'Justin... don't, please,' he begs.

'Really? You actually expect me to keep your dirty little secret quiet after all you've put me through. Go on, Rob, tell your precious Grace what you threatened to do if I didn't leave her?'

73

JUSTIN
NOW

'We've no news yet,' says the detective coldly.

'So Garth's not dead?'

DC Gorman sits back down. 'Like I said, no news.'

'And Daniel?'

'Nothing's been confirmed.'

I can't take this not knowing, this helplessness. I bang the tabletop with both palms and lean across. 'I need to know... now! He's my son.'

DC Gorman leans forward too, his face just six inches from mine. 'Not on paper he's not.'

I flop back and rub my stinging eyes. I desperately need sleep, and a growl from my stomach reminds me I've not eaten anything for over twenty-four hours. Despite an urge to stop co-operating, my physical needs, along with my burning desire to find out about Daniel and Garth, override it.

'Okay. You asked me about the night Grace told me she was pregnant.'

'The night you left,' he says.

'Yes, the night I left. About two months before that...' I pause,

251

thinking how to put it. 'About two months before, I slept with Candice.'

He looks up from his notes. 'You had an affair with Grace's cousin.'

'No, not an affair. We had a stupid one-night stand. I was drunk, she was teary... you know, the usual cliché.'

'Why was she teary?'

'Had a fight with her husband. They were always at it. He'd gone off in a huff. She phoned to say she was desperate, needed to talk to someone. Usually she'd talk to Grace, but she was on a girls' night out, staying over at a friend's.'

'So what made you go?'

'She said she felt like ending it all. I had to.'

'And when you got there, who made the first move?'

The question takes me by surprise. 'What does it matter?'

'Did you, did she?'

'She did. She's always had a thing for me, always making sexual innuendos and trying to get me to come round to the house whenever Rob was out.'

'But this was the first time anything happened, physically I mean?'

'Yes. She was crying, and like I said, I was drunk, so...'

'And after you'd slept with her?'

'She said she was in love with me and wanted me to leave Grace. I told her no way, that it was a stupid mistake, should never have happened.'

'And then?'

'She got mad, tried to hit me, told me to leave.'

'Did you tell Grace?'

'God no. It would've crucified her.'

'And Candice? How was she after the *one-night stand*?' He draws quote marks in the air.

'She wouldn't leave me alone. Kept phoning me day and night. Then suddenly she stopped. I thought that was it, didn't hear from her for a few days. Then I got a text that ruined my life.'

74

JUSTIN
2 YEARS AGO

Why the hell is she being snappy with me? All I wanted to know was if she wanted normal mash or cheesy mash. I'm not asking her if she wants a mansion or a palace. As I trudge back down the stairs, I pause at the framed photos lining the staircase wall. There's a black-and-white one of the two of us, Grace standing behind me with her arms around my neck. She's kissing my cheek as I laugh, a look of mischief in her eyes. That's how it used to be, both purposefully winding each other up, then immediately laughing it off. Now look at us. Still winding each other up but no hint of laughter. How did we get to this?

I guess it emerged from the difficulties of trying to start a family, each of us silently apportioning blame on the other while simultaneously trying to provide support when that self-blame broke the surface. That's when the gaps in our relationship started to emerge, when I started to lose her.

Back in the kitchen I peer through the oven door at the fish pie starting to bubble and brown. *Looking good*, I think, but these days there's nothing I can do that seems to make Grace happy. In some ways it's no wonder I succumbed to one night of ego-boosting appreciation with Candice. But what a nightmare that turned into. At least Candice has stopped mithering now.

And then, right on cue, my phone buzzes and my stomach drops. Only the text is not from Candice, it's from Rob, and the message is far more worrying than those his wife was sending:

I know everything. If you don't want Grace to find out, meet me now.

I hear Grace thundering down the stairs. She bursts into the kitchen.

'Oh my God, Justin, I'm...'

And then, what should have been the best news of my life is blurred in the despair of what is going to happen when Grace finds out about my night with Candice. *Shit, shit, shit.* 'Sorry, what was that?'

'I'm pregnant,' she says.

A child. Our child! But all I can think about is Rob threatening to rip everything apart and expose me for what I know I am, a fraud. Grace gags, puts a hand over her mouth and dashes to the bathroom. I can think of nothing but what Rob is going to do. I need to know how much he actually knows.

Rob sits at a corner table of the Wheatsheaf. We eye each other without greeting. I place my Guinness next to his half a shandy and perch on a padded stool opposite.

He takes a sip, calmly places the glass back on a beer mat, and sits back, arms folded. It feels like he's revelling in the moral high ground. 'I thought we were friends,' he says, finally.

Truth is, we're couple friends, and it's Candice who both Grace and I prefer. Rob is boring, a whining waffler. 'We *were* friends... I mean we are.'

'You slept with Candice.'

I hide my shock behind a sip of Guinness. *Shit!*

'Friends don't do that. Friends don't try to steal a mate's wife,' says Rob in a patronising tone, as if he was trying to explain morality to a child.

'I'm not trying to steal Candice. It was a one-off, a stupid, drunken mistake.' I feel the weight of guilt, but not for this sanctimonious prick in front of me, only for Grace.

Rob leans forward, stabs at his phone. 'That's not what you said in your text messages with her.' He turns the screen round. 'I took a screenshot.' He smirks, waiting for my response.

Candice: *Do u love me Justin?*

Justin: *Yes*
Justin: *It's the truth*

Candice: *U and me are meant to be together, we both know that*

Justin: Without a doubt

'Pretty compelling evidence that it's more than a one-night stand,' says Rob.

'Wait. That's not what was said. Stuff's been deleted!' I argue as I finish reading it.

'Show me what you said then, on your phone,' says Rob.

'I deleted everything.'

Rob snorts. 'How convenient.'

'Listen, she asked if I loved her and I said, *no, I love Grace*,' I say, running my finger along the lines in the text. 'Then she said something like, *you still love Grace after last night*, and I said, *yes*. And when I said, *without a doubt*, she'd asked me if I thought last night was just a mistake. She's just deleted lines to make it look like something different.'

Rob has his eyes closed, shaking his head. 'It's all here in black and white. You can't deny it.'

'I'm telling you, Candice has deleted half of the conversation. It went nothing like that.'

'And I'm telling *you* I'm not losing my wife to some cheating lowlife, so this is how it's going to work. You're going to leave Grace, your house, your phoney life, and never come back.'

'I'm not disappearing. Grace is pregnant for God's sake.'

Rob holds his glass suspended between table and mouth. 'Grace is pregnant?'

'Yep. So there's no way I'm leaving my unborn child.'

He takes a sip, processing the news. 'Well, that's even more reason to leave. If Grace finds out about you screwing Candice, she might have a miscarriage. Do you want that on your conscience too?'

'I can't just leave. That's crazy. They need me.'

'Justin, let's be honest here now. *Nobody* needs you, believe me. Look at you! You're a weak, lying philanderer with no prospects, no skills and no morals. You work on a fairground for God's sake! Not exactly a perfect role model for a new child, are you? What are you going to give them? How will you provide? And all the time you'll have it in the back of your mind that any day, at any moment, it could all come tumbling down if your dirty little secret comes out. Is that what you want?'

I wish I could argue back, but I have nothing, no foundations on which I can build a denial. I'm not father material even though I'm aching to have a child. Even that's probably a selfish motive just so I can right the wrongs of my own childhood by proxy.

'And it would be such a shame if the child ended up in care,' Rob continues. 'You know what that's like moving from care home to care home. And Grace is hardly the most stable person at the moment, so between you... I'm sure you know what I'm saying.'

I feel the heat rising. 'What do you mean by that?' I snarl.

Rob leans closer. 'You know she'll probably do something stupid again. Remember last time she hit rock bottom?' He sneers as mimes being unconscious. 'And if her mind's not on the job at my practice because of your infidelity, she'll make mistakes, could even get fired. Difficult to concentrate when you've got that much on your mind. Can't put patient's lives in danger now, can we?'

I stare at him in silence, dumbfounded by how low this meek and mild-mannered man that I thought I knew could go. There's pure hatred in his voice, his intentions. This is not just about punishing me for sleeping with his wife, this is about destroying me and my life. But he's not finished yet.

'You know in my line of work, we often see babies and young kids with signs of abuse, both physical and mental. It's our duty to report that to social services. One phone call. It's that easy.'

I jump to my feet, grab his collar and pull him over the table. Guinness and shandy cascade off the table in a frothy stream. 'You're sick,' I hiss. I pull back a clenched fist ready to strike. Rob puts up no defence despite the fear in his eyes. He wants me to punch him, wants the Sunday drinkers to see how violent I am, to this 'respectable' well-known member of the community.

'I could have you arrested for assault, right now,' he says calmly. 'Plenty of witnesses.' He nods his head towards the bar.

I look around at the pub full of onlookers, all quiet, staring anxiously at the drama unfolding. I release my grip but remain standing.

Rob wipes at his wet jeans with a handkerchief. 'Leave now,' he says, eyes focused on mopping up, 'And I give you my word Grace and the baby will be well taken care of, and so will you.'

He reaches inside his jacket and slides a bulky envelope towards me.

'What's that?' I snap.

'Incentive,' he replies coolly.

'You're paying me to leave Grace!'

'I'm helping you. I'll deal with Candice and make sure the truth never comes out. She doesn't know I know and I'll keep it that way. It's either that, or I'll make sure yours, Grace's *and* the baby's life will be a living hell. I'll tell Grace everything. You're not worthy of her, Justin. They're better off without you. You know that.'

I clench my teeth, my fists. I've never wanted to inflict pain on someone as much as I want to batter Rob right now, to see him squirm and plead and bleed. But he's right. Instead, I turn and stride out of the pub, ignoring the envelope, and the disdainful looks from the corners of drinkers' eyes.

75

JUSTIN
NOW

'Rob obviously knew at the time that Candice was pregnant as well, and that the baby wasn't his. I remember him telling me once they hardly ever slept together.'

DC Gorman scribbles something in his notes, then looks up, tapping the pen against his cheek. 'So why did Rob not tell you his wife was pregnant?'

'He must have thought that if I knew Candice was carrying my child, I'd want to be with her, or at least want to bring the child up. I guess he didn't want to risk that.'

'And Candice? If she wanted to be with you, why didn't she tell you she was pregnant herself?'

'She didn't realise till after I'd left. I found out yesterday that she'd been rushed into hospital the morning I met Rob. She'd started bleeding. That's when she found out she was pregnant, Rob too. He must have known straight away it wasn't his but, I guess with me out of the picture, Candice told him the baby was his and he chose not to speak up about it.'

'So Rob knew the baby wasn't his but how did he find out it was yours?'

'Went straight on her phone and checked her messages. Put two and two together.'

DC Gorman leans back, hands behind his head. 'If he knew Candice had been unfaithful, why was he still so keen to save the marriage?'

'I don't know. He used to have a thing for Grace, but now it's pretty obvious he worships Candice, even though she walks all over him.'

'Treat them mean and all that claptrap. Some blokes love it. Listen, Justin.' Gorman straightens up and fixes me with a stare. I sense the shift in dynamics. Suddenly, I'm no longer the enemy. 'Do you think Rob might have something to do with Daniel's disappearance? If he thought he was about to lose him, is it possible he did something to stop that from happening?'

The implication turns my stomach.

'If that arsehole has done anything to my son, I'll kill him!'

76

GRACE
1 DAY EARLIER

There are too many questions I need to ask but none of them will formulate properly inside my head, let alone come out my mouth. In truth, I'm still devastated from learning that Justin and Candice have slept together; that Daniel is the product of their betrayal – the little boy who I've dedicated my whole life to for almost two years, who I've cradled in my arms and sang lullabies to despite my heart constantly aching for Noah. God... Daniel is Noah's brother! The realisation hits me like a punch to the stomach.

'Grace, you have to believe I only ever wanted Justin out of the picture,' says Rob, breaking the fraught silence. He glances over at me, nervously. 'I wanted to save my marriage, yes, but also for you to never feel the way I did.'

Justin sneers through the driver's window. 'Come off it, Rob. Tell her the truth.'

'Yeah,' adds Candice, her eyes awash with excited anticipation. 'Tell her, Rob.' She's enjoying it I realise; it's little more than a game to her. Under the light of the pale moon she resembles a werewolf – sleek glossy hair, top lip curling revealing sharp white teeth. I turn away, can't bear to look at her for a second longer, to see how easily I've been fooled by her shows of loyalty. How could she do this to me? To sit there, night after night in the days following Noah's death, consoling me, holding me upright when I no longer could. How could she allow my tears to soak her skin when all the time she'd betrayed me in the worst possible way? Did she care for me at all? Or did my tears simply water her amusement?

In contrast, Rob's face is flushed with shame, though why I still don't know. What I do know is that like me, he has been let down by the person who was meant to love him the most, only for him it's worse, because he's carried the burden of betrayal for two years, all the while knowing he was bringing up another man's child. I guess that's true love. Or stupidity.

'Grace, please.' His eyes are everywhere but on mine. 'I need you to know that I acted on impulse. I never meant a word. You know I've loved you since we were kids.'

'Sure you have,' says Justin, his voice dripping with sarcasm. 'Loved her so much you threatened to destroy her if I didn't disappear.' He glares at me, anger now flashing in his eyes. 'I'll tell you the truth, Grace, seeing as though he's not got the balls.' He breathes in, steeling himself. 'Rob, here, threatened to phone social services and report our baby as being neglected. He obviously knew Candice was pregnant with my child and he was prepared to do whatever it took to make sure I was out of the picture, including having Noah taken off you.'

I glare at Rob, shock and pain curdling to anger. 'How could you do that?' I choke out the question.

'Grace, I'm sorry.' He hangs his head. 'I offered him money at first. I just wanted him gone.' His eyes flick to mine, though only fleetingly. 'I didn't want the truth to come out. Then Justin said you were pregnant, and I knew I had to really scare him to make him leave. I couldn't risk losing Candice, no matter what she'd done. I couldn't bear to think of her with him, the both of them playing happy families when he's destroyed my life.'

'Grace, you have to know I knew nothing about this, I was as much in the dark as you,' whines Candice, as though she's the injured party. 'That day Justin left you I'd been in hospital that morning remember, with stomach pains. They said I was pregnant. I was bleeding, too, and I thought I was going to lose the baby. I didn't even know Rob had found out about the affair. Not until yesterday.'

'It wasn't an affair for God's sake!' Justin breathes in slowly, as though fighting with himself. 'Grace, please. It was just a stupid one-night stand that I've regretted ever since.'

'You regret fathering that child in your arms?' snaps Candice, expressing genuine emotion for the first time since the truth came out. 'You wish he was never born?'

Justin falters. 'I didn't say that.'

'Daniel isn't his child,' snaps Rob. 'Biologically perhaps, but it's me who's brought him up, so give him to me, now!'

Justin's eyes narrow. 'That was you, too, wasn't it? The note on my car? *You* said Daniel wasn't my son!'

'Yes.' Rob's confession hits the air as a cloud of warm breath. 'You sent me a voice message one morning, a few days after I'd sent you the warning message. You shouted something about me not taking your son. I panicked, thought you must have done the dates, figured out Daniel was yours. I just wanted you to clear off.'

'As soon as I discovered the truth at the spa,' interrupts Candice. 'I wanted to get it all out in the open with you both, at the house. Only I didn't get to do that, did I?' She turns and glares at Rob. 'Seems somebody was still as desperate as ever to keep the truth buried.'

'You?' I turn to Rob, feeling the ground being ripped out from underneath me. 'It was you who attacked Candice?'

GRACE
1 DAY EARLIER

The colour drains from Rob's face. 'I didn't mean to. It was an accident.'

'How can battering your wife unconscious be an accident?' I say, incredulously.

His gaze flits between the three of us as though unsure where to land. 'I thought I was going to lose everything... my business, Daniel. I panicked,' he gabbles, guilty eyes now settling on Candice. 'I honestly never meant to...'

'Honestly never meant to do what, Rob? Leave me out cold?' she retorts, spitting her words at him. 'Gotta give it to you, doc, I didn't think you had it in you.'

'You threatened to ruin my practice. Said you'd have me arrested for blackmail. That you were taking Daniel away from me and shacking up with Justin.' His voice is shrill and breathy. 'I tried to make you see sense, but you wouldn't stop hammering on Grace's door. I just wanted to stop you from ruining me.'

'I thought you had no memory of the attack,' I say to Candice, remembering this morning's conversation with Grandpa. 'You told the police it was all a blur.'

'Wanted to see if he had the balls to admit it first.' She snorts, shaking her head. 'Should have known he'd try to worm his way out of it – point the finger at Justin.'

Rob removes his glasses and wipes his eyes. 'I was going to ring the ambulance, honestly. And then I saw you, Grace. You were getting Daniel out of your car. I knew you'd help her so I ran.' He sniffs up loudly. 'I'm a coward I know.'

In the distance, blue flashing lights illuminate the night sky. I shoot a look at Justin who frowns. 'What?' he says quietly.

'The police,' I mouth. 'The police are coming.'

'Ahh, here comes the cavalry,' announces Candice. 'Now what should I tell them?' Slowly she runs her tongue over her top teeth, intentionally toying with Rob.

'Candice. Don't. I'm begging you.' Rob holds his hands together as if in prayer. 'I'll lose everything. It was an accident.'

'Sorry, but I have to.' She shrugs theatrically. 'I can't trust you around Danny, can I? Unless, well, let me think.' She's dangling him by a string, the master manipulator and her wooden puppet. Hasn't it always been that way? Him dancing to her tune. Despite everything, my heart goes out to Rob. He believed he was about to lose everything – his career, wife, child. Aren't we all capable of violence if pushed to the limit?

'Anything, Candice. I'll do anything you want.'

'Anything I want?' She makes a show at considering this. 'Nope. Sorry. The damage is already done. At least you like porridge, every cloud and all that.'

'I've heard enough,' I snap. 'You want to tell the police it was Rob then do it, but remember you're far from innocent.'

'What have I done?' she asks incredulously. 'Okay, so me and Justin fell in love but that's hardly a crime, is it?'

'We did *not* fall in love!' shouts Justin, 'I slept with you once for Christ's sake!'

'So what are you saying? You don't want me and Danny in your life? Because we *only* come as a package, remember that.'

Justin's eyes flash with fury. 'You're sick, you know that? Both of you.' Justin turns the ignition. 'Them lunatics are not taking my kid! They've already taken everything else from me, they're not having him too.'

'Justin! Don't...' My words are drowned out by the sound of wheels screeching on the tarmac.

'Give me my son, you bastard!' Candice runs after the car then stops dead as she realises it's futile. 'This is all your fault, Grace!' She marches back towards me, her finger jabbing at the air between us. 'I swear to God if anything happens to Danny...'

'Don't even pretend you give a shit.' Burning rage hisses through every word. 'I have more love for that boy than you've ever had. Don't pretend your tears are for Daniel. They're for yourself – because Justin doesn't want you.'

'He wanted me that night though, didn't he?'

'Get away from me.' I step away from her, a flame of hatred curling in my stomach. 'I'll never forgive you for this.'

'You're just jealous because I gave him what you never could,' she snarls, now inches from my face.

Suddenly I'm on the floor, my face pressed into the ground, my arms about to break.

'Hands behind your back, now!'

I'm disorientated, as though submerged in deep, murky water. Where am I? What's happened? I cry out, taste the damp earth on my tongue. Spit it out. Fight. I can't breathe.

'Stay down!' A deep voice reverberates in my ear, a heavy weight pushing into the small of my back. I play dead. Close my eyes. Something cold and sharp bites into my wrist.

I hear Candice's shrill voice; 'I think she's broke my nose, the psychotic bitch!'

I'm yanked up, see Rob glowering at me. Candice is wrapped around him, crying theatrically.

I spin around, come face to face with the officer who only last night sat on my sofa drinking tea. 'What the...'

'I'm arresting you on suspicion of assault,' he barks, bundling me towards a waiting police car. 'You don't have to say anything unless you wish to do so, though whatever you say may be given in evidence.'

'Rob!' I shout, but he doesn't acknowledge me. He's too busy comforting his wife.

78

JUSTIN
1 DAY EARLIER

My anger needs a release, and for now it's discharged through knuckles squeezed white on the steering wheel and my right foot jammed hard to the floor.

For too many years I've been pushed around, letting others decide what's in my best interests – from social services to Jack and Caroline, and more recently, Rob. Today that stops. There's absolutely no way I'm letting that happen to Daniel. And I'm not letting that happen to me anymore.

Simply due to the lack of any other plan I speed towards Prestbury, to Jack and Caroline's house, a natural go-to when things got tough previously, but even in my fog of fury, I suspect the police will also anticipate where I'm headed.

Sure enough, it's not long before I spot the distant flash of a blue light in my rear-view mirror. 'Hold tight, matey,' I say, and swerve off the main road down a country lane. Who knew my days of joyriding Jack's car when I was a teen would come in so handy in adult life? I know all the side streets, shortcuts and hiding places within a twenty-mile radius.

Parked behind a hedgerow, I watch as the police car races

past. 'You okay, mate?' I ask, turning around to Daniel. He looks confused, frightened.

'Mama,' he mouths quietly.

'Yeah, we'll see Mummy soon.' Shit, it dawns on me he means Candice, not Grace. How am I ever going to get my head around Daniel being Candice's son? I still don't understand why Grace lied to me. Why not just tell me the truth about Noah? Tears sting my eyes at the thought of my child, and for Grace. She went through that alone, abandoned by my cowardice. 'First, you're going for a little drive with Daddy. Is that okay?'

He doesn't answer, just stares wide-eyed, his beautiful face as pure and pale as the full moon that casts a silvery glow over the surrounding fields. I pat his knee and turn around. I need a plan, or more urgently, I need somewhere to go. I can't drive around with Daniel all night waiting for something to happen. But it needs to be somewhere that the police, Grace and the others wouldn't guess, and there's only one person I can trust when I need an idea so random that no one else would think of it.

'Hi, Garth. Me again. Fancy an adventure, like the old days?'

79

GRACE
NOW

I sit hunched on the stone-hard bed, hands clasped between knees which are barely touching. I've lost so much weight in the last three weeks it's scary. A plastic tray of, now cold, soup lies at my feet but, despite my stomach growling, I can't bring myself to eat it. The night is turning in on itself and Daniel is still out there, alone and afraid. He hates the dark, will be cold and hungry. What if somebody has him? Will they know he needs his night light, that he'll not sleep without it? His dummies, too, one isn't enough, he needs three, one for each hand and the other in his mouth; how will a stranger know that? The panic builds like a cluster of spark plugs in my chest. I take a slow, calming breath, close my eyes, hear the clicking of his fingers against the teats, his soft, milky breath on my chest as sleep takes hold. 'I'm so sorry, baby boy, this is all my fault.'

The station has fallen silent now, the drunken girl in the cell opposite seemingly comatose after a ten-minute protest of hammering the cell door and slurring obscenities to herself. She sounded young, late teens, early twenties. It makes me wonder what kind of betrayals she's suffered in her short life to become a person who's inebriated on a Tuesday teatime. Neglect? An abusive relationship? The loss of innocence at the hands of a predator? *There but for the grace of God go I.* Mum loved that saying, drilled it into me from an early age. *Every one of us is susceptible to sin, Grace.* I'm lucky that in my darkest days I had good people around me; Grandpa, Rob and even Candice at the time, and later, Justin. It's why, even now, despite everything, I can't bring myself to hate them. I guess that's what hurts the most of all – I still care for them all.

I stand, unable to sit doing nothing for a moment longer. The hard floor is icy cold beneath my bare feet. The officers took my shoes when I arrived, my belt too. What do they think I'm capable of? It's been almost twenty-four hours now since they arrested me. I've watched enough crime documentaries to know they'll soon need to charge or release me. Weirdly, confessing to Sally has helped me to piece everything together, as though I arrived at the station with a loose jigsaw puzzle that she tipped out in front of me and helped me to solve. The pieces were there all along, I just had to find the outline.

Only there's one piece still missing, and that piece lays at the heart of the jigsaw. Why? Why did Justin cheat on me with my own cousin? Why did Candice never confess the truth when Justin left? And why did I feel the need to lie to Justin over and over again, despite knowing there could never be a happy ending? I guess I'll never truly know the answers.

I bang my fists against the wrought-iron door, the panic creeping higher now, covering my nose and mouth. 'Sally! Let me out. I need to speak to you.'

I listen. Nothing. Bang again, harder this time. 'Please let me out! I need to know if Daniel has been found.'

Dark thoughts accelerate in my head. What if he's been abducted? Killed? What if he's stuck some place with no way out? I know I need to breathe but I can only gasp, the air too stuffy, choking me. I'm going to black out. The room spins and I squat on the floor, feeling sick. 'Please let Daniel be all right. Please let him be safe.' I hold my hands together in prayer – one final time. 'Please God, just this once. Not Daniel too – please not him as well.'

The sound of footsteps draws closer, quickly followed by the clanking of metal. The door hatch opens. 'What's the matter, Grace?'

I look up at Sally, only her eyes and nose visible.

'Daniel, I need to know if he's okay, I have to know he's safe.' My words echo off the four stone walls. 'Please tell me you've found him.'

Sally releases the lock and opens the door. She stands over me, her eyes red and dry as though she too hasn't slept for a week. She doesn't answer immediately. 'We do have news Grace.' She looks at me for the longest of times. 'We've just had a call from the station in Buxton. It's about Daniel.'

80

JUSTIN
10 HOURS BEFORE

'Morning, mate.'

Garth looks remarkably bright and fresh for once. He must have been up for ages.

'What time is it?' I grunt.

'Precisely...' He picks his phone up from the draining board of the kitchenette. Unsurprisingly, it's dripping wet. 'Shit,' he says, wiping it with his hand. 'Seven minutes past nine.'

Jesus. How the hell could I have slept so well on the floor of a caravan? I sit up suddenly.

'Where's Daniel?'

'He's fine, chill. He's outside playing with Sandy and Scar. Had his breakfast, black pudding sandwich. Loved it, he did. Brew?'

I don't know what to question first, that Daniel is playing with someone called Scar, or that black pudding is not the healthiest thing to feed a one-and-a-half-year-old. I decide against raising either point. I have enough to think about with all that went on last night. My mind is in turmoil. On the one hand, I should be ecstatic as hell with the confirmation that Daniel is my son, but that's overshadowed by the fact that his mum is not Grace, who now knows I was unfaithful, and also that Noah, the child we did have together, died, and I wasn't there for her.

But there's no time for self-pity. My focus from now on is to make sure my son is safe and happy.

'So, you kept this Sandy quiet,' I say to Garth, now throwing on some clothes. 'You been seeing her long?'

Garth winks. 'Friends with benefits, mate. She ain't no looker, but she knows what's she's doing, know what I mean?'

'Love's young dream then,' I joke. I leave Garth happily rolling a joint and head outside.

A lady, who I assume is Sandy, sits in a flimsy deckchair that strains in all directions as it battles to contain her voluminous frame. A boisterous pit bull sprints back and forth at full speed from an adjacent caravan. As soon as it sees me it changes path and leaps up. I can't tell if it's trying to lick my face or chew it off.

'He's only playing,' says Sandy as she raises a flabby arm and bellows, 'Scar! Leave it!' The dog takes no notice until Sandy makes as if she's going to stand. It cowers momentarily, then goes back to making mad dashes between the other twenty or so caravans on the grassy park.

'Sorry if we woke you up last night,' I say apologetically.

Sandy dismisses my worry with a wave of her chubby hand. 'Didn't hear a thing. When I've gone, I've gone.'

I smile.

'Garth says you've had a bit of a rough time of it lately,' she continues.

'You could say that. Had a bit of a problem with my son. Speaking of which,' I glance around, looking for Daniel. 'Where is he?'

Sandy shades her eyes from the morning sun and makes a show of looking for Daniel. She shrugs. 'Was here a minute ago.'

I spin a full three-sixty. 'Danny mate? Where are you?'

A sense of déjà vu washes over me, the same numbing panic, and an overwhelming fear in the pit of my stomach.

Garth appears from the caravan and struggles to lower himself onto the grass. 'Blinding headache. Need a hair of the dog, I reckon.'

'Mate, you seen Daniel?'

'No, why? He done a runner.' Garth grins. 'Takes after his old man, eh? Ow!' He winces and holds his head. 'Can't handle the drink these days.'

Realising I'm going to get zero help off Garth or his 'lady friend', I take off, shouting Daniel's name at the top of my lungs.

A middle-aged lady with a full head of rollers waddles over from one of the nearby caravans. One end of her dressing gown cord trails through the mud behind her like a snake in pursuit.

'Sandy!' she squawks. 'Scar's crapped in my hydrangeas again.'

I grab her by the sleeve. 'You seen a little boy? Two-year-old? He was here like... when, Sandy?' I shout over at her. 'When did you last see him?'

She shrugs unhelpfully. 'Can't have been more than twenty minutes ago.'

'Twenty minutes? Christ! You were meant to be watching him.' I do another scan of the caravan park but aside from the lady in rollers it appears everyone else is still in bed.

'Oh give over, it's safe as houses here.' Sandy heaves herself up and waddles over to Garth, who is now slumped over on the grass. She shakes him by the arm and then calls his name. 'Think he's dropped off,' she directs over at me. 'Garth, come on, lovey, you're panicking me.' She shakes him more violently and her pleas for him to wake up become increasingly frantic. 'Justin, you better get over here,' she yells, 'he's gone all weird.'

Jesus, this is all I need. I sprint back over to Garth and gently slap his face. 'Mate?'

Garth turns his head to look at me. As he does, his eyes roll to the top of his head and he flops backwards.

'What's up with *him*?' says the lady in rollers, having now caught up with us.

'I dunno. He's like passed out or something,' remarks Sandy. 'Garth! Wake up, love.'

Beneath Garth's eyelids, I can see his eyeballs moving erratically. 'Call an ambulance,' I shout. 'Quickly!'

Sandy tries to heave herself up from her crouching position, but by the time she does her neighbour has already shuffled back to her caravan and re-emerged on the phone.

I continue calling Garth's name, patting his cheeks, but there's no response. *Come on, mate, don't do this to me. I need you.* His body jolts suddenly, making me jump back. His eyes have stopped twitching. I lean in, ear to his mouth.

'He's stopped breathing,' I shout. Kneeling beside him, I feel for a heartbeat. Immediately I start pummelling his chest. I've never done this before, don't know whether I'm doing it right. 'What's that song?' I ask a confused Sandy and the roller lady. 'The song, for doing this? The rhythm?' They shake their heads as if I'm speaking a different language.

'Come on, mate, come on,' I plead, still pounding. 'Daniel!' I shout, suddenly remembering. 'Sandy. Go look for Daniel. Where's the exit to this place?'

She puts two chubby hands on her cheeks, a horrified look on her face. 'Is he dead?' she asks, staring at Garth. 'He's gone awful still.'

More people have emerged from other caravans and stand watching from a 'polite' distance.

'Daniel!' I shout, still pounding Garth's chest. Blood is trickling out of the corner of his mouth. 'Somebody please find my son!' I roar. 'He's missing!'

My mind is in a frenzy over whether to stay with Garth or go to find Daniel, both potential life and death decisions. *What do I do, what do I do?* But there's no time for a logical analysis. 'Does somebody know how to do this properly?' I shout to the gathering crowd.

A shirtless man with tattoos covering his upper body strides forward. ''Ere, move over. You gotta do it harder,' he grunts.

As he takes over the resuscitation, I put a hand softly on Garth's pale cheek. 'I'm sorry, mate. I need to go and find Daniel. You understand, yeah? Don't you dare go anywhere now. I'll be right back.' My eyes mist as I force myself to stand. 'Love you, bro,' I add, my own heart hammering in panic as I race to find my son.

81

JUSTIN
NOW

DC Gorman has been away for at least ten minutes now. I glance around at the plain, empty room, devoid of any features or character apart from the digital recording device, and the bare-bones table and chairs. The silence, the blandness, the isolation wreak havoc with my mind as it scrambles to conjure up every possible scenario of what might be going on beyond these four walls with Daniel, Garth, Grace and Candice. Naturally, the worst possible outcomes are the most vivid and replayed scenes.

The door opens and the detective walks in, head bowed slightly. He avoids eye contact. I steel myself for the worst.

'I have some bad news,' he says.

Of course he has. That's the only kind I get in my life. I promise myself I won't break down, but the lump in my throat has already risen, the muscles in my eyes straining to hold back the tears.

'I'm afraid your friend, Garth, has died. Hospital says it was a brain tumour.'

The knockout blow sends my gaze to the floor and my heart crumbling to its knees. Garth, my brother in arms, gone for good. How can I live with not seeing his stupid, grinning face ever again? I suddenly feel alone in a way I've never felt before, as if half of my whole being has gone forever and I'm left to carry the weight of our past.

'And Daniel...' he continues.

I take a gasp of air.

'... has been found, safe and well.'

I look up. 'He's okay? My son is okay? Is he here? Can I see him?'

'Erm... yes, he's here, but no, you can't see him. Your name's not on the birth certificate so you need his mother's permission.'

'But I'm his dad.'

'Not on paper.' He almost looks sorry for me. 'But the other good news is that Candice has decided to drop the child abduction charges. Which means...'

'I can go?'

'Yes, you're free to go.'

Suddenly the banal interior seems to have colour. No longer does it feel like a space of confinement and repression, it feels more like a gateway to opportunities. Beyond that drab door lies freedom, possibilities – my son – and before DC Gorman invites me to leave, I'm through it and looking for Daniel.

The duty sergeant unlocks a heavy door and I step into the fluorescent light of liberty. It feels like I've been contained for weeks, though it's been barely nine hours.

'Justin!' calls a voice.

I hadn't noticed Candice and Daniel sat on a row of black, plastic chairs. She stands and throws her arms round me as I go to pick up Daniel. I keep my hands by my side, unwilling to reciprocate.

'I love you,' she whispers in my ear, still squeezing.

I desperately want to push her off, to grab hold of my son

and hold him so tight. Finally, she lets go, slides her hands down to mine.

'Are you okay?' she asks.

'Actually no,' I mutter. 'I've just found out my best mate, Garth, has died. He was like family.' I try to release my hands, but she grips them harder.

God, this woman never knows when to give up!

'Oh, that's a shame,' she says dismissively. 'But we can be a family now. Just you, me and Daniel, like it should be, flesh and blood together,' she says.

I glance over her shoulder at my son, so small, innocent and vulnerable in this adult environment. He shouldn't be here. This is not his world and never will be. I need to make sure of that, to protect him, guide him, show him he's loved so very deeply, that he has a family that will always be there for him, no matter what. A family. It's what I've always needed. Can I deny my son of that, even though it's Grace I still love? I know she hates me now, but this isn't about me. It never can be again. I have a son, and this is about him. He has to come first in everything from now on. I force a smile at Candice.

'Yeah, a proper family.'

82

GRACE
NOW

'They've found him, Grace. He's alive and well.'

'Oh, thank God!' I bury my head in my hands and allow the tears to come. 'Is he all right? Where was he?'

'Still on the caravan site, would you believe? Seems some older kids took a shine to him and he was happily playing in a wood nearby.' Sally rolls her eyes. 'Christ only knows where their parents were.'

The relief is as palpable as the four walls that imprison me. I realise I'm no longer concerned what happens to me. For all I care now, they can charge me and throw away the key. Daniel is safe, and that's all that matters. 'Have you told Justin?'

'We have. He's relieved, to say the least.'

A sudden rush of emotion catches me by surprise. 'Justin's a good man, you know,' I say, the confirmation as much for myself as for Sally. 'He messed up, but his heart's in the right place.' I fall silent.

'What is it, Grace?'

'Candice and Rob know Daniel's all right, yeah?' Despite everything, I know they love their son. Him being missing would have been torture for them.

'Yes. They were the first to know. Candice is here now to collect him.'

'Good.' I look down at the ground, guilt still gnawing away at me. 'I take it you're going to charge me with assault?'

The events of last night are still sketchy. One minute Candice was up in my face, goading me about Noah and Justin, next thing I knew I was being restrained.

'You know something, Grace?' Sally's voice is little more than a whisper. 'I probably shouldn't say this but I'm going to anyway. I've met many people in my line of work. Nearly all of them sit across from me in the interview room because they've messed up, some pretty royally.'

I glance up at Sally. 'Like me you mean?'

'Like you.' A half-smile pulls at the corner of her mouth. 'We record all our interviews as you know. But what's said in a police interview is rarely the most important.'

'No?'

She shakes her head. 'Truth or guilt lies in a person's eyes. Of course, we can't acquit, or convict based on eyes. Probably for the best really. The prisons would be chock-a-block.' She laughs softly. 'What I will say is that eyes always hold the truth that the mouth tries to hide. You may have been arrested on assault charges, and your cousin is, of course, innocent in the eyes of the law, but over these last twenty-four hours I've sat opposite you both and I know who the real victim is in all of this.' She purses her lips as though holding in a smile. 'I've just got off the phone to the CPS. They're not pressing charges.'

I gasp. 'You mean I'm not being charged with assault?'

'Nope. Seems your brother-in-law remembered that it was his wife who struck you first.' Sally raises an eyebrow, the implication clear. 'I reckon you owe him a pint.'

'Rob? But... I don't understand.' The last time I saw Rob he was throwing me a death stare while cradling Candice in his arms. 'So what? I'm...'

'Free to go.' Sally leans back against the cell door. 'Go on, get out of here. Though you might want to wait a few minutes. If Candice is here, I don't fancy breaking up round two. You gave her quite the shiner.' Sally smirks, as though me lumping Candice wasn't such a bad thing.

A minute later I find myself in reception, the harsh strip lights stinging my eyes after hours of being holed up in a dark cell. The desk sergeant gestures me over. 'Just need you to sign for your stuff.'

'Gayce!'

'Oh my God, Daniel!' Instinctively I crouch down and hold out my arms. 'I've missed you so much.'

Daniel runs towards me, a huge chocolaty grin lighting up his face.

'Danny. Get here!' Candice marches over and pulls him back.

'Gayce!' Daniel wrestles his way free.

'Candice, I...' My voice dies in my mouth as I catch sight of Justin stood behind her. He nods an acknowledgement.

'You okay?' he asks.

I force a smile. 'Fine.'

'Come on, Danny. Give Gracie a cuddle.' I beckon Daniel back over to me, determined to hold him one last time. I expect Candice to protest again but she doesn't. 'I love you so much, Danny boy, remember that.' I hold him close, breathing him in – so innocent and pure. I know it's likely the last time I'll see him, for a while at least. The thought of not spending my days with him anymore is more than my heart can take. Gently, I prise him away from me. 'Go give Daddy a big cuddle now. I reckon he needs it.'

'Candice, give us a minute, will you.' Justin picks up Daniel and kisses him on the forehead before passing him over to Candice. I'm shocked when she complies without argument.

'How the hell do you do that?' I feign a half-laugh, determined to make light of the situation despite every part of me wanting to curl up and die.

Justin shrugs. 'She wants us to be a family, a proper family with a live-in dad. I can't not be there for him, but I still love you, Grace. I don't know what to do.' He looks at me with pain in his eyes, desperate for my blessing.

I take his hand in mine. He grips it tightly, as though he's drowning and I'm his life raft. 'You have to do what's right for Daniel,' I whisper, forcing the words out not because I want to say them but because I know Justin needs to hear them. 'You're his dad, his dad! He needs you.'

'I'm so sorry,' he says, his voice choked with tears. 'For everything.' His eyes are softer than I ever knew eyes could be. Instantly I remember Sally's words.

'I know you are, Justin. I know.'

'Come on, Justin, Danny's tired.' Candice wanders back over to us, sits Daniel on the reception desk and wraps her arms around Justin's waist. 'I think he wants his mummy and daddy to read him a bedtime story.'

The snipe is as clear as the discomfort on Justin's face, but I choose to ignore it. 'Sorry things had to end like this, Candice. I do hope you'll be happy.'

'Yeah, sorry, cus. I really never meant to hurt you,' she says while resting her head on Justin's shoulder. He looks me deep in the eye, an ocean of regret wordlessly passing between us.

If only things had been different.

83

JUSTIN
NOW

G race holds the door open and looks over her shoulder one last time. A cold chill sweeps through the station reception. Our eyes meet, sadness reflected in both our faces. Then she turns, and is gone, leaving me with my 'real' family, that forever elusive dream, my happy land beyond the treetops.

In a second my mind flashes back to all the moments when I was desperate for the loving embrace and protection from my own parents, the two things that never came. I picture the betrayal of my dad while I lay in bed; the psychological battering of my mum's slurred words repeatedly telling me how I was just a 'bad mistake'; the day I was wrestled from my own home by social services, kicking and crying, knowing then that those deep, dark feelings that suffocated my every waking moment were not in my imagination, that they were real and they had names – 'rejection' and 'abandonment'.

I look at Candice, her perfect hazel skin glowing, her full lips sharing a victorious smile. And Daniel, sat on the reception counter – my beautiful boy, a miracle of sweetness and innocence that makes me feel reborn, like my life can start all over again, my journey finally written as it should have been, with the fairy tale happy ending it never had.

That dream is here in front of me. All I need to do is reach out and embrace it.

'Shall we go?' says Candice, lowering Daniel to the floor and hooking her arm in mine.

'Go where?' I ask, suddenly aware that I don't know where this new life starts. But Candice has no hesitation. She's already worked it out.

'My house.'

'And Rob?'

She smiles again, only this time it's a different smile. 'Rob who?'

I narrow my eyes and tilt my head, refusing to play her game. 'Your husband?'

'We won't be seeing him again.'

'Oh?'

'Let's just say we came to an arrangement,' she says, smirking. 'He walks away and leaves me the house and our savings and I don't tell the police who really attacked me.'

'You blackmailed him?'

She weighs up the thought. '*Blackmail* is a bit harsh. I prefer to think of it as setting us up for life. It's not for me obviously, it's for Danny. Rob owes him that after purposefully keeping him from his real daddy.' She looks down at Daniel and pats his head like a pet dog.

Immediately that vision of a rebirth vanishes. This isn't how a perfect life starts, founded on extortion and loveless parents. Family love is supposed to be like a solid chain, an impenetrable barrier of protection. This chain has a broken link, and only now do I realise that it's irreparable without Grace.

I unhook my arm. 'I'm sorry, Candice, I can't do this.'

84

GRACE
NOW

By the time I leave the station it's already gone nine. Rain hammers down from a black sky, soaking me to the skin. I don't care. I doubt I'll care about anything ever again.

Houses and cars pass in a blur as I make my way home by foot. I don't even have any money for a taxi. In the last twenty-four hours I've lost everything; my family, a job I adore, the only man I've every truly loved. I feel like crying but why bother? What's the point in crying when there's nobody left to comfort you?

My phone vibrates in my coat pocket.

'Grandpa?'

'Grace, I've just heard Daniel is safe. Thank the Lord.' I hear him expel a shaky breath. 'I've been so worried.'

'We all have,' I say flatly, not in the mood for conversation. A harsh wind whips my soaked hair across my face.

'Where are you?'

'Walking home.'

'Lord, child, you'll catch your death.'

I don't respond.

'They're not pressing charges then?' asks Grandpa.

'No. Candice decided not to in the end.'

'Good.' His voice weakens. 'I know I ought to have told you myself.'

'You did know then?' I ask, the bitterness I feel inside seeping into my voice. 'About them sleeping together? Rob's blackmail? That's what you meant when you said I had to ask Justin for the truth.'

'Rob confessed to me,' admits Grandpa after a beat of silence, his voice little more than a whisper. 'When Noah died. He was eaten up with guilt. He thought perhaps Justin leaving in the way he did had contributed to the stillbirth.'

My insides tighten. Do I believe that too? 'Well I guess we'll never know.'

'I wanted to tell you, Grace, but I didn't see what good it would do.' Regret interlaces every word. 'I believed you were better off without Justin. What he did to you, betraying you like that, I despised him for it.'

I scoff. 'And what about Candice? You didn't appear to despise her.'

'She made a silly mistake, that's all.'

'Seems pretty contradictory to me.'

He blows out. 'I'm not perfect either, you know. I struggle with sin just like anybody else. I really am sorry. Forgive me?'

A heavy silence hangs on the line. 'There's nothing to forgive,' I concede, knowing in my heart that I can't blame Grandpa for what's happened. 'You did what you thought was right. Although I still don't fully understand why you were in the house yesterday morning?'

'Rob told me to collect Daniel, that was the truth. He thought Justin might be at the house and he didn't want a confrontation. I didn't know then that Rob had attacked Candice.'

'And you do now?' I ask, wondering how he knows.

'Rob told me a few minutes ago when he updated me on Daniel. Seems for a non-believer, that one sure likes a confession.' He laughs, though it sounds tinged with regret. 'I told him to hand himself in to the police.'

'Probably for the best.' Despite everything, I feel a stab of empathy. Rob isn't a bad person, he just made an already bad situation a million times worse.

'But why didn't you take Daniel yesterday? You left without him.' I think that if Grandpa would have just taken Daniel like he was supposed to then none of the rest would have happened.

'Candice messaged me while you were busy bandaging your hand. She told me to keep Daniel with me, to not allow Rob anywhere near him. I didn't know why then but I thought I'd best do as she wished. Only I haven't the first clue how to look after a toddler, so I figured he'd be best off with you.'

'Right.' I walk a few paces in silence. What is there left to say? 'I best be going. I'm almost home now.'

'Okay. May the Lord keep you from harm. I love you, Grace, darling.'

I hang up, the words I desperately want to say lodged in my throat. *I love you too, Grandpa.*

Cold rain continues to hit me head-on as I turn onto the main road. Burying my chin against my chest, I press on, my head and heart pulling in different directions. Was I right to leave Justin with Candice and Daniel at the police station? It was obvious that he wasn't comfortable being with Candice, that it was Daniel he stayed for. Should I have fought harder for him?

I glance up, see Rob's car slowing to a stop beside me. He rolls down the window a fraction. 'Get in, you're soaked.'

I shake my head, unable to look at him. 'I don't think that's a good idea.'

'I know you're angry with me.' His voice is only just audible over the buzz of traffic. 'If you just hear me out, give me a chance to explain.'

'You can drive me home, that's it.' I climb into the passenger seat and fold my arms.

'You're soaked.'

'It's raining.'

Rob drums his thumbs on the steering wheel. 'I want to explain,' he mutters. 'Properly like.'

'Where were you going anyway? This isn't your way home.'

'To the station. Your grandad told me to confess to what I did. He's right. Candice is already trying to blackmail me, wants the house, my money, the lot.' He shakes his head. 'Justin's welcome to her. Poor man doesn't know what he's letting himself in for.'

'He's doing it for Daniel,' I say, more for my own benefit than for Rob's.

We drive in silence for a minute or so, neither of us knowing what to say. So much has changed in the last twenty-four hours, we're different people to who we were, and yet I know in my heart that Rob is still the man who saved me all those years ago, who spent night and day nursing me to health. Doesn't he deserve a second chance? 'Look, I don't hate you, okay. I'm just angry.'

Rob's shoulders relax, the tension inside of him visibly deflating. 'Candice never really loved me, you know,' he admits. 'Said she always wanted to be with Justin. Right from the moment she met him all those years ago in the pub.'

I nod, not having the words to reply. I still can't get my head around the two of them together, perhaps I never will. 'The station can wait until tomorrow,' I say, pushing thoughts of Candice and Justin to the back of my mind. 'I reckon we both need a stiff drink.'

~

Removing my sodden jacket, I place it on the adjacent bar stool and wring out my hair. As I glance around at the walnut panelling and brass picture frames, I realise that Rob and I came to this very same pub eighteen years ago on our first date. What would life have been like if I'd married Rob instead of Justin? Would I have been happier than I am now?

Rob returns from the bar with the drinks, a pint for him and a glass of red for me. 'Did you see Daniel when you were released?' he asks, passing me the wine. 'I wanted to go and see him but Candice refused.'

My heart goes out to him. 'She'll come round,' I offer, though in truth I doubt she will. If Justin sticks around, which he will if only for Daniel's sake, then she'll have no use for poor Rob. 'Danny was absolutely fine though,' I add, forcing a smile. 'And that's the main thing, right?'

'It is,' says Rob. 'All I want is for Daniel to be happy.'

'Me too,' I reply, meaning every word.

85

JUSTIN
NOW

Candice's eyes darken. 'What do you mean you can't do it?'

'This... pretending to be a happy family. I love Grace, not you.'

'It's you and me now,' she barks. 'And Daniel,' she adds as an afterthought. 'Forget Grace.'

'I can't just forget her. We were together ten years!'

'How can you still want her over me?' Candice is screaming now. 'She's a nutter who used my... *our* son to trick you.'

'Me and you made a mistake, Candice, a huge, one-night mistake. That's all it was.'

'But you just said we were a real family now, remember?'

'I know. I thought we could, but there's nothing real about it.'

'You said you loved me.'

'You said I loved you. I've just realised I don't even like you, never mind love you.'

'And our son?'

'I will do everything for my son, *everything*.'

'Then you'd better make the right decision, right now. Is it me and Daniel, or is it her?'

'It'll never be you, Candice. Get that in your head.'

'Then say goodbye to Daniel.'

'You can't stop me from seeing my own son.'

'Oh no? Watch me.' She scoops up Daniel. 'Say bye to Justin, Danny. This is the last time you'll see that arsehole.' She grabs his arm and waves it at me. 'Bye-bye, Justin, bye-bye,' she mocks.

I look at Daniel. Unable to comprehend the words, his eyes and ears try to decipher what's going on by the tone of voice and the facial expressions. He looks helpless, abandoned. In those beautiful brown eyes I see me – lost, confused. I can't leave him again, I just can't. I look back at Candice. It's here, family, staring me in the face. All I need to say is 'okay'. *For God's sake, take it.*

I open my mouth, but nothing comes out. I crouch down and squeeze Daniel. 'Daddy loves you, son. I just need to do something.' I kiss him on the forehead and stand up, Jack's words resonating in my head like the tolling of bells – *the right thing to do is rarely found on the path of least resistance.* Candice stares, open-mouthed, as I turn and walk out the door.

86

GRACE
2 MONTHS LATER

I tape up the last remaining box, marking its contents with a black marker. This morning, I repainted the nursery walls a bright white. Painting over the stencil of Noah's name brought a lump to my throat, but it's time to move on. The baby boy I lost will forever remain in my heart, but I realise holding on to the past was stealing my present. For the first time since Noah died, I'm not only content, I'm also looking forward to the future, whatever that may hold.

Yesterday, I attended church for the first time since Andrew's memorial. God remains an enigma to me but the look on Grandpa's face when I walked through the doors was a blessing enough. Over the last two months, he's apologised profusely for keeping Rob and Justin's secrets. I don't hold it against him. Rob placed him in an impossible position and, as a pastor, Grandpa believed he was doing the right thing. Whether he was right or wrong is debatable, but I've chosen to forgive him. One thing that the last few months has taught me is that everyone is capable of doing bad. *Only by the grace of God go I.* Mum had it right all along.

'Grace, do you think Daniel would prefer spaghetti or penne

with the bolognese?' Justin stands at the open nursery door, a burnt tea towel draped over his arm and a panicked look on his face.

'Whatever you think. He'll likely get the whole lot down him anyway.'

'I've chucked a load of mushrooms in as well and then I thought, shit, can eighteen-month-olds even eat mushrooms?' he says.

I laugh. 'Yes, they can eat mushrooms. Calm down, he'll just be happy to see you.'

'God, I hope so.' He crosses the room and peers out of the window. 'I'm so nervous. Supposing he doesn't remember me?'

'He will, Justin. You're unforgettable.'

It took me precisely twenty-four hours after being released from the police station to realise that I still loved Justin. Of course, I still hated what he'd done, how he'd humiliated and betrayed me. Yet I knew in my heart that I could forgive him, that he was deserving of a second chance. There's a famous saying that if you truly love a person, you have to let them go. I don't buy into that. I believe that if you truly love someone then you have to fight for them.

I place the cardboard box full of Noah's things on top of the rest. Tomorrow I'll donate them to charity. It gives me a sense of joy to know that his possessions won't go to waste. 'I can't wait to see Daniel either. I've missed him.'

'Do you honestly think she's going to bring him?'

'Too right.' I join Justin at the window and lean my head against his chest. His heart is pounding. 'With Rob facing a six-month stretch, Candice will be pulling her hair out with Daniel all by herself.' I smile at the thought of Candice having to deal with the terrible twos all by herself. Despite the way she's treated me, I don't hate her. If anything, I'm indifferent, not giving her much thought at all. 'Candice is no single mum, Justin. I expect we'll be seeing a lot of Daniel from now on.'

Justin pulls me in close and kisses the top of my head. 'I hope so. I need to be with my boy.' The last few months haven't been easy on Justin. Candice has done everything in her power to make things difficult for him, for weeks using Daniel as a weapon. It was only when Justin threatened to take court action that she changed her tune. With Rob filing for divorce and having refused her any financial backing, she wasn't prepared to risk her own money.

A swish of headlights slicing through the darkness announces their arrival. 'Told you.'

Justin blows out a huge sigh of relief. 'Do you want to go and get him? He'll feel more comfortable with you.' I can feel the nervous energy radiating off him.

'No, you do it. You're his dad.' I still find it mind boggling that Justin is Daniel's dad, but I know it's something I'll have to get used to if our relationship is going to work. 'As long as you promise to bring him straight up here. I'm dying for a cuddle.'

I wait until I hear the sound of the front door opening before making my way through to the bathroom. The pregnancy test lies face down on the edge of the bath. It was this morning, while packing away Noah's vests and Babygros, that I realised I haven't had a period in over two months. Excitement flutters in my chest as I pick it up.

'Holy shit!' I collapse down onto the toilet seat, staring at the solid pink line in the test window.

'Gayce!'

'Hello, mate. Wow, look at you. You're so big!' Tears prick my eyes as I wrap Daniel in my arms, two thoughts colliding. The first is that he's going to make the best big brother.

'Grace? What's that in your hand?' Justin is standing at the bathroom door, his eyes glued to the test.

'Surprise!' I hold it out to him, finally witnessing the reaction I've waited a decade to see.

'Oh my God! You're pregnant?'

'Yep. You're going to be a dad – again!'

Shit! The words are out before I have a chance to catch them.

I've regretted sleeping with Rob since the moment it happened. I was drunk and upset, had just spent twenty-four hours in a police cell. Rob had lost his son and wife. I had lost Justin and Daniel. I guess we both needed comfort that night and found it in each other. Thankfully, Rob agreed that it had just been a silly mistake, and that Justin should never find out.

Of course, now I might not have a choice.

The dates stack up – Rob or Justin's? A fifty-fifty split.

'Grace, you have no idea how much this means.' Justin kisses me hard on the mouth. 'I promise to do everything right this time. I love you so much.'

'I love you too,' I say, deciding that the truth can wait until tomorrow, or the next day, or maybe I don't ever need to tell him.

After all, what harm is a little lie?

THE END

To find out more about Gemma and Joe, and the trials of writing a book together, follow them at their blog, hesaysshesays.net

ACKNOWLEDGEMENTS

No story, no book, no literary journey is accomplished without the support of many others. For me and Gemma, this includes many people in a myriad of ways.

So we want to start with those who provided the wind with which we could set sail.

Without Betsy, Fred, Tara, Ian and the rest of the Bloodhound gang, our book would still be bobbing aimlessly in a sea of other unpublished work.

We also want to show our appreciation to beta readers, Wendy, Joanne and Danni, for privately pointing out our foolishness before it became public.

To Sally and Caroline at The Olive Garden in Tenerife, we owe you big time. Not financially, we *think* we paid all our bills, but for allowing us to use your fantastic restaurant as our second office, and for keeping us fed, watered and caffeinated while we demanded electricity, Wi-Fi and the removal of other patrons from our favourite table.

And of course, there are our families. Huge thanks (and apologies for our self-absorption) to our respective partners and kids – Joe's Joy, Molly and Sam; Gemma's Danny and Jude.

Lastly, thanks to everybody who's got this far in the book. Especially to those who enjoyed it.

A NOTE FROM THE PUBLISHER

Thank you for reading this book. If you enjoyed it please do consider leaving a review on Amazon to help others find it too.

We hate typos. All of our books have been rigorously edited and proofread, but sometimes mistakes do slip through. If you have spotted a typo, please do let us know and we can get it amended within hours.

info@bloodhoundbooks.com